The CHILDREN OF THE WIND quartet is a sweeping Irish–Australian saga made up of Bridie's story, Patrick's story, Colm's story and Maeve's story, four inter-linked novels for 10- to 14-year-olds, beginning with the 1850s and moving right up to the present.

Bridie's Fire

Becoming Billy Dare

A Prayer for Blue Delaney

The Secret Life of Maeve Lee Kwong

KIRSTY MURRAY is a fifth-generation Australian whose ancestors came from Ireland, Scotland, England and Germany. Some of their stories provided her with the backcloth for the CHILDREN OF THE WIND series. Kirsty lives in Melbourne with her husband and a gang of teenagers.

OTHER BOOKS BY KIRSTY MURRAY

FICTION

Zarconi's Magic Flying Fish

Market Blues

Walking Home with Marie-Claire

NON-FICTION

Howard Florey, Miracle Maker

Tough Stuff

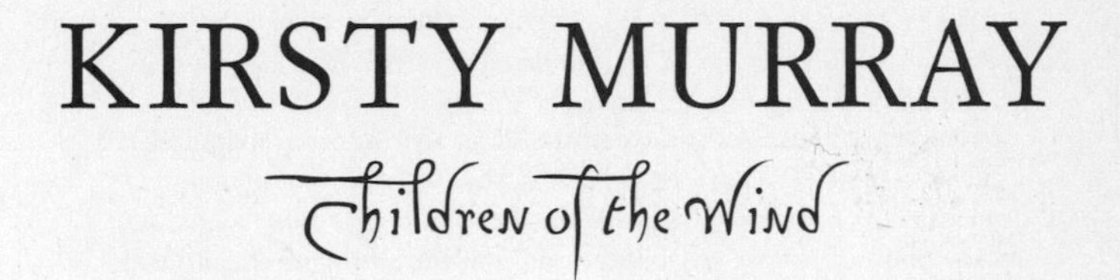

ALLEN&UNWIN

First published in 2003

Copyright © Kirsty Murray 2003

All rights reserved. No part of this book may be reproduced or transmitted in any form or by any means, electronic or mechanical, including photocopying, recording or by any information storage and retrieval system, without prior permission in writing from the publisher. *The Australian Copyright Act* 1968 (the Act) allows a maximum of one chapter or ten per cent of this book, whichever is the greater, to be photocopied by any educational institution for its educational purposes provided that the educational institution (or body that administers it) has given a remuneration notice to Copyright Agency Limited (CAL) under the Act.

Allen & Unwin
83 Alexander Street
Crows Nest NSW 2065
Australia
Phone: (61 2) 8425 0100
Fax: (61 2) 9906 2218
Email: info@allenandunwin.com
Web: www.allenandunwin.com

National Library of Australia
Cataloguing-in-Publication entry:

Murray, Kirsty.
Bridie's fire.

For children.
ISBN 1 86508 727 0.

I. Title. (Series: Murray, Kirsty. Children of the wind; bk. 1).

A823.3

Australia Council for the Arts

This project has been assisted by the Commonwealth Government through the Australia Council, its arts funding and advisory body

Designed by Ruth Grüner
Set in 10.7 pt Sabon by Ruth Grüner
Printed by McPherson's Printing Group

1 3 5 7 9 10 9 8 6 4 2

Contents

Acknowledgements

Bridie's story is the first of four novels in the CHILDREN OF THE WIND series. In both Ireland and Australia, countless kind souls generously provided me with their time, their knowledge, their family stories, their understanding of themselves and their connections with the past. Many people have helped these stories come to life over the past few years, but for the moment I will confine my thanks to those who helped with *Bridie's Fire*. I would also like to acknowledge the support of the Australia Council in funding this project; without its support, none of these stories would have been told.

In the West of Ireland I am grateful to Father Pádraig Ó'Fiannachta for his wisdom and insight; Con Moriarty of Lost Ireland for some fabulous yarns; Gerry O'Leary of the Kerry Historical Society for a wealth of information; Tim Clarke, Heidi and Fionn O'Neill for their generous hospitality; and especially Alice and Shanthi Perceval for their love, support and companionship.

In Dublin I thank Margaret Hoctor, Elaine Ryan, Con Sullivan and Ruth Lawler for their time and their kindness, and also the staff of the National Library of Ireland for patiently answering a convoluted list of questions.

In Melbourne I am indebted to Judy Brett and Graham Smith, Mairead McNena, Catherine O'Donoghue, Alice Boyle, Val Noone and the Celtic Club, the Caroline Chisholm Library, *Clann an Ghorta*, the La Trobe Library at the State Library of Victoria, and my ever-reliable local favourite, the Yarra Plenty Regional Library Service.

Special thanks to Peter Freund of Her Majesty's Theatre, Ballarat, for his fabulous insights into the history of theatre on the goldfields, and the wealth of material he provided. And to Trevor McClaughlin for his commitment to reconstructing the lives of the orphan girls.

I am also very grateful to Rosalind Price for her continuing faith, and to Sarah Brenan, John Bangsund and Penni Russon for their persistent clarity and annoying attention to detail.

And of course, most importantly, there are the people who have had to live with this project and still have more blarney to suffer before it's finished: Ruby, Billy and Elwyn Murray, and Ken, Romanie, Isobel and Theo Harper. Thanks, guys.

To Ruby Joy Murray,

my brave and fiery girl

1

Ride a wild pony

'Bad scran to you, evil prince,' said Bridie, thrusting her stick at Brandon. 'Pick up your weapon and I'll kill you three times over!'

Brandon waded out to where his driftwood sword floated on the waves, while Bridie leapt nimbly from one black rock to another until she stood on the one that jutted out furthest into the ocean.

'C'mon, boyo, the great warrior Queen Medb is ready for battle!'

Brandon looked up at her and grinned. 'That's two times you've let me kill you,' he said, 'and I've only had to die this once. So, you know, I'm thinking I'll not risk another thrashing.'

Before she could reply, he ran down the pebbly beach to join the other boys.

Bridie watched him for a moment and then turned to face the sea. She shouted a victory cry, her voice ringing out across the waves. Her friend Roisin glanced up from where she was gathering shellfish from the rocks. 'What are you shouting about now, girl?' she asked.

Bridie stretched her arms wide, as if she could embrace

the wind. 'Do you ever feel, on a summer day like this,' she said, 'that if you sing out they'd hear you calling on all the islands, hear your voice all the way to America?'

Roisin tucked a wisp of red-gold hair behind her ear.

'All I'm feeling is my empty belly. Mam will be wild that I've spent the morning larkin' about with you and not gathering shellfish to thicken the pot.'

Bridie jumped down from the rock, sending a spray of seawater into the air.

'I've a sack full of periwinkles and I'll give you the lot, girl.'

'I can't be taking them from you.'

'But I'm wanting you to take them,' said Bridie, running across the beach and picking up the small hessian sack that she'd left near the base of the cliffs. She pushed the bag into Roisin's arms. 'There are more little ones in your house than in ours.'

'You'd best be taking them,' said Brandon, joining them. He was followed by Roisin's small brothers, Mickey and Jim.

'You never know what I'll do if you cross me, Roisin O'Farrell,' teased Bridie. 'Why, when I was a strip of a girl, I was so mad at our dad for going out in the currach without me that I jumped off the cliffs at Dunquin.'

Roisin laughed and slung the bag over her shoulder. 'I know that old story. My mam told it to me. She says there's no one as wild in the whole of Ireland as Bridie O'Connor in a rage. God bless you, girl.'

Roisin and Bridie walked along the beach, calling for their brothers to keep up. Mickey and Jim straggled behind, picking up coloured pebbles. They were scrawny boys with round pale faces and thin gold hair. Brandon looked big and sturdy beside them. Bridie watched him with pride as he showed them how to skip stones across the surface of the ocean, his curly red hair bright against the blue water. The wind picked up, making the pebbles skitter off course, but Brandon stepped into the waves and sent a purple stone skimming smoothly out to sea.

They were turning onto the cliff path when, out of nowhere, a black pony came charging up the beach, with surf churning white about its hooves. There was no time to get out of its way. It skidded to a halt, rearing up so close that Bridie could smell the hot scent of horseflesh as its black hooves scraped against her shoulder.

'It's the pooka!' she shouted. 'Run!' She stumbled backwards, trying to herd the other children behind her, but before she could stop him, Brandon slipped past, stretching out his arms to the wild pony.

'It's only a frightened beast,' he said, glancing back at Bridie. 'If we're still, she'll know we're her friends.' The pony lowered its head and nuzzled his chest, as if it understood his words.

Roisin reached out for her little brothers. They stood a short distance up the path, poised to run, but Bridie took a step closer until she felt the pony's breath warm against her cheek.

'If it is only a frightened beast and not the devil's own mare, why don't you prove it, boyo,' she said. 'Why don't you get on her back and take her for a ride. I dare you!'

'You come away from it, Brandon!' shrieked Roisin, grabbing her brothers' arms and dragging them further away. 'You climb on its back and it'll take you into the surf and drown you. You know those stories, Bridie – why, you told them to me yourself! The black pony will take you across the sea to the fairy folk or bring the devil to your door. How can you be daring your own brother to risk it!'

Bridie and Brandon looked at each other, and they both laughed as their thoughts entwined.

'Man alive, Roisin, you don't think I'd be daring him and not taking the dare myself?' She turned to Brandon and gave him a leg up. The pony stamped its feet and snorted anxiously, shying away.

'What are you doing?' shouted Roisin. 'You O'Connors, you're both flaming mad!' She ran up the cliff path, with Mickey and Jim chasing behind.

Brandon sat astride the black pony, stroking its neck with long, gentle movements, and all the while whispering sweetly until the animal grew calm again. Then he gave the signal and Bridie carefully guided the pony to an outcrop of rocks so she too could climb on its back. When they were both securely mounted, Brandon leaned forward and coaxed the pony into a walk. It shied into the surf until the waves washed against its flanks. Bridie felt a ripple of alarm.

'Are you sure she won't take us out to sea?' she whispered.

'She won't be doing that. I'm thinking she's a runaway from Lord Ventry's stables,' he answered quietly.

The pony broke into a canter and they rode along the water's edge with the wind biting their cheeks, the animal swift and powerful beneath them. The surf roared in their ears as they rounded the point. Bridie wrapped her arms tight around her brother and felt the excitement in his taut body, his heart beating as if it were her own.

They'd only just sent the black pony on its way, and were walking homewards along the beach when Bridie spotted their father's currach riding the crest of the waves, heading towards them. She cupped her hands and shouted, and their dad waved back. He beached the boat and jumped out, clasping three shimmering fish hooked together. Brandon held the catch while Dad and the other men dragged the currach high onto the beach, and then together they set out for home. Dad whistled all the way up the steep cliff path.

Inside the house, Mam was busy scraping hot potatoes from the embers of the fire. Bridie hurried over to help, rescuing her baby brother, Paddy, from the mess he was making in a small pile of cold ash. He laughed at the faces she pulled when he tugged at her dark curls. Shifting the tiny boy onto her hip, she took him into the late summer twilight.

They sat on the bench outside the whitewashed house and Bridie shared her potato with Paddy, feeding him small mouthfuls with her fingertips. Brandon came out and joined them, hungrily scooping out the hot sweet flesh from the skin.

Her mother put her head around the door and smiled at them. 'Thanks be to the great God who spared you to me, Bridie. The O'Farrells are paying us a visit this evening and I'm hoping you'll be minding the little ones so Kitty and I can have a fine old gossip while we sew.'

'I can tell them about the great hairy ghost that lives under that lump of stone by the lane.'

'Don't you go frightening Roisin,' said Mam.

'It's true,' said Brandon, with his mouth half-full of spud. 'Bridie's already given her a death of fright this morning.'

'What's the boy talking about?' asked Mam.

Bridie reached over and cuffed Brandon on the head. 'Never you mind, Mam. I'll tell some fine old fairy stories that will keep the lot of them out of trouble.'

Half an hour later, Roisin came running up the path to their house, clutching a handful of bright flowers, her long red plaits bouncing as she ran.

'But sure I'm glad to find you home,' she said. 'I thought you'd be under the sea by now.'

Behind her were all the O'Farrell family – Kitty O'Farrell with one of her baby twin boys on each hip and a crowd of small red- and golden-haired children milling around their father.

'Blessing o' God on ye, Seamus O'Connor!' said Mick O'Farrell. His tired face lit up with pleasure as Bridie's father pulled a long-necked bottle of whiskey from the cupboard and set it on the table.

Bridie loved these evenings, when the house was full of people, the warm scent of whiskey and tobacco, and the sound of lively talk and music. When Bridie's mother sang, Bridie thought her voice was the loveliest in all the west of Ireland. The room grew still as she sang the story of a beautiful girl with a broken heart, whose love had gone across the sea to America and was never heard from again.

'One day I'll be going across the sea to America, like Uncle Liam,' said Brandon, when the song was finished.

'Now why would you be thinking such a thing?' asked

Roisin. 'No one's ever heard from your Uncle Liam.'

'To be sure, he's rich and living in a grand house,' said Brandon.

'But you'll not really be wanting to do that, Brandon,' said Bridie, putting an arm around her little brother. 'You'll be wanting to come and live with me in my house, not with Uncle Liam. I'll have my own little house, and one half of it will be red gold and the other half, the lower half, it'll be silver; and I'll have me a red door, and the threshold will be copper, I think, and the thatch will be so lovely, like the wings of magic, white-yellow birds, like you've never seen, not even in your dreams. And you and me, we'll live there together for ever.'

Brandon grinned shyly, glancing across at the O'Farrell children with pride in his eyes. There was no other girl that could tell stories like his sister. But Roisin folded her arms across her chest and glared at Bridie.

'You and your fairies!' she said. 'First you tell me that if you ride a pooka, it will take you out past the ninth wave, to hell or the otherworld. Then you and Brandon go riding on that beast, and here you are, safe and warm. And then you tell me that fairies are living in the mounds near the beehive huts. I went like you told me, girl, and I waited in the dawn, like you said I should, until the cold crept into my bones, and not one fairy did I see, nor any magical folk.'

Bridie looked from Roisin to Brandon and laughed. Then she put on her most serious expression. 'But sure I've seen them, my darling girl. With my own eyes, I've seen the fairies weaving *pishoge* over by St Brendan's hut.'

Brandon nodded. 'I own to God, she speaks the truth.'

Roisin looked suspiciously from sister to brother, and then suddenly she laughed.

'Devil a lie, Bridie O'Connor,' said Roisin, 'but I want to believe every word you say.'

The grown-ups grew louder as the whiskey took hold, and their talk became more troubled. They spoke of the crops that were failing again on the other side of the mountain and of the terrible suffering that all Ireland was enduring. The children snuggled down together in front of the hearth, watching the last embers flicker while Bridie whispered stories of all the magic things she'd seen in the hills and fields around their homes. In the glowing turf Bridie could almost see the vision she described: a beautiful faerie queen in a shimmering gown with feather-white pieces of fabric floating about her and dewdrops like tiny pearls on every fold of her dress. Even Roisin was entranced by the description, and when Bridie looked down into their bright faces she could almost believe that every word of the stories she told was true.

She nestled down closer to her brother and began another tale.

2

The hunger

The next morning was bright and clear. Bridie woke with Brandon and Paddy a tangle of limbs and tousled hair on the pallet beside her. The O'Farrell children were gone. Someone must have woken them quietly and then moved Bridie and her brothers to their bed.

The chicken that they kept in the cupboard was scratching and clucking, anxious to be out in the day. Bridie padded across the pressed-earth floor, reached in between the wooden bars of the cage under the cupboard and drew a warm egg from beneath the hen.

The door to the cottage was open, and the fire was smouldering on the hearth. She wondered why Mam and Dad hadn't woken her when they left and why her mother hadn't let the chicken out. Still clutching the warm hen's egg in her hand, she stepped over the threshold. Pale dawn light crept across the morning sky. Bridie walked around the back of the cottage to where the family potato plot lay. Her parents were already at work in the field, but there was something odd about the way they were going about it, a frenzied desperation in their movements. Then Bridie saw that the leaves of the plants looked strange, limp and wilted. The day before they had been a thick tangle of stalks and rich green leaves.

Then, as her father dug his hands into the black soil, he moaned, a horrible low growl like a wounded dog.

'Da, don't!' she called, frightened.

He looked up, his face white and contorted with despair. 'It's the blight, girl.'

Bridie caught her breath and pressed her fists against her cheeks. She knew what this could mean. She had seen the gaunt and desperate men and women, turned out of home when their crops failed and they'd been unable to pay their rent. They drifted across the land and wound their way around the peninsula, begging at every door, driven by a hungry wind. All across the country, first in the north, and then rapidly spreading south, the potato harvest had been hit by a terrible cholera, but the O'Connors had been spared – until now.

Bridie slipped the egg into the pocket of her dress and set to work alongside her parents, separating the good potatoes from the bad. Some were no more than black pulp, with a stench that burnt her nostrils. Others showed a row of small spots, like tiny weeping sores.

At the end of the day, a day in which they barely stopped for a moment from the grim work, Dad leaned against the whitewashed wall of their house and looked out across the ravaged field. 'There's just enough good spuds to half-fill the pit. We'll take care with these, and God save us, there'll be enough to tide us through the winter.'

They filled the store-pit with what they'd salvaged, and laid straw across the top. Mam said a prayer over the pit and Bridie knelt beside her with head bowed, whispering the words with anxious longing.

That evening, Bridie and her father walked down the narrow white path to the O'Farrells' house. Mam and the boys were already in bed, but both Bridie and Seamus O'Connor were restless. It was a sombre gathering at the O'Farrells'. Their crop was blighted as well, and not even the whiskey could break through the chill that settled on the room. Bridie was in no mood to tell fairy stories to the O'Farrell children, so instead she sat beside her father, nestling in against his strong body and listening quietly as he and Mick discussed what had brought the disease to their crop.

As they argued back and forth, Bridie shrank closer to her father, her mind consumed by guilty imaginings. Had she brought this ill luck on Dunquin by riding the black pony? She remembered Roisin's screaming that the pooka would bring the devil to their door. And now it had come true. She frowned and concentrated hard, trying to make sense of what the men were saying.

Mick thought it was the summer storms or the easterly winds or maybe even the moon, but Seamus O'Connor shook his head, adding, 'Whatever cause brought this upon us, you can be sure the English will make it no easy cross to bear. There'll be no help for the likes of us, Mick O'Farrell. The hunger has the whole of Ireland by the throat. My blood shivers when I think of the poor widows and orphans flung out of their homes, the men working and dying on the public service for a handful of cornmeal while good butter and oats and the best Ireland has to offer is loaded onto boats bound for England.'

'And here you were telling me only a few years back that our man Dan O'Connell would change it all for us,' said Mick. 'But to be sure he can't change the will of God, boyo.'

Seamus slammed his hand down hard on the table. 'Mick O'Farrell, I tell you these troubles and the hunger they will bring are man-made and not the will of God!' Bridie could feel the tide of rage rising in her father's body. He shook his head angrily, pushed a handful of curly black hair away from his face and reached for another mouthful of whiskey. 'Whatever becomes of us, I'll not have you slack-jawed about the Great Liberator,' said Dad. 'They've laid him low, and he can't talk for us now, but if he could, he'd put a stop to their mischief!'

The first bite of chill autumn was in the air as they walked back home that night. Bridie felt her whole body aching with grief and guilt. She couldn't put the thought of the black pony from her mind. When Seamus noticed her slackening pace, he hoisted her up onto his broad back and carried her the rest of the way home. The coarse fabric of his coat scratched her cheek but she wrapped her arms tight around him. When he set her down outside the cabin door they stood for a moment, looking up at the swirling stars. Bridie slipped her hand into her father's and he squeezed it firmly.

'Dad,' she whispered. 'I did a wicked thing. And I've brought the curse upon us. It's all my fault that the praties turned black.' She wiped a tear away from her cheek with the back of her hand. Dad knelt down and swept her up into his arms, bringing her face close to his.

'Husha, what's this you're saying?' he said, his warm, whiskey-scented breath against her cheek.

'I rode the pooka, with Brandon. A wild black pony on the beach near the *cuisheen*. It's an evil sign, isn't it?'

Dad laughed and brushed his hand against Bridie's hair. 'If it was the pooka you were riding, you'd not be here in my arms, girl. No, it was only a black pony and you can be sure of that. You've no cause to go blaming yourself for anything.'

He sat down on the bench outside the house and settled Bridie in his lap.

'You're frightened of what lies ahead, aren't you, child?' he said softly. Bridie nodded.

'Wisha, sweet child, if I could spare you the grief of this world, I would. But I know you're a match for the devil and all his mischief. When you were born, just a fresh babe, and I held you in my arms for the first time, I knew that we had to call you Bridie, after the blessed St Brigid. I knew because the moment I set eyes on you, I saw you had holy fire in you, exactly like our own St Brigid.'

'But Mam said St Brigid had golden hair, like the flame. Mine's as black as soot,' said Bridie.

Her father laughed and tugged at one of her black curls. 'But you've got the markings, girl. St Brigid was scarred on her lovely face too. It's a sure sign.'

He traced the long pale scar that ran across Bridie's face from temple to chin with his fingertips. 'I'll never forget the day you won that. There I was rowing to the Great Blasket Island, and when I look back what do I see? My own darling girl running along the high cliffs and then, like a bird, launching her sweet self into the air, red petticoat flying. I tell you, child, my heart was in my mouth as you fell. I've never rowed so hard in my life. When I found your little crumpled body lying on those sharp rocks and the spark still in your heart, I knew it was a miracle.'

'Will there be a miracle to save us from the hunger, Dad?'

Bridie felt her father sigh. He drew her closer to him, folding his jacket around her to keep her warm.

'I'll tell you a story. A story about your own sweet saint,' he said.

Bridie shut her eyes and let the sound of his rich, deep voice wash over her. She loved the way she could hear his words with her skin, not just her ears.

'When St Brigid was a baby and her mother was living with the druid, they left her sleeping in the cradle and set out to work in the fields. But when the druid looks up the hill to his house, he sees great licks of flame leaping from the windows and his own home a-blazing. He comes running up the hill to save the little baby, and as he runs closer, the flames stretch from earth to heaven. But when he reaches the babe, there she is lying in her cradle, smiling the sweet smile of the innocent, and the flames all around her are leaping from the holy presence of the little babe herself. And the druid's house wasn't burnt to the ground, for the flames were the fire of God. St Brigid was never harmed because the fire burnt within her, in her heart and her soul. And I swear, when I first held you, Bridie, I saw that fire in you, darling girl. You make sure no one ever puts it out. That angry fire will keep you strong against all the evil the world can bring.'

'So the evil will come?' said Bridie in a small voice.

'There's always evil to battle, but the O'Connors have fighting spirits. No matter what lies ahead, nothing can put that out, not the wind, nor the sea, nor the sharp rocks of Dunquin. Nor least the English and their famine. But it's time you were asleep, my darling, you'll be saying your prayers and curl up with your brothers in your little bed. It's off to dreams of *Tír na nÓg* for you.'

He swept her up in his arms and carried her inside.

It was the stench that woke Bridie, even worse than the smell of the black potatoes that they had grubbed from the soil yesterday. The cottage was rank with it. Brandon woke up too and whispered, 'What is it, Bridie, what black curse is it?'

In the dark, they heard their parents stir to waking and fling the door open to the night. They listened to their father's voice rising in despair.

'Rotten, black and rotten the lot of them, rotting in the pit, they are!' Their mother wailed in the darkness, keening as if there had been a death in the house.

Bridie and Brandon went outside and stood beside the pit in the moonlight, shivering even though the night was warm. The air felt thick and heavy and Bridie tried not to breathe too deeply so that the rank and bitter smell wouldn't get inside her. It smelt of death and misery. She reached out for Brandon's hand and drew him closer, so close that she could feel his heart beating as hard and fast as her own.

The hunger came sooner than they'd expected. Before the month was out, there were no potatoes to be had anywhere on the Dingle Peninsula. Brandon and Bridie and the O'Farrell children spent hours every day scouring the beach for tough little periwinkles, and scraping limpets from the rocks. All the cockles and mussels had been taken long since. Soon the rocks were stripped bare. Even the dulse and sloke seaweed that they raked up with their hands was sparse, for now there were crowds of hungry villagers trying to harvest what they could from the shores.

One day the children came home, and Mam was at the hearth, cooking up a mixture of gruel and nettles in the pot over the stove. She took the limpets from Brandon and set them to roast on the fire. Then she spooned a little of the nettle brew into a wooden bowl and handed it to Bridie.

'Here, girl, take this to the poor wretch out by the side of the house,' she said. When Bridie looked doubtful, her mother waved her outside. 'Remember, we're never so hungry that there's not someone hungrier than we are,' she said.

Bridie found the man propped against the wall of the cottage, his breath coming in short gasps. She squatted down beside him and offered him the bowl but the man just stared back at her with glazed eyes. She tried to spoon the porridge into the man's mouth, but it ran back out again. She wiped a bit of it away with the hem of her dress.

'Mam,' she called, stepping away from the man. 'Mam, come quick.'

'Jesus and sweet Mary,' said her mother, kneeling down beside the man and taking his hand. 'Will there be no end to it?'

That night, Bridie heard her parents arguing in fierce whispers. '*Erra*, woman, you can't be going hungry now with the state you're in. You've got more than your own mouth to think of feeding.'

'But if they catch you, man! Think of it! What will become of us all if they send you to New South Wales? I couldn't be doing it alone. There's no money for thread and besides that, not a soul who can afford to have their finery mended. You must think of the children and not your pride.'

'Husha, girl. It's the children and yourself that I am thinking of! Whatever way the wind blows, I'll not watch my family starve. I'll be a rogue for as long as I need and no longer. And I swear I'll never take a penn'orth from a poor man, but I'll feel no grief for the ill-bred upstarts that can afford to lose a lump of loot. And who are the real rogues, when there's food a-plenty in the land but none for the starving? When a fine man like Mick O'Farrell is forced to the public works, working like a dog for a bag of coarse meal that won't feed his starving children?'

In the small glow from the embers, Bridie saw her father pull on his boots and slip out the door. She listened to the wind howling off the sea and shuddered at the thought of her father taking the currach out on those wild waters. She'd heard of small parties of men making raids along the coast and disappearing into the dark night. The embers flickered and then grew dimmer and Bridie closed her eyes and prayed for the fire inside her to grow stronger, strong enough to keep the darkness from swallowing up each of the people she loved.

3

St Brigid's Eve

Bridie sat on the threshold of the cottage with the door at her back and her lap full of rushes, making St Brigid's crosses. Her fingers were numb and aching from the cold but she kept on knotting the rushes, turning them over and binding the centre until each cross was perfect. Out across the sea, dark clouds were gathering on the far horizon. She wished her father would come home. She'd woken in the dark of night to the wind howling off the sea like a banshee. She heard the anxious whisperings of her mother and felt the cold winter air blasting into the cottage as her father opened the door and slipped out into the blackness.

Brandon struggled up the steep path from the *cuisheen* and then turned onto the pathway to their house. He dropped the sack he was carrying and sat down beside her on the step, panting. His knobbly red knees stuck out through his ragged trousers and he rubbed them for warmth.

'They're only empty shells, Bridie. The rocks, they're scoured clean. There was nothing to gather. Do you think they'll work, even though they be empty?'

Bridie didn't answer. She stared out over the green fields to the sea, the St Brigid's crosses in her lap, unable to look into Brandon's anxious face. Ever since she could remember, they'd scattered shells in the corners of their home every St Brigid's day, and prayed to the saint to keep them safe from hunger for another year. But last year, St Brigid hadn't listened.

'This year, we'll shout to make her hear us,' said Bridie, tightly knotting another cross.

That afternoon, Bridie and Brandon walked down to the small clutch of houses that stood above the *cuisheen*. Bridie carried a basket filled with the rush crosses. There were other Brigids at Dunquin, but none of them had wanted to help deliver the crosses this year. When Bridie had asked Brigid MacMahon to join her, the little girl had simply stared and turned away to face the fire again, too exhausted by hunger to move. They trudged down into Dunquin with heads lowered against the driving wind. Their bare feet were blue with cold and icy needles of rain soaked their worn clothes.

'I don't see that crosses and shells can keep us safe,' argued Brandon.

'For heaven's sake, boyo. Sure, our prayers will be answered one day,' said Bridie.

'They haven't done, have they?' he said, kicking at a clump of grass by the road. 'Mam's always a-praying and it doesn't make anything come right. I'm still hungry most of the time. Even with the food our dad brings home that we hide in the hole, there's never enough.'

'Cut the sign of the cross on yourself and ask God to forgive you. The Devil will hear you and we'll lose what little we have left,' she said sharply. Then she looked at the boy and her heart leapt with pity. He looked so small and sodden, with his red curls plastered darkly against his pale brow. 'Darling boy, I know what you're saying. Sometimes I feel mad as a bull with our St Brigid. I'm thinking, isn't it a saint's business to guard her people? Especially when that saint knows so much about the hearth and the home? But then I'm reasoning, I've got you and our dad and Mam and baby Paddy and together we make a grand family so even if there isn't food, there's plenty of heart. So c'mon, bucko. We'll go down the *cuisheen* to see if Dad's coming home in the corrach, and we'll give each of the men a cross to take home with them.'

The sea was wild, foaming white and churning, the sky like black slate. Except for the swirling movement of the ocean, it was hard to tell where sea and sky met. There was no sign of the little boat.

'He won't try and come home across that, will he? He'll stay on the Great Blasket Island, to be sure?' asked Brandon, suddenly anxious.

Bridie pulled at the strands of black hair that whipped across her face and stared out at the wild sea. She knew their father wasn't out on the Great Blasket Island. She was sure he had gone on a foray further along the peninsula. She scanned the sea and shoreline, willing the currach to come into view. The waves rose up on the sea, like walls of water, as if it was boiling, the Devil himself stirring its heart.

Further down along the pebbly beach, a group of people gathered around something. It looked like a seal that had been washed onto the shore, its black body humped on the beach. Brandon and Bridie took the narrow path along the clifftops towards the village, keeping apace of the crowd that was moving along the beach. Bridie's basket grew sodden in the driving rain, the little crosses unravelling as the water swelled the rushes. Doggedly, the two children pushed on through the wind to the village.

They went from door to door, offering a rush cross to anyone who opened. Half the houses were empty now – so many people had left, taken by death or gone to America to escape the hunger. Some people didn't even open their doors, and those that did had nothing to offer the children in exchange.

It was in Muiris MacMahon's house that they found the party of people who'd come up from the beach. The door was open to the road and a single candle illuminated the small front room. No one spoke as the two children entered the house. Laid out on a door, his wet clothes gripping his still limbs, lay a giant of a man with a sharp, craggy face. For a moment Bridie didn't recognise him, and then it was as if her heart froze and the cry that was forming in her throat was stilled by horror. Brandon ran to the body and took a cold, swollen hand in his own, but Bridie backed away and stood in the doorway, staring at her father's corpse.

'Stay, child,' said an old woman. 'Muiris has gone for your *mamai*.'

Bridie looked down at the water pooling in the bottom of the basket and the swollen, useless crosses. The women all began to keen, their voices rising in a spiral of grief. Bridie turned and ran. The cobblestones of the village bruised her heels as she raced to the cliffs. She stood face to the wind, fighting to hold her feet on the narrow winding path, and flung the basket of crosses out into the churning sea, roaring with rage and misery. Brandon reached her side and took one of her trembling hands in his. They stood watching as the basket swept skywards in an updraft before it plummeted into the ocean, the crosses scattering in the wind and water.

'Oh Brand, I heard the banshee keening last night – heard it in the wind, and didn't stop our dad from stepping out! I never thought we could lose our dad!' She pushed her fists against the front of her worn dress as if trying to stem the pain.

There was no one at home when the two children returned, but the door was open. Mam must have run, with baby Paddy in her arms, down the long, bleak slope to the road. Bridie pushed the door shut, closing out the wild night and huddling close to the turf fire. She put her face so close to the smoking embers that her eyes stung and the tears ran free, coursing down her numb, cold face.

For months after her father's death, Bridie felt as if the fire that flared inside her had been turned inside out, and her skin was alive with heat and flame. Most mornings she would leave the house at dawn and scurry across the wet grass. She scoured the beach and hillsides for food with a wild fervour, searching in the hedgerows for nests and nettles – anything that could be thrown into the pot to stretch out the last of their stored meal.

Spring began to unfold, with tufts of green in the drystone walls, pale yellow primroses in the lanes, and foxgloves spreading their velvety leaves across the damp ground, but none of it was beautiful to Bridie. At night she lay in bed with Brandon and listened to the wind off the

Atlantic battering against the stones of her house, but it sounded with a different voice. The hearth she sat beside, the brown and green landscape with the clouds hanging low over Mount Eagle, none of it was the same without her father in his place. Her *dadai* was underneath the earth, underneath the crowds of snowdrops pushing up through muddy soil and Bridie found no joy in seeing new life sprouting in the fields, no pleasure in the birdsong from the hedgerows.

On a cold spring morning she walked along the beach, staring down at the speckled pink, purple and mauve of the pebbles. Brandon sat on the shore, curled into a little ball, staring out to sea. Beside him was a small pile of limpets that he'd scraped from the rocks.

'Why do you sit here every day, doing nothing but staring out at the sea? We've got to keep moving, you've got to keep searching for something for the pot, boyo.'

'The island out there, the Sleeping Giant. It's not an island. It's our dad out there, see.' Brandon traced the outline of the dark island with his finger. 'See, that's just what he looked like when he was laying on the lid. His spirit's gone out to the island and he's there. The magic is in it and it's singing out to me.'

Bridie sat down beside him and followed his gaze to the island Inishtooskert, a wild, dark shape rising out of the Atlantic.

'That's not our dad and there's no magic in it. You'd best be believing there's no magic in this place any more. There's only misery and hunger,' she said, scraping his small pile of limpets into her skirt and turning her back on the sea.

4

The going away

On a bright May afternoon, Bridie set out with the last of her father's possessions, his boots, his nets and his good knife, hoping to find a buyer. The earth was warm beneath her feet, but the lanes were too quiet. There were no children's voices any more, not even the low, whining sound of the dying. Nearly everyone was gone. Mick O'Farrell had died on the public works, building walls and roads that led nowhere while his family starved. All six of the O'Farrell children had died one after the other, their bellies swollen with hunger, their eyes too big for their faces. There had been no funerals. The last three had died within days of each other and Mrs O'Farrell had waited until she could wrap all three of the little wizened bodies in sacking and take them to the cemetery to be buried together. One day Bridie had seen Mrs O'Farrell sitting huddled on the doorstep of her home, and then a week later the door was blowing open.

All along the laneways, houses lay empty, as if the people had gone out for an evening walk but then never returned. In some houses, the dresser stood with the crockery still upon it. Every day, a steady stream of people climbed over Mount Eagle or took the rugged road around the coast to Dingle.

In the end Bridie had to walk halfway around the peninsula before someone would give her a few pennies for her dad's things. Bridie went home to find Mam sitting close to the fire, rocking Paddy as he moaned in his sleep, with Brandon curled up near her feet. Paddy was starting to look like an O'Farrell child; his cheekbones were too big, his cheeks too sunken, and there was no softness to his little limbs. He didn't want to play any more. Mostly he just slept in Mam's arms.

'We'll have to leave, Mam,' said Bridie. 'We'll have to go like the others or we'll starve, right here in our home.'

'There's no cure for misfortune but to kill it with patience,' said her mother, laying Paddy down on the bed that she'd once shared with their father.

Bridie couldn't stop the words and the fury spilling out. 'The devil sweep your soul, you fool of a *mamai*, the hunger will kill us before patience can win!' she shouted.

'Can we go to America?' asked Brandon, sitting up. 'If we go to America, we could find Uncle Liam.'

Bridie looked at her brother and scowled. 'And bad cess to him, it's never a word we've heard from him since,' she said. 'No, we'll go to Dingle, to Aunt Mairead's house. We'd be cracked to stay here. I've heard there's a soup kitchen in Ventry. We can go through there on our way.'

'That's enough of your slack-jaw, girl,' said her mother quietly. Though her words were stern, her whole body spoke of her exhaustion.

'Your dad always said, "No matter how hungry we get, we'll never stoop to taking the soup",' said Mam, stroking the pale curls away from Paddy's brow.

'But it's the Quakers, Mam! They're not asking anything of us. They're not like the Church of Ireland. I wouldn't go over to the Devil for a bowl of soup, but I'll not watch my brothers die for want of it. I won't be putting our boys in sacks like Kitty O'Farrell. We'll be going to Dingle tomorrow,' said Bridie firmly. 'Blood knows blood, so Aunt Mairead will take us in – and the Quakers will feed us on the way.'

Mam looked at Bridie as if she hardly knew the fierce girl who stood at the end of the bed. 'God help us,' she said, putting her face in her hands.

Brandon wanted to go straight over the top of Mount Eagle, but Bridie said they had to take the coast road. Perhaps they'd be able to beg something from the folk along the way, and besides, none of them had the strength to carry the last of their possessions and Paddy over the high hill.

The last time Bridie had travelled this road with her father, they had set out in the morning and reached Ventry by noon. But this time it took them a day and a half to walk the rutted track, stumbling behind the carts making their way around the peninsula. Bridie took a wooden bowl and begged a morsel at as many doors as would open to her, but most folk were as hungry as the O'Connors. At night she lay curled up against her mother and thought of the man she had tried to feed with nettle soup before he died. Her dreams were full of dark images.

They reached Ventry late the following day to find the soup kitchen closed. A great mound of empty cockle and mussel shells lay piled beside the door. Brandon squatted down and sifted through them with his fingers, sighing wistfully.

Mam wanted to seek shelter in the shadow of Rath Fhionnain, the fort that lay above the town, but Bridie encouraged her to walk a little further to the other side of the village, so that Dingle would be in sight. They stopped in the shade of the Giant's Bed, a huge dolmen like a table made of three slabs of limestone. The space beneath the dolmen was black and still. Some said it was an ancient grave and others thought it the entrance to a fairy world. Brandon climbed onto the biggest flat stone, but Bridie called for him to come down.

'That's the Munsterman's Grave, boyo. You don't want to go waking him now,' she said. 'Come sit beside me, here, and I'll tell you a story about the great giant that lives under these stones.'

Brandon climbed down slowly and snuggled close to their mother.

'I want Mam to tell me the story,' he said.

Bridie put her hands on her hips and glared at Brandon. 'Don't you go bothering our mam. She should be saving her strength for the morrow.' She took out the sticks and turf she'd pilfered along the coast road and set about lighting a small fire to warm her family. The harbour looked blue and inviting in the summer afternoon, yet it was cool in the shelter of the Munsterman's Grave.

'What's that mountain, over there to the north, Mam?' asked Brandon, pointing.

'Why that's Mount Brandon,' she answered, smiling. 'After his blessed self, our own *St Brennain*.'

'Am I like St Brandon, Mam?' asked Brandon, staring up at the mountain.

'Well, he was a great adventurer, like you, my darling. And he sailed to the Promised Land with his brothers and they found the Paradise of Birds and other wonders and that's how the Irish discovered America.'

Bridie sat on the far side of the fire, feeding it with twigs and watching Brandon gazing at Mam's face, and Paddy, like a kitten curled against her side. She longed to crawl over and lay her head in her mother's lap, to shut her eyes and listen to a story. She willed herself to be strong, strong enough to made sure her family reached Aunt Mairead.

Bridie woke early the next morning. There was a mist across the landscape and the Munsterman's Grave looked silver-grey in the half-light. Bridie looked into the face of her sleeping mother. Every line seemed to have grown deeper, her features more careworn than ever. She lay with one thin arm around each of the boys and her hand resting on her swollen, hungry belly. Bridie felt a pang of fear that her mother would be too weak to travel any further.

As her family slept, she hurried across the green fields towards a cluster of houses. Even if she could only beg a crust of bread to start the day, at least that might give her mother enough energy to walk on. She knocked on the first door of the village but no one answered. The quiet chilled her. She hugged her arms around her and walked to the next door. At the end of the lane, the top half of a doorway stood open. She peered into the dark room. A sickly, sour smell wafted out and there was no glow from the fire. In the corner lay a heaped pile of rags. Bridie pushed the door open and stepped into the gloom. She put her fist in her mouth to stifle the scream that swelled inside her. The pile of rags was a group of bodies, huddled together in their last moments, a whole family, their stick-like limbs entwined. Bridie turned and ran, the slap of her feet on the ground echoing through the empty houses.

Dingle was teeming with homeless folk, many of them as ragged and desperate as the O'Connors. People pushed past each other without greeting as if they weren't even there. Bridie tried not to look into their haunted faces. A man stepped out of his shop and waved away the crowds, shouting at them in a language she couldn't understand. 'What's he saying, Mam?' she said pulling at her mother's ragged dress.

'He's speaking English, girl. I'm not sure of the words but you can take his meaning,' she said.

They turned into the laneway where Aunt Mairead lived, where the narrow houses were already cast in shadow. Bridie felt the barrenness of the place before they'd even reached Aunt Mairead's door. The windows and entrance were barred over, and the inside was dark and empty. 'She's gone to America,' said the neighbours. 'Left for Tralee months gone by.'

Mam slumped in the doorway, folding her thin arms around Paddy. Brandon squatted down beside her, uncertain if she was going to cry and whether he should keen with her, but Bridie stood looking up and down the length of the lane, trying to think what their next move should be.

'Mam, we should go to America too,' said Brandon quietly. 'We could go to Tralee and get on a ship and go to find Aunt Mairead. I'd like to go to America.'

'Husha,' said Bridie, angrily. 'Can't you be quiet about America. We none of us want to go there.'

'I do,' said Brandon. Bridie scowled at him and put one arm under her mother to help her stand again.

'There's a hut, down the other side of the town, I saw it when we came in. We'll take the boys back there, Mam.'

As they walked out of town in the late morning sunshine, they saw a man lying dead on the side of the road. Mam put her hand over Brandon's eyes and steered him away from the sight, but Bridie stared hard. She never wanted to forget. The man's mouth was stained green and Bridie looked up at the fields and swore to herself that no matter how hungry she became, she would never eat grass.

The hut had been made in the side of a bog, just four walls cut clean into the dirt. It was eerily still, just like the village of the dead that she'd run from that morning. Bridie looked about for some turf to make a fire with. She didn't want to think why the owners had left the hut.

When she had settled her mother and brothers, Bridie walked back into the village to beg their supper. She stopped and stared again at the dead man with the green mouth. No cart had come to take his corpse away. Around his neck was a small pouch and on his feet a pair of worn boots. Glancing either way along the road, Bridie squatted down beside him and with one swift jerk she pulled the pouch away. Fighting off her disgust, she knelt back down and checked the pockets of the dead man to be sure that was all he had on him. Then quickly, before revulsion could stop her, she pulled the boots from his stiff, cold feet and put them on her own. She walked away swiftly, prying open the leather pouch. The big boots slapped against the road as she walked. Inside the pouch was a single bright shilling. Bridie stopped and stood staring at the coin for a long moment, her mind whirling, her heart on fire. Why had he eaten the grass before spending his last coin? Why had the desperate soul been wearing boots? Was it stealing to take a coin from a corpse?

'Before God,' she said to herself, 'I don't care if I'm a liar and a thief, I'll not have my brothers starve.'

Later that evening, when she'd returned to the hut in the bog with some bread and oatmeal that she'd bought with the shilling, Bridie glanced across at her mother, sitting with Paddy in the crook of her lap. She'd told Mam a kind man had given her both the food and the boots. She knew she couldn't tell Mam what she'd done to the corpse by the wayside that afternoon. Nor would she ever tell her about what she'd seen at the death village that morning. It suddenly made her feel grown old too quickly. She set to work making a small, smoky fire to keep the cold of the night at bay.

5

Fever and changelings

Paddy took ill with the fever that evening. He couldn't even take any of the bread that Bridie had brought back from the town. Mam chewed the crusts and took a tiny morsel out, balancing it on the tip of her finger, trying to feed him as if he was a baby bird and not a boy any more, but he lay limp, his eyes unseeing. That night, his fever grew. His body was a tiny brazen furnace, and his pale gold curls were plastered to his forehead. Mam rocked him in her arms. When she looked too weary to hold him any longer, Bridie took him. His body was like a little bird's, all fine brittle bones folded in her arms. Bridie curled down on the ground and sang to him, a babble of mouth music. She woke to find him cold and stiff. She knew even before she was properly awake that his soul had flown away while they slept.

Mam just wanted to hold Paddy. She sat huddled by the little turf fire that Brandon had rekindled that morning, the small boy in her lap. Bridie took Brandon and led him away from the dirt hut.

'Listen, we have to help Mam,' she said. 'We have to leave her be with Paddy for a while and go down to the marsh. Have you got your little knife?'

Bridie sat on the edge of the marsh while Brandon gathered rushes. At first he only brought her handfuls but when he understood her purpose he worked with a fury, staggering across the marshy ground with armfuls of the dry gold rushes and laying them beside his sister. Bridie wove them together swiftly, fashioning the rushes into a golden basket.

'This can be for Paddy, to hold him for the last. You see, I'll make the sides high so he'll feel safe inside there and the cold breeze won't get to our darling boy,' she said, not even feeling the tears that streamed down her face as she worked. Brandon stared at her with bright eyes, his mouth twisted with grief, and then sat down on the damp ground beside her and put his facc in his hands.

When Bridie had finished, she carried the basket back to the bog and set it before their mother. Mam looked up at her as if Bridie was the grown-up and she the little child. Bridie reached down and took Paddy's still body from her mother's arms and laid him tenderly in the rush basket. Mam bent over the basket and kissed him and then turned away.

Brandon followed Bridie up to the famine cemetery that had been set up high on the hill behind the town. A cart laden with bodies trundled up the *bothereen*, the rutted track that led to the graveyard. The wind was at their back as they trudged behind the death cart. The graveyard was just a field with a low drystone wall around it. Dirt was turned over in great heaps everywhere, piled high above the trenches where the bodies were stacked, dozens and dozens of them.

When Bridie saw the careless way the man took the basket from her, she wanted to strike him. But she turned away, took Brandon's hand and ran back down to the village, taking breaths of air so sharp she felt her lungs would burst. She didn't want to see Paddy laid in the ground, to see the small basket flying to its final resting place. When they were out of sight of the famine pit, she fell to her knees by the roadside and prayed. Brandon knelt beside her, his lips moving soundlessly and together they keened, in a voiceless grief.

After Paddy died, Mam wasn't herself any more. It was as if a strange woman had moved into her thin body. Every day she crawled to the top of the nearest dune and sat staring out across the sea, her eyes the same deep blue as the waters of Dingle Bay. Then early one morning, she stood up and said, 'We're not staying here. The fever is in this place. I'll not watch my babies die one by one.'

They followed her back into the town where thousands of other displaced people wandered aimlessly and squalor and chaos met them at every turn. They stood on a corner for a long while that morning, holding out their bowls, begging. Bridie shut her eyes. She couldn't bear to see the pity on people's faces. No one gave them anything. There were beggars on every corner and people lined up outside the priest's house crying to be fed.

In the late afternoon, they passed out of the town and headed towards the beach. On the far side of the dunes, by the roadside that led up towards the cliffs, they found a ditch where the wind off the harbour couldn't reach them. They huddled down for the night. Bridie lay awake for a long while, staring up at the stars. She couldn't understand why she wasn't weary. Streaks of pale pink and green light began to appear in the sky above her. 'Maybe the world is near an end,' she thought. She crawled across to where her mother and brother lay and snuggled in close against her mother's back.

That night, as they slept in the open air, Bridie woke to the sound of her mother gasping in pain.

'Mam, Mam, what is it? What's wrong?'

Her mother's eyes were wild and dark in the moonlight and she pushed Bridie away from her.

'The baby, the baby's coming, Bridie.'

'The baby?' Bridie held her mother's sinewy hand and shut her eyes and prayed, prayed as she'd never prayed before. 'Take the baby, sweet Jesus, but leave us our Mam.'

When it came, at last, just before dawn, it was a tiny thing, small enough to fit in the palm of Mam's hand, and its skin was a strange pale green colour in the half-light. A changeling, too small to be human; a girl child, but too strange to be Bridie's own sister. Bridie stared at it as it lay curled on Mam's shawl, so still. Her prayer had been answered. Mam's brow was damp with sweat, her skin clammy to touch. She folded her shawl over the baby and pushed it away from her.

While her mother slept, Bridie carefully gathered up the tiny changeling and climbed out over the side of the ditch. She walked down to the sea. When she reached the shore, she wrapped the baby in seaweed, winding thick dark strands of kelp around the tiny body. She didn't hesitate when she reached the water's edge, walking straight into the icy water. The dark bundle bobbed and weaved on the waves as she released it, floating out to sea, out to the mouth of the harbour, and on to the deep waters of the bay.

6

Road into darkness

Bridie woke on damp sand, and in a cloud of whiteness. A thick fog had rolled in over the water and covered the beach while she slept. When she held her hand out in front of her, she could barely see the outline of her fingers. She sat up and drew her knees against her chest. She was chilled to her marrow, and her ragged clothes were heavy with dew. The sound of the waves rolling in and her own jagged breathing was muffled by the fog; and yet she could hear voices – her father, the O'Farrells, little Paddy, and even the strange changeling baby. It was as if they were all just out of her sight, but she felt their presence so strongly that she could almost imagine the touch of their hands on her skin. For a moment she wondered if she too was close to death. Maybe this wasn't a fog at all, but the dream place between living and dying. Maybe she had been washed away, beyond the ninth wave to a new world. But the cold sand beneath her felt rough against her skin and she could hear her own heart beating, blood pounding at her temples. She stood up slowly. Like a blind girl, one hand stretched before her, she walked into the swirling mist. She could still hear voices in the fog, but now they sounded real and warm and firm, not the voices of the dead. She couldn't decide which direction they came from. It was the brightness that caught her eye and guided her forward. She stared at the point of light, a small flicker of orange and gold in the still, heavy mist.

There were a dozen people gathered around the blaze. Bridie stepped into the ring of light cast by the fire. No one spoke to her as she drew close to the flame and warmed her hands. It was as if life was flowing back into her. She gazed into the embers, not speaking, a strange calm spreading through her as the warmth crept into her body. She'd been cold for so long.

'You'll join us for something to warm the cockles of your heart as well, won't you, child?' asked a woman. She looked at Bridie with sharp blue eyes, and a network of little wrinkles creased her face as she smiled. Bridie stared disbelievingly and drew her wooden bowl and spoon out from under her dress and held it up. The woman nodded approval.

The big pot was taken off the fire and everyone gathered round. The delicious smell made Bridie feel faint. The woman ladled out the rich broth.

'Now you mind, little one, not to eat too much nor too swift. When you've been fasting, your body's not used to the shock of a good feed. Some poor souls kill themselves trying to eat too much too fast.'

Bridie took tiny little sips of the broth and felt the warmth of it through every part of her body.

'And now you've supped with us, you'll not tell anyone what you've had,' said the old woman.

'It was a stolen sheep, wasn't it?' asked Bridie haltingly. 'Can I take some for my mam and my brother? Just a peck of something. If you give me a bone with a bit of meat left on it, I could fix something for them.'

'Are you the little girl from the hut, west of the village?'

'To be sure, but we're from Ballyickeen, above Dunquin,' said Bridie, finally finding herself again. 'We came to Dingle to be with my Aunt Mairead but she'd gone to America. Then my little brother died and Mam wouldn't stay in the hut 'cause she said it's where Paddy caught the fever and surely we'd all die if we stayed there, so we're sleeping in a ditch up beyond the dunes.' The words tumbled out in a rush.

'Bridie?' came a voice through the mist. 'Bridie O'Connor?'

Mrs MacMahon stepped around from the far side of the fire. Bridie hardly recognised her. They'd not seen each other since the day her father had lain on the lid in the MacMahons' cottage at Dunquin. 'Where's your mother, girl?'

The fog was lifting and the harbour was azure in the morning sun as they walked over the dunes. Bridie led Mrs MacMahon to the ditch by the roadside. Curled in a huddle of rags at the bottom lay Mam and Brandon.

Mrs MacMahon knelt down beside Mam and stroked her hair. 'Maire, it's Kitty MacMahon. We're going to Tralee, Maire. You and your little ones must come along with us. There's nothing here in Dingle for any of us, nothing but misery and grief – but the workhouse in Tralee might take us all in.'

Mam gave a short cough, almost like a laugh. 'Heaven help me, Kitty, I couldn't walk to Tralee, I'm bound for the long road. But the children must go. Take the children. If I should get my strength back, I'll follow you. You're a fine friend to me, Kitty, a fine good woman, you are,' she said, and then she lay back down in the dirt, trembling.

Mrs MacMahon rested one hand on Mam's brow and stroked it tenderly. 'Now, you lay there a minute longer and rest yourself, Maire. Muiris and I won't be leaving until all the mists have cleared. If you find your strength, you could join us.'

Mrs MacMahon took Brandon by the hand and tried to lead him up out of the ditch, but he looked wild and tore his hand away, kneeling down beside his mother and burrowing his face against her side. Mrs MacMahon looked down and shook her head.

'We'll wait on the beach for the children,' she said, moving away from the edge of the ditch.

Bridie knelt beside her mother and looked straight into her dark eyes. 'Mam, we can wait until you're stronger. Then we can go together,' she whispered.

Mam turned towards Bridie as she cradled Brandon's head with one hand.

'No, Bridie, I want you to go with Mrs MacMahon. I want you to take Brandon and for you both to go to Tralee and find shelter. There's nothing for us here.'

'But we don't want to leave you,' said Bridie, her voice rising.

Mam reached up and touched Bridie gently on the cheek to calm her.

'Bridie, you know what you must do.'

'I won't,' said Bridie, angry tears pricking her eyes. 'You'll come with us. You'll come now.'

Bridie forced one arm under her mother's back and tried to make her rise. 'Help me, Brandon. Help Mam,' she said through gritted teeth, trying to take her mother's weight on her shoulder.

'Bridie, girl, no,' moaned Mam, a shudder coursing through her as she sank to the ground.

Bridie knelt down to make Mam try again but suddenly Brandon reached across and slapped Bridie hard across the face.

'Leave her be, leave our mam alone,' he shouted.

Bridie stepped away from them both and sat near the edge of the ditch, staring down at her mother and brother. Mam was stroking Brandon's face and whispering to him as he lay nestled against her. The day grew bright and clear with only a touch of autumn cold. Bridie felt as though a storm should break over them, like the storm that was raging inside of her, but nothing more than a light breeze came drifting off the water.

It seemed they'd been sitting for hours when Mam called to Bridie, stretching one hand out to her. Brandon climbed up to take Bridie's place, gazing out to sea.

Bridie pressed her face against her mother's neck and wrapped her arms tight around the thin, fragile body. 'It's my fault, Mam. I never should have made us come here. We'll go home now,' she wept, fiercely. 'I've brought the bad luck to us. I've lied and I've stolen from the dead and I've brought my family to this bad place. Mam, Mam, we'll go home again and somehow things will come right.' She choked back the tears, gasping as she spoke.

'My little lamb,' said Mam, taking Bridie's hands and folding her thin, hot fingers around them. 'There never was a brave woman who was not crooked and straight, and better we look for hope in the world than die lonely by our own hearth. Don't you have a care for your mam. I'll quench my thirst from the Stream of Glory before too long. Now, you'll be my brave, fierce girl and do as your mam asks.'

Bridie wept until her face and throat were raw. It was as if her heart, which had been aching for so long, had finally been torn apart.

'God direct you and give you courage for the long road, darling child,' said Mam.

Bridie kissed her mother on the brow and then, gasping at the pain inside her, she staggered up out of the ditch.

Brandon walked beside Bridie, not looking at her as they made their way down to the beach. Bridie felt frightened by how still and quiet he was, his face fixed in an inscrutable expression. 'Brandon,' she said, trying hard to keep the bitterness from her tone. 'This is what Mam wants us to do.'

Brandon turned and looked at her with his pale blue eyes and Bridie realised he was not accusing her. 'We'll have our little house, one day, won't we, Bridie? The one half-gold and half-silver, and our mam will watch over us there, won't she?'

Bridie slipped her arm around her brother. 'To be sure, darling boy,' she said, though the future stretched out before her like a road into darkness.

7

The death-house

The small crowd of ragged travellers moved steadily up the road away from town. Bridie didn't look back, but she prayed, her lips moving fervently as they followed the path up to the Connor Pass on the road to Tralee. Hundreds of men and women were labouring to build a road over the mountain. Their shoulder bones stuck sharply through the thin fabric of their clothing and their eyes were glazed as they dug or hauled stones up the steep hillside.

It took all of the long afternoon to climb to where the path cut through the mountains. Bridie turned and gazed back at the land laid out behind them, at the arms of the peninsula wrapped around the harbour. Brandon said nothing as they all sat resting at the summit, but she could hear him humming quietly to himself, a strange, lonely tune.

Low clouds lay like fairy mist over the landscape and Bridie felt a stab of grief that somewhere so beautiful should be so cruel. She prayed for all the people she was leaving behind, her father at Dunquin, Paddy in the cemetery behind the town, and the strange changeling sister in the waters of the harbour. Most of all, she prayed for her mother, closing her hands and forcing hope against hope from her heart into the blue sky.

It seemed the whole of Ireland was on the move. Bridie didn't look at the crumpled bodies by the wayside. She looked ahead, at the long road that wound its way around the peninsula and led to Tralee.

The adults didn't talk with Brandon and Bridie often. Even Mrs MacMahon said little to them, as if any word spoken would take away from the energy she needed to take the next step. They slept by the roadside, huddled together for warmth, and rose early in the morning to continue the journey.

At Tralee, the streets teemed with people. There were soldiers in uniform, fat merchants, fine ladies in bonnets and full skirts; so many people who looked prosperous. Bridie found it hard to understand how some could be so well-fed when Dingle was full of wraiths. Brandon clung to Bridie's arm, pressing himself against her. She tried not to show how overwhelmed she felt as people jostled them in the crowds and she struggled to keep up with the MacMahons.

When they reached the workhouse gates, they discovered a swelling crowd waiting outside. People jostled for a place and argued in whining tones. The air reverberated with the babble of English and Irish, the low wail of some child, the cry of its mother, as scores of people waited to be taken into the workhouse.

Bridie kept a firm grip on Brandon's wrist and stood behind the MacMahons as they approached the porter of the workhouse. The man looked exasperated at Mr MacMahon's questions and answered them in English.

Even though she couldn't understand what he said, Bridie knew by his expression that it didn't augur well for them. She tugged at Mrs MacMahon's dress.

'What's he saying?'

'He's saying there's no place for us here,' she said wearily, not meeting Bridie's gaze.

Bridie felt her scar burn hot as she flushed with anger. She pushed her way forward and stood defiantly before the porter.

'We've come from Dingle,' shouted Bridie, as if raising her voice would make it possible for him to understand her better. 'We've walked all this way because they said in Dingle that you'd take us in. My brother and me, we left our mam because she said you'd give us shelter.'

The porter turned away as if she were invisible.

'There'll only be room if more of them die,' whispered a thin, dark man sitting hunched by the steps. 'In the morning, when they take away the dead, then they let some of us who's waiting in.' The man looked close to death himself. 'I'm praying they'll find space for me inside before the day is out. 'Tis a terrible fate to die in the gutter.'

Bridie and Brandon sat down with the MacMahons and waited. As the day wore on more people arrived and milled outside the workhouse gate. A tradesman fought his way through the raggedy, starving crowd and the porter let him in, shouting at people to stand back. Bridie looked along the line. The thin, dark man they'd talked with when they first arrived had closed his eyes, and Bridie knew he wouldn't get his wish to die inside the walls of the workhouse.

Bridie had caught a glimpse of the inside of the building.

It looked like a big stone prison with dark figures moving about in the rank stillness. Something about it reminded her of the death village. The terrible wails of the crowd seemed to echo inside her head. Bridie drew her knees up against her chest, shut her eyes and covered her ears with her hands, not wanting to hear their cries. Suddenly, she felt Brandon's small hand reaching for hers. She grasped it, and turned to look at her brother with gratitude, as if he'd brought her back from the brink of hell.

'We're not waiting here,' she said. 'We're not ready to die.' She stood up, pulled him to his feet and dragged him to the end of the street.

Mrs MacMahon glanced up and raised a hand to beckon them back, but Bridie moved away quickly, weaving through the crowd and out into a wide street.

'Where are we going?' asked Brandon, frowning. 'Mrs MacMahon says they might have room for us tomorrow if we'll be patient. She says Mam would want us to wait and that she promised she'd come after us.'

'If she promised you that, boyo, then she promised a lie. Mam won't be coming after us and that place is a death-house, not a workhouse. This wasn't what our mam meant for us.'

Brandon flinched. Bridie felt a wave of grief and guilt break against her as the weight of her words made him hunch over in pain. How could he have not understood what leaving Mam had meant? He said nothing more, and his silence hurt her more than any accusation. Suddenly, it struck her how much more like Paddy he looked, each day, closer to becoming an angel. He folded his thin arms around himself and his face fell into the shadow of a swathe of red hair. She wanted to take him in her arms and comfort him, to hold him close and whisper lovingly, but the idea of it made her feel as if she'd unravel around him. She reached out and grabbed his wrist, dragging him onwards through the crowded streets. Bridie wasn't sure where she was going, but she knew she had to get as far away from that death-house as she could, and movement fuelled her will to live.

Suddenly, they found themselves down by the docks, where the masts of great ships stood black against the blue morning sky. People lined the quays. Soldiers stood guard, their bayoneted guns ready to fight off the crowds as great sacks of meal and grain were loaded on board ships bound for England. Everywhere she looked, there were soldiers standing guard over the food supplies.

Further along the quay, a boat was casting off. As it moved away from the dock, the passengers lined up along the deck reached out their hands and called to those they were leaving behind. There was a tumult of weeping, grieving families, crying out for their departing relatives. An old woman fell to her knees beside Bridie and Brandon, keening as if death was all around them, crying out for her children who were sailing to America, knowing that would be the last she'd see of them.

Brandon stood staring up at the masts.

'Are we going to get on a ship, to take us to America?' he asked, and for the first time his voice had a spur of hope in it. 'We could go to Aunt Mairead. We could find Uncle Liam. I want to go there, Bridie. I want to go to America.'

Bridie wanted to box his ears, even if he did look like an angel. 'Those ships, you know what they call them?

They call them coffin ships. You want to go and be buried in America?' she said scornfully. She grabbed him by his scrawny wrist and dragged him away from the quay.

'Where are we going?' asked Brandon.

'We're going to find shelter,' she said, taking the road out of Tralee.

8

Black dogs and broken houses

Ragged people were pouring into the town. Bridie and Brandon passed hundreds of people, like ghosts, drifting along the roadways. Some just sat by the wayside and stared vacantly into the pale sky. Others were wild-eyed, moving their gaunt limbs with fierce intent.

Bridie felt better just being away from the town, with the open sky above her head and green fields and drystone walls stretching out before them. In the late afternoon they came to a roadside inn, a lone building at a crossroads where the road forked in three directions.

'Let's try our luck,' said Bridie. 'We'll beg a crust from the innkeeper.'

They crept around the back of the building and looked in through the kitchen door. A big cauldron of mutton broth was cooking in a pot over the fire. Bridie stood patiently in the doorway, but as soon as she realised there was no one about, she put a finger to her lips and whispered to Brandon, 'You've got your spoon, boyo?' He nodded and pulled the spoon out from under his clothes.

'Then we needs both be quick.' The two children tiptoed into the kitchen and dipped their spoons into the hot broth. There was no time to blow on the spoonful to cool the soup. Neither of them cared if their mouths were scalded. Bridie looked around frantically, searching for something else to take away with her, but then the kitchen door swung open and a big woman stood glaring at them.

'Please, ma'am,' begged Bridie. 'It was just a taste we were after.'

The woman sighed and pushed the two of them towards the door. 'Not safe in my own kitchen, from thieves and beggars.' She looked down as she was about to slam the door and suddenly she softened. She darted back inside and came out, thrusting a small loaf of bread into Bridie's hands.

'Be gone with you,' she said.

Bridie thanked her and slipped the loaf into the front of her ragged dress as they walked away. The crust felt warm against her skin. Carefully, she broke a little piece for herself and Brandon.

'We're going to make this last and last,' she told him.

They didn't make much progress that day. They spent a long time picking blackberries from a bramble that sprawled over a fence by the roadside. The juice stained their lips so their faces seemed even paler with their dark mouths.

They came to the broken village as the evening came down around them. There was nothing left of it. Someone had torn the lintels from the doorways and the houses had collapsed in on themselves.

'Do you think there are ghosts in this one?' asked Brandon, looking around at the ruins of the hamlet.

Bridie swung a leg over the remains of a cabin wall. There was still some peat beside the fireplace. She pushed through the pile of ashes in the hearth.

'It's not that long since there were folk living here,' she said. She knelt down in the ruins of the house, raking through the debris. Strewn among the rubble were dozens of St Brigid crosses, fallen from the rafters. Bridie picked one up and cradled it in her hand. All those crosses, from years and years of prayer and hope. All the promise of a safekeeping come to nothing.

They found a corner of the ruins where there was just enough shelter to keep the night damp from settling on them, and curled up together among the stones. Brandon fell asleep quickly with his head on Bridie's shoulder, but Bridie lay awake a long while, gazing between the splintered rafters at the cold and distant stars. She thought of the night she'd gazed up at that same sky by her father's side, and puzzled at how quickly all the wonder could drain out of something so beautiful.

In the morning, they ran through the village and climbed down to a nearby brook. They knelt on its banks, their hands cupped, and took long drinks of the cold water. Bridie broke some more off the loaf and they sat listening to the peaceful flow of the brook.

Next morning, they reached another village, but there the lintels were still in place. They'd been walking for only two hours and already they felt weak with exhaustion. Bridie looked across at her brother and knew they couldn't keep travelling like this. They sat side by side on the edge of the road. She'd nearly given up hope of their moving anywhere that day when she noticed a small cart laden with barrels moving slowly down the main street.

'Here's a chance for us, bucko,' she said. While the carter was waiting for the crowds to thin, Bridie gave

Brandon a leg up onto the back and then scrambled up after him. She prayed no one would alert the driver. They slipped in between the barrels, which smelt strongly of oily tar, and each found themselves a little pocket of space. The wood chafed against their skin, but the slow rhythm of the cart gradually lulled them to sleep.

Bridie was struggling to wake up, struggling to free herself. In her dream, a banshee was dragging her down into a dark, murky pool, but when she woke it was the carter, pulling her out from between the barrels, shouting crossly at her in English.

He dragged a struggling Brandon out as well and held them both by their ankles. Bridie kept her arms wrapped tight across her chest to keep her loaf of bread secure but Brandon yelped and struggled so the man dropped him in a heap. Slowly, the carter lowered Bridie to the ground.

She brushed at the dirt on her ragged dress and tried to stand tall before the broad-shouldered man.

He said something else in English. When Bridie and Brandon looked at each other and shrugged sullenly, he tried again, this time in Irish.

'So what were you hoping for other than a hiding, sneaking into my cart like that?' he asked.

'We're going to the east,' answered Bridie. 'To find a workhouse.'

'But there's one in Tralee.'

'They wouldn't have us. They're full to bursting – with dying people. It's not a workhouse, it's a death-house. They've got the fever bad there. Things might be better in the east. Dan O'Connell is in the east and my dad said he'd tried to make Ireland a better place for all of us.'

'He did, did he?' said the carter. 'Well, I don't know that Dan O'Connell will be able to help you. There's a workhouse I know of that maybe's got a place for two fleas like yourselves. But we can't be standing here all the day, jawing on like this. The road's a dangerous place these days and I've got to get this load to town before dark, so let's be moving along now.'

They climbed up and sat either side of the carter on the bench.

'You're not carrying anything that thieves would want to steal, are you?' asked Bridie.

'Desperate men will do desperate things in desperate times,' he said. 'Why, you can't leave poor old Nellie for a moment. Only yesterday, I found some men sticking thorns in her and sucking out her blood. I should have beaten them for causing my Nellie grief, but the buggers were a whisker away from death anyway. As if drinking the old nag's blood would save them.' He shook his head disbelievingly.

As the afternoon wore on, a low mist settled over the road. Up ahead, dark animal shapes moved mysteriously in a bank of fog. The carter moved the reins across to one hand and reached beneath the seat to draw out a big, thick stick with a hard knobbly end on it.

'What's the matter?' asked Bridie.

'Wild dogs,' said the carter, his face set hard.

He climbed down with his staff and took the horse's halter, leading her into the fog. The dogs began to howl.

'They won't harm us, will they, Bridie?' asked Brandon. 'We're Ó*Conchobhairs* and they're our friends. Dad always said that's what our name meant – friend of the wolves.'

Bridie ignored him and kept a firm grip on the reins.

The driver called back to them. 'You two keep jawing, they don't like the sound of us talking – make as much noise as you can.'

'Should we sing?' asked Bridie.

'That's a grand idea, girl,' said the driver.

Bridie began to hum one of the songs her mother had taught her. Then she sang of the beautiful girl whose true love was stolen by the fairy queen and who then had to search all of Ireland for him. Brandon sang too. Their voices sounded eerie, muted by the heavy fog. Every now and then they could hear a low growl from the wild dogs circling the cart. In the short silence that followed the end of the song, the first dog took its chance and leapt out at the carter. He was ready for it; the knobbly end of his stick met the dog's skull with a sickening crack. Then other dogs came out of the fog, leaping at the horse and snapping at her throat. The carter was swinging his stick wildly now, standing in the middle of the roadway and knocking the rangy hounds to the ground. Nellie whinnied frantically and shied away. Bridie pulled hard on the reins and gave the horse no head, but it was straining to break free. Suddenly, Brandon scrambled past Bridie and jumped lightly onto the horse's back, murmuring into her ear and stroking her head. When the carter had beaten the last dog away and two lay dead by the roadside, he turned and looked at Brandon with astonishment.

'Well, if you two haven't turned out to be a bit of luck for me,' he said cheerfully, lifting Brandon off Nellie's back and hoisting him onto the bench.

Brandon looked at Bridie, aglow with pride, and for the first time since they'd left Dunquin Bridie laughed out loud.

9

Pilgrim souls

Bridie saw it from a distance: a long, tall building, four storeys high, with tiny windows all along its length. She tried to make herself feel glad that they were at last going to find shelter, that their fortunes were changing.

There was a crowd of people gathered around the gate of this workhouse too, though not so many as at Tralee. As the cart drew closer, Bridie saw a tall, thin man in a black coat, followed by two helpers, crossing the workhouse yard to the gate where the people were waiting. A chain bound the gates shut. The black-coated man turned a big key in the lock and opened the gates.

'There you go,' said the carter. 'Just in time, they're taking some in.'

Bridie jumped off the cart, but Brandon didn't follow. 'Climb down, then,' she said. Brandon didn't move. He stared ahead with a hunted expression.

'Can't I keep with you a while longer?' he asked, turning to the carter. 'I could help you with Nellie. I wouldn't be much trouble.'

The carter's face suddenly closed over. He gave Brandon a little shove.

'You'll have to get off here, boy,' he said, looking away.

'Brandon,' Bridie said crossly. 'This is what our mam wanted, for us find a safe place, and now we've found it. Get down.'

'But what if they won't take us and we die in the ditch?' asked Brandon.

The carter sighed and leapt down from his vehicle. Grabbing each of the children by the wrist, he pushed his way through the crowd to the front of the gate.

The man in black was shouting at everyone, gesturing for some to come in and others to wait, but the carter pushed Brandon and Bridie ahead of him and shouted at the workhouse porter to get his attention. They stood arguing with each other fiercely.

Bridie couldn't understand what they were saying. It seemed the whole world spoke this ugly language. She looked from one face to the next as the carter angrily pointed at the porter and then at the children. In the confusion, a tall, fair-haired girl sidled up and smiled at Bridie, resting one hand on her shoulder. She felt too bewildered to shrug the girl off. Suddenly, the carter was pushing them towards the porter and mumbling a hurried goodbye. The big gates of the workhouse started to swing shut again and Bridie and Brandon and the fair-haired girl were swept down the path towards the workhouse.

Inside the big doors, another man in a black coat was asking questions of the people and scribbling things down in a big ledger. Bridie listened carefully, trying to guess what the questions were by listening to the answers that the people ahead of her gave.

'Name?'

‘*Bríde ÓConchobhair, agus dearth____ir Bhréanainn ÓConchobhair,*’ said Bridie, drawing Brandon beside her and pulling herself up to her full height.

The man looked up from his ledger and sighed.

‘Speak English, girl,’ he said.

Bridie didn’t answer. She wasn’t sure how to answer. She’d heard so little English that she couldn’t think *how* her own name would sound in that strange tongue. Suddenly, the tall pale girl stepped up behind Bridie. She said something that Bridie recognised as her own and Brandon’s names. Bridie realised the girl must have understood the argument between the carter and the porter and joined her because of it.

Bridie looked up at the girl, bewildered. She looked to be a couple of years older, perhaps thirteen, and she wore her hair in a long golden plait down to her waist. She was so fair that even her eyebrows and eyelashes were a pale silvery-gold colour that merged with the whiteness of her skin. Her bones showed through the worn fabric of her clothes, and her fragile hands and feet were suffused with blue. Bridie listened carefully to the girl’s answers and understood her name was Caitlin Moriarty.

When the questions were over, Bridie tried to thank the girl for her help, but she simply shrugged.

‘You made it easier for me to slip through the gate, so I’m paying my debt. You’ll have to learn English. The Irish won’t serve you well in here.’

Bridie couldn’t imagine making sense of the new language. Caitlin saw her distress. ‘You will learn,’ she said, repeating her reassurance in both English and Irish. Bridie mouthed the new words, trying to fix them in her mind.

‘You’ve been here before?’

'Not this workhouse, but others. First with my family, and now, I'm on my own,' said the older girl grimly.

They passed through the big, dark entrance hall of the workhouse. The flagstones were cold beneath their bare feet. Another tall man in a black coat stood watching the new arrivals with a stern expression.

'Who's that?' asked Bridie.

'The Master of the workhouse,' whispered Caitlin.

'There'll be no talking,' snapped a thin woman in an apron. 'You, with the lads,' she ordered, shoving Brandon towards a group of dishevelled boys. 'You girls, with the lasses.' She pointed Bridie in the opposite direction.

'I have to keep with my brother,' said Bridie, following her.

'Out of my way, girl. Get in line,' snapped the woman.

Caitlin put out a hand to draw her back. 'You must mind what they tell you and do as I do, or there'll be nothing but misery for you here,' she said.

Bridie watched Brandon as he followed the other boys up a flight of stairs. At the top, he looked back at her. Their eyes met and that moment was like a thorn in Bridie's heart. She took a fold of Caitlin's ragged skirt in her hand and hung onto it as the girls walked in single file to a long, open courtyard, where they were made to strip off their clothes and scrub at open troughs of cold water in the fading afternoon light. Then they were given the workhouse uniform. Bridie tried to keep her spoon, the last remnant of her old life, but it was swept away with her clothes. An angry-looking woman led them from one part of the workhouse to another, explaining the rules in shouted English. The words washed over Bridie in an incomprehensible tide.

Towards the end of the afternoon, they were marched into a room with a long table and given a bowl of stirabout, a thin porridge full of yellow meal, and a piece of dry bread. Some of the girls ate like wolves, but Bridie tried to savour every mouthful and ate the bread slowly, dipping it in the porridge so her gums wouldn't bleed when she ate it.

The girls climbed another flight of stairs that led to the top floor of the workhouse. Inside the main room was a long walkway, almost like a trough, with raised wooden platforms running along either side. The platforms were covered with a scattering of straw and hundreds of women were already crammed onto them. The room was full of coughing and whimpering as the women tossed and turned. Bridie and the other new girls were herded to the end of the room, where a small area of fresh straw lay waiting for them. Every second girl was handed a thin blanket to share. Bridie stayed close to Caitlin so they got to share a blanket. As they lay beside each other in the straw, Bridie stared up into the rafters and wished she had the open sky above her still. Even though it was good to be warm, the air here was close and thick with noise and rank smells.

'Things are getting worse,' said Caitlin. 'They gave us each a mattress and a blanket last time I came to the workhouse. I lay with my sister then.'

'Where is she now?'

'Dead of the fever,' said Caitlin brusquely, turning her back on Bridie and hiking the blanket up to her chin.

'And your mam and dad?'

'Dead. I told you. They're all dead.'

'Do you miss your mam most or your dad or is it your sister?'

'Do you have to ask so many questions?' said Caitlin.

Bridie curled into a ball with her fists clenched and her eyes shut tight, and wished sleep would come, but her body was trembling and her mind whirling with thoughts of Brandon. Was he lying in the dark afraid? Who would watch out for him among all those other boys? Would she lose even him, as Caitlin had lost everyone?

'Can you stop your quivering, girl?' said Caitlin, sighing and sitting up to look at Bridie.

'I'm thinking of my little brother, God help him.'

Caitlin reached out and rested one hand on Bridie's shoulder until the warmth of her touch stilled Bridie's shivering. 'God direct you,' she said softly. 'The boy's not lost to you yet. There's nothing for it now but to put the thought of this evil day on the long finger.'

10

Riot

Morning sun streamed in through the tiny window panes, catching motes of dust and fragments of straw. Bridie was pushed along by a crowd of girls to the end of the dormitory. Women with brooms swept fetid straw into the long troughs and then another woman unlatched a door so the straw could be swept out into the yard below. Bridie watched it float down through the wintry air, and wished she was falling with it. She sneezed and shuffled after the other girls to start the working day.

Bridie had lost track of the number of days since she had arrived at the workhouse. The weeks had stretched into months, and she'd only glimpsed Brandon at a distance. She hadn't been able to talk with him once. Boys and girls were kept completely separate from each other.

The first days had passed in a blur of confusion as she struggled to learn all the rules of the workhouse. New girls were set to tasks each morning, scrubbing first the big flagstones in the hallway and then the long flights of wooden stairs, black with trodden muck. Bridie's hands grew red and raw from being constantly in water. The only compensation was that she worked alongside Caitlin.

Caitlin insisted she learn more English but sometimes Bridie would beg her to speak in Irish for a while so she could hear the warm rhythms of their mother tongue. Mostly Caitlin refused. 'I'm doing you a grand favour, girl. The sooner you learn the English, the better,' she would say.

As much as she resented it, Bridie knew Caitlin was right. Slowly, the orders of the Matron stopped sounding like a babble of sound and began to have meaning, though sometimes knowing what was being said was worse than wandering in a fog of ignorance. There was never any kindness in the Matron's remarks.

One day, Bridie was working on the stairs that led to the Master's rooms when she heard shouts. The door to the dining hall downstairs was forced open and a stream of shouting men and boys poured out into the forecourt. Behind them came dozens of policemen and warders beating the men across the shoulders with batons, herding them into the yard. Bridie leaned over the balustrade and stared down in amazement at the tumult beneath.

Suddenly, among the crowd of crazed men and boys she saw Brandon's flame-red, tousled hair as he was thrown against the wall directly beneath her. He had one arm raised to shield himself from the fierce blows of a policeman.

'Brandon! Brandon!' called Bridie, but her voice was lost in the roar of the rioting men. Frantically, she reached for the bucket behind her and heaved it over the balustrade, drenching a policeman with filthy, grey water. She was about to fling the bucket down on the policeman's head as well when an iron hand caught her wrist.

'No you don't,' said the Master, dragging her up the last few steps to the landing.

That night, Bridie lay in the darkness weeping with rage and despair. Her hands and back ached from the beating Matron had inflicted on her, but the pain in her heart was worse. She couldn't drive away the image of Brandon cowering beneath the policeman's baton.

As if she could read Bridie's thoughts, Caitlin shifted and put her arm gently around Bridie, whispering, 'There's hope from a prison, but none from the grave.'

Bridie discovered that the men had been rioting because a fever was taking hold of their wards, and the bodies of the dying were being left among the living. After the riot, those who fell ill were taken across the fields to the empty cotton mills. Bridie shuddered to think of what it must be like there. No one came back. The faces in the wards changed from one day to the next as the fever-struck were taken away and still more paupers were let in at the gates. Some mornings, the body of someone who had died during the night would be carried out of the dormitory. Bridie heard of a chamber they called the Black Room where the bodies were kept until the corpse-gatherers came to take them away.

Bridie was scrubbing the workhouse steps when the death cart drove up outside, having collected its first load from the cotton mills. She hardly noticed the clatter of wheels as it pulled into the courtyard. It was the silence of the other girls that made her look up. In the grey morning, men were loading dead bodies, emaciated men, women and children, onto the cart like old sacks. The last body they slung into the cart was that of a woman, her dark hair a tangle, her face a sunken white mask. For a long and terrible moment, Bridie was frozen with horror, thinking of her mother, of her face warm and alive but ravaged by the fever. She turned back to her work, wishing she could scrub away the images of the dead that filled her mind.

That evening, before they lay down in the straw, Bridie pressed her face against the cold glass of the window and stared out into the darkness, imagining the big, ugly courtyard and the dark black fields beyond. She tried to make herself feel the fire inside, the fire her dad had told her would never stop burning, but it felt like nothing more than dying embers.

'What are you looking at?' asked Caitlin, coming up behind her and staring out into the black night.

'Nothing,' said Bridie despondently.

11

Angel, go before me

Caitlin never missed an opportunity to make things easier for herself and Bridie. Bridie told Caitlin what a fine seamstress her mother had been and how she missed those mornings when they sat in the sun outside their cabin and sewed together. When the Matron came looking for girls to do needlework, Caitlin stepped forward, dragging Bridie along beside her. Each morning they were taken downstairs to sew in a small room alongside several other women and girls. Bridie had a quick, deft hand and could make beautiful stitches but she soon realised Caitlin knew next to nothing about sewing. Bridie covered for her as best she could, leaning across and whispering helpful instructions and Caitlin quickly learnt how to make her needle fly.

When summer came, Bridie heard the potato crop had failed yet again and the queues at the workhouse gates grew even longer and more desperate. Sometimes she would hear the wails of paupers waiting for the gates to be opened. The portions of bread in the workhouse grew smaller, the soup and porridge as thin as water. On hot summer nights, the smell of death and disease lay like a heavy blanket across the girls' ward. Bridie's chest felt tight with anxiety that perhaps the boys' ward was the same and that the fever would take Brandon away. Occasionally Bridie had seen him at a distance, hoeing the ground in the workhouse gardens with other boys, but it was months since they had exchanged a word.

One chill autumn day, nearly a full year after Bridie had first passed through the gates of the workhouse, the men in black frock-coats arrived. The girls had just finished breakfast when the men strutted into the dining hall with the Master of the workhouse like a flock of black crows.

'All orphan girls aged twelve to sixteen, please line up against the west wall and curtsey to the Guardians,' called the Master. The rest of the women and girls were dismissed.

The Guardians walked up and down the length of the row, stopping now and then to scrutinise a particular girl.

'Matron, are these girls of good character?' asked one man.

'To the best of my knowledge,' said the Matron. 'Some of them haven't been with us long, some have been here more than a year, but they all seem a decent set of girls.'

'We are only interested in females in good health,' said one of the Guardians sharply.

'They are none of them ill,' said the Matron defensively.

One of the Guardians stepped forward and addressed the girls in a loud voice.

'Girls, I have been appointed by the Emigration Board to choose young females of good character and in good health to emigrate to Australia. Who among you would be willing to emigrate to Australia? Step forward, please.'

Caitlin grabbed Bridie's arm, dragging her along. The whole line of girls moved at the same time.

'You will have free passage,' the man continued 'and the Board has agreed to pay the expenses to outfit each of you for your new lives in the colony. Upon arrival, you will be indentured to employers.'

'Have these girls wait outside the Master's quarters for interviewing,' said the man, turning on his heel.

When the Guardians had left the dining hall, Bridie whispered to Caitlin in a low voice, 'But I don't want to go to the other side of the world.'

'Do you want to stay here? Or go back to Dingle? Back to your family's graves?'

'But there's Brandon. I promised my mam I'd take care of him.'

'You can't take care of him, Bridie. It will be years before you can, and who knows what might happen in that time? He might have to go from the workhouse and leave you behind. If you get discharged, it will only be to go into service with someone and you won't be able to take Brandon with you then either. Don't you understand, girl? You'll never be able to take care of him while you stay in Ireland. The only way you can help him is to leave. He'll get a place when he's bigger, working as a labourer for someone, and you'll be able to send money.'

Bridie said nothing. She folded her arms across her chest.

'Why would you want me to go?'

'I don't care if you do or you don't,' said Caitlin coolly, 'but mark my words, girl, you'll never get this chance again. Free passage! You know, there are girls lining up to get into the workhouse just to be offered a prize like this.

If we were in the New World together, we could get good places, save our pennies and then one day get our own little house together and sew together and live like sisters. Maybe one day you could send Brandon the fare and he could come and live with us too.'

Bridie thought of all this as she sat on the long wooden bench outside the Master's office. It had been so long since she'd spoken with Brandon that sometimes she felt as if he too had died, even though she knew that every morning they woke up in the same building. She found herself struggling to think what his voice sounded like, trying to remember his small, quiet gestures and the way he looked at her with his pale blue eyes. The picture that Caitlin had painted, of the two girls in their own little house, made her giddy with desire, but what would Brandon say when he found out she'd abandoned him?

From the moment the girls were chosen for the venture, everything changed for them. They were taken downstairs to sleep in a separate room and preparations for their departure began. There were thirty-two girls from all across Kerry. Some were Protestant and some were Catholic, but all were orphans, and the prospect of the New World held less fear for them than having to make their own way in Ireland.

Bolts of fabric arrived and the girls were set to work sewing new outfits for the journey. Bridie wanted to shout with joy at the feeling of the new fabrics between her fingers. There was calico for their shifts, plaid for their cloaks, flannel for petticoats and yards of cotton for handkerchiefs. There was twilled linen and bright gingham for their aprons, wool and printed calico for their gowns, and worsted and cotton for their stockings. There was so much to be done. Bridie sewed swiftly, finishing Caitlin's work for her when the older girl fell behind. Each of the girls was given a wooden trunk to keep all her things in, with her name on the top. Bridie had never owned so much clothing in all her life.

Prayer books and Bibles were provided as well. Bridie turned the books over and over in her hands. She'd never owned a book before and the small black marks on each page were unfathomable to her, but when Caitlin received hers she immediately crossed over to the window and began reading the Bible, her expression full of concentration. Bridie stood beside her and watched.

'You can read?' asked Bridie.

'Yes,' said Caitlin, turning the page without looking up. And then, in a low voice she read, 'Behold, I send an angel before thee, to keep thee in the way and to bring thee into the place which I have prepared.'

Autumn sunlight cut through the small panes of the workhouse window, making Caitlin's pale hair shimmer like spun gold, a halo above her white face. Bridie could almost believe Caitlin was her very own guardian angel.

'It's from the book of Exodus, in the Old Testament,' said Caitlin, thumbing the pages. 'You know, the one about Moses.' Bridie shook her head. She knew her rosary and all the prayers and parables and stories of Jesus that her mother had told her, but she knew nothing of the Old Testament stories.

That night, as they lay together in the room set aside for the girls of 'The Scheme', Caitlin read the story of Moses out loud to Bridie. Some of the other girls crept closer to listen as well, their eyes bright.

Bridie liked to hear that the people were chosen by God, just as the girls were chosen by the Guardians to go to a new land, but her favourite part of the story was when the Red Sea parted and all the people of Israel walked across to their new home.

That night, Bridie dreamed of the journey. She was walking between great columns of water, red as blood and towering hundreds of feet above her. Beside her was Caitlin and ahead all the other orphan girls from the workhouse. Silver fish squirmed in the puddles of red water at their feet and they lifted the skirts of their new dresses to step across, and laughed. Bridie felt her heart beating faster and faster as she hurried between the walls of red seawater to reach the land ahead. They scrambled up the black rocks of the new land and then turned to stare down the long tunnel of waves. She could just make out the figure of a boy, a small boy, running between the walls of water towards them. As he drew closer, Bridie could see it was Brandon, calling to her as he leapt over the writhing fish. And then behind him, the sea began to fold back in on itself. She opened her mouth to cry out to him but no sound came. The roaring of the sea filled her ears as waves crashed down upon the small figure, sweeping him from her. She woke in a cold sweat, her heart pounding. Beside her Caitlin slept soundly but for the rest of the night Bridie lay awake, staring at the play of moonlight on the ceiling, trying to rid her mind of the image of Brandon drowning in a blood-red sea.

12

Land of forever young

Bridie tiptoed up the winding stairs, her body wired, tense. If they caught her, they'd never allow her to go to Australia. They'd probably throw her out of the workhouse, a bad girl like herself, sneaking into the boys' quarters in the dark of night. She moved like a shadow, swiftly, quietly from one doorway to the next. She hoped desperately that the boy drawing water from the well in the courtyard had given Brandon the message that she would come to find him.

She peered into the long boys' dormitory. There were rows and rows of boys huddled together in the straw, a mass of indistinct shapes in the dim moonlight. There was no way of knowing which was her brother. She dropped to her knees and crawled along the boards, peering through the darkness at the humped forms, whispering his name. A small boy sat up and watched her with curiosity. Finally, right near the end of the row, she was answered by a boy throwing his arms around her.

'Brandon, is it you?' she whispered hoarsely, though she knew that it was. She could hardly make her voice work, the tears were so close. Brandon gently touched her cheek.

'To be sure, blood knows blood,' he said softly. They knelt in front of each other, their hands gently moving across each other's faces, feeling the familiar features.

'We're going to run away? That's why you've come for me, isn't it?' asked Brandon with barely suppressed excitement.

Bridie took his hands, entwining her fingers with his, and prayed for the courage to tell him the truth.

'No, darling boy,' she whispered. 'I've come to say goodbye.'

'Goodbye?' Brandon's eyes looked black in the half-light.

Bridie swallowed hard and tried to make what she had to say sound ordinary.

'I'm going to Australia. Tomorrow we leave for Dublin and then a boat will take us to Plymouth, in England, and then we'll sail right across the sea for months and months to reach the colony.'

'I never dreamed one of those girls would be you. How can you be leaving me?'

'You would have left me if the carter would have had you.'

'I would have made him take us both!'

Though she couldn't see his face in the darkness, she knew as she knew her own heart that his face was streaked with tears.

She moved closer and put an arm around him.

'I've missed you, Bridie,' he said.

'I've missed you too. I've missed you every day since we've been parted.'

'We shouldn't have come to this place,' said Brandon.

'It was the workhouse or dying in a ditch by the roadside, boyo,' said Bridie, trying to sound stern with him though her heart was breaking. 'And now I've got this chance, I'll get to the New World and then I'll send for you.'

'Like Uncle Liam?' said Brandon with a bitterness that she'd never heard in his voice before.

'Brandon, you know I'll come back for you. You remember the story of Ossian? Remember how our dad used to tell it? How even though the most beautiful fairy princess in all the worlds took him beyond the ninth wave to the land of wine and honey, and loved him forever and kissed him with honeyed kisses, still he never forgot his brothers. And remember how the love of them brought him back to Ireland? I'll be like Ossian, but I'll bring you to me, to the Land of Forever Young, like in the stories except it will be Australia, and there'll be sun-bowers and maybe palaces and we'll have a home there together. We'll have our silver and gold house right there.'

'I remember Ossian,' said Brandon in a small voice. 'I remember that Ossian stayed away for three hundred years and when he came home everything had changed.'

'But if I stay here, we'll never have anything, Brandon, don't you understand that?' She pulled Brandon close to her and cupped his face in her hands. She could feel sobs racking his thin body, and she leaned her brow against his until he grew still.

'You listen, Brandon O'Connor, and you listen well. I promise you this. You'll sail across the sea too. Just like the blessed *St Brennain*, that Dad used to tell of. And you'll cross all the waters to come to me and you'll see all sorts of wondrous things like the Paradise of Birds and then we'll have our house, one day, just like I always told you, I promise. We'll have our silver and gold house.'

The carts pulled up in the workhouse yard and the girls' boxes were loaded on board. Bridie felt cocooned in the layers of her new clothes as she stood in the yard with the other girls. Her new boots were unyielding and painful, and the hard leather bruised her heels. She felt she was someone else, not the Bridie O'Connor who'd run wild across the cliffs at Dunquin, nor the Bridie who'd buried her baby brother and changeling sister and left her mother dying in a ditch, nor the Bridie who'd walked for days across Kerry looking for a safe haven for her brother and herself. She looked up at the windows of the workhouse, wishing that Brandon's face would materialise in one of the panes, but they were blank and dark.

'Here, Bridie O'Connor,' called Caitlin from the back of the cart, her eyes bright with excitement. 'Take my hand.'

She pulled Bridie up into the cart beside her. The gates of the workhouse swung open and the cart turned into the road, taking them away from the workhouse, away from their old lives, away from Brandon. The other girls were all chattering among themselves but Bridie sat completely still, her hands folded in her lap, and stared at the road ahead.

Bridie had never even seen a train, let alone climbed aboard one. The girls were herded into third-class carriages. Some of them shrieked as the train pulled away from the platform, and Bridie felt her stomach lunge and her heart beat faster.

After their long journey and the heat of the city, the

cool sea breeze from the Dublin wharves washed over them like a blessing. Bridie took a deep breath, and even though the air around the docks was sour, not fresh like the wind that swept off the Atlantic at Dunquin, she felt a thrill of recognition.

Hundreds of girls milled about on the wharves, all in almost identical clothes. Further along the docks, some women were keening for their departing families. There was no one to keen Bridie O'Connor's leaving Ireland, no one to call her name and bind her heart to the old world, nor was there for any of the other orphan girls.

The water was flat and grey as they sailed out of Dublin harbour and into the great open sea. Some of the girls wept as Ireland disappeared from view, but most simply looked numb. Bridie and Caitlin leaned over the side of the boat and stared at the waves breaking against the bow. The steamer was so crowded that the girls were piled into every corner. They spent most of the night standing on the deck of the steamship, pressed tight against each other. By the time they reached Plymouth, they were all wretched and bedraggled and their beautiful new cloaks were heavy with seawater.

A plump matron came on board and herded the girls down the gangplank. It was like being in a strange dream. They were taken to a big brick building and shown into a dormitory where they could change their damp clothes. They even had tubs of warm water to wash in and a doctor inspected each of them, to ensure they were strong enough for the voyage to Australia.

That night, there was an endless flutter of conversation among the girls. Bridie lay in the dark listening to the ripple of voices that moved up and down the length of the room, but Brandon's parting words wouldn't stop echoing in her head.

When at last they filed up the gangplank of the *Diadem*, the ship that was to be their home for the next four months, all the girls were strangely silent. There were over two hundred of them. Bridie's cheeks flushed pink from the bite of frost in the air. Sailors were everywhere, on the decks and in the rigging. Three matrons shepherded the girls to a hatch that opened into the lower decks. Everywhere, people were shouting instructions. Bridie looked at the open hatch that led to the decks below. She wanted to turn and run back down the gangplank, but she reached out and grasped the folds of Caitlin's cloak and followed her into the darkness below.

13

The voyage south

Bridie sat on the end of her bunk and turned the knife and fork and two spoons that she'd been given over and over in her hands. Piled up beside her were a new mattress, bolster, blankets and counterpane, a large canvas bag for holding linen and clothes, a metal plate, and a drinking mug. Bridie had never owned so many things. She found it hard to believe they were hers to keep.

The girls were divided into groups of eight for their meals. Three of the girls in Bridie and Caitlin's mess were from the same workhouse, but there were also three new girls who'd come from Dublin. One of them, Biddy Ryan, couldn't stop talking. The words bubbled out of her. She spoke in English, but it wasn't the sort of English that Bridie had learnt from Caitlin. Every day, Bridie picked up new words from Biddy and practised them, saying them again and again until Caitlin stamped her foot and blushed angrily.

'You don't need to say those words out loud. You don't even need to be knowing them,' scowled Caitlin.

'They make me laugh,' said Bridie. 'I know they're rude but there's nothing wrong with a bit of fun.'

'There's nothing right with that Biddy Ryan. You know how I've been counting our provisions each morning. Well, there's a mite too much going missing. If you're going to listen to that girl, then you can watch her too and make sure you tell me if you see any mischief.'

Bridie couldn't see that it mattered whether Biddy was stealing a handful of currants. Most of the girls couldn't keep their food down anyway, and those that could weren't eating much. As they sailed through the Bay of Biscay nearly everyone was vomiting except Bridie. At night and for most of the day, the other girls lay in their bunks, groaning, calling out for their mothers or praying as if they were near death's door. Caitlin and dozens of other girls were constantly leaning over the side of the bunk and throwing up into a bucket. Often the girls would miss the bucket, and the decks below were awash with bile. Bridie stayed with Caitlin some of the time, but after a while the smell would overwhelm her. She had found her sea-legs quickly and she loved being on deck, listening to the cries of the sailors mingling with the call of the seabirds. When the big sails unfurled and billowed in the wind she felt her heart swell with happiness.

Ten days after leaving Plymouth, they came into warmer weather. Bridie went up on deck and gazed out at the coast of Spain. Caitlin joined her, looking thin and wan. When Bridie slipped her arm around the older girl's waist, she could feel how frail she'd become. Caitlin took a deep breath of the warm air and smiled for the first time since they'd left Plymouth.

'Four months!' said Caitlin. 'But then, when we get to the colony, I tell you, girl, things will be good for us.'

'I hope so,' said Bridie. She couldn't imagine the life that lay ahead.

'It will be grand. We'll both get jobs and save our pennies and then have our own little house together. Like two sisters.'

Bridie looked into Caitlin's pale face and knew she had never had a friend like this before. Her thoughts were interrupted by a cackle of laughter.

'Will you look at those two,' muttered Caitlin, frowning at Biddy Ryan and Margaret O'Shea. Biddy and Margaret were flirting with a pair of sailors, even though every girl knew it was forbidden to even speak to the men.

'It's just a bit of fun they're having,' said Bridie, bewildered by the ferocity of Caitlin's disapproval. 'They've each had their head in a bucket for a week. They're probably trying to be sure they haven't taken on the look of it.'

Caitlin laughed, but Bridie could see from her sharp expression how much she disapproved of the other girls.

Now they had all found their sea-legs, the Matron in charge announced that lessons were to begin and asked all the girls who could read and write to step forward. Bridie was left sitting on a bench with Biddy and Margaret. The matrons and two of the lady passengers who had volunteered to help began opening trunks of books and organising the girls into groups.

Bridie couldn't believe her good luck when the Matron appointed Caitlin to instruct illiterates. But when she looked at the pages of small black print, her heart sank. Learning to speak English had come to her quickly, but learning to read it seemed a huge and impossible task. How could she possibly make sense of all those little marks on the page?

Even though Caitlin was encouraging, Bridie made small headway. Most of Caitlin's time was taken up arguing with Biddy Ryan, and Bridie was left to unravel the mystery of the printed words alone. One sultry morning, while Bridie sat hunched over her Bible, tracing the words with her fingers, Caitlin and Biddy's conflict took a turn for the worse. Biddy lost her temper and threw her book at Caitlin.

'I've had enough of this useless studyin',' she shouted.

'Well you'll never make much of yourself in the colonies if you've got no learning, Biddy Ryan.'

'Oh, I'll make myself useful. I'm going to find myself a husband good and quick, and he'll find uses for me.' She laughed a low, throaty laugh and nudged Margaret. Caitlin snorted her disapproval and turned her attention to Bridie.

Biddy Ryan was always in trouble but she didn't care. After breakfast and chores, at half-past ten every morning, the Surgeon-Superintendent inspected each mess and every girl. Nothing was allowed to be left damp, and no hole or corner escaped his notice. The Surgeon made each of the girls hold her hands out, and if anyone had dirty nails his reprimand was cruel. It was always cruellest for Biddy Ryan, but when the Surgeon turned his back she'd pull faces at him and wink at the other girls. Bridie wanted to dislike her, to feel exasperated with her for making it so much harder for all the girls in their mess, but she couldn't help admiring Biddy's daring, and her jokes always made Bridie laugh, much to Caitlin's disgust.

At half-past twelve the ship's bell rang, and pies or cakes were served out to the messes in turn; then the girls studied or sewed until teatime at half-past five. Bridie loved it when she was allowed to put her pencil down and take up a needle. The needle responded to her touch in a way she felt the pencil never would, and she quickly became known for having the finest needlework on board, despite being one of the youngest girls.

At dusk, lanterns were hung on deck and between-decks as well for those too shy or too ill to go above. At first, Caitlin and Bridie sat on their bunk together in the evenings. Bridie would sew while Caitlin read to her and the sounds of music would waft down to them from up on deck. After several weeks, Bridie finally persuaded Caitlin to join the others. Eliza Dwyer had a fiddle and another girl a concertina and yet another a tin whistle. They played all sorts of songs and then a lively dance reel that brought the other girls to their feet. Bridie couldn't resist the music.

'C'mon, darling girl,' she said to Caitlin, offering her arm, but Caitlin looked away. Suddenly Biddy Ryan was beside her, threading an arm through Bridie's and dragging her out into the circle of dancers. Bridie swung in time to the music, her feet moving swiftly, the warm sea air like balm against her skin. Biddy waved at the sailors in the forecastle who were watching but Bridie paid them no attention. At that moment the dancing mattered more to Bridie than anything.

Then the Matron caught sight of Biddy blowing a kiss in the sailors' direction, and in a moment she'd dragged both Biddy and Bridie from the dance area.

'Biddy Ryan,' she snapped, shaking Biddy by the shoulders, 'you are altogether too free with your attentions. This is not the first time I've had to send you below decks for this sort of flagrant wickedness but I hope it is the last.'

Bridie went back to stand beside Caitlin, annoyed at the flush of knowing triumph on the older girl's face.

The day they crossed the Equator, all the girls were keen to be on deck for the ceremonies, even Caitlin. There were shouts of laughter as someone cried out that Neptune was being hauled up the side of the ship. It was the cook, his big belly hanging over a scrag of seaweed and scraps of green cloth. Beside him one of the younger deckhands was dressed as his wife, Amphitrite, and several other sailors paraded the deck as his attendants with their shirts stripped off and their bodies rubbed with something that lent a peculiar greenish hue to their skin. They grabbed several of the first-time sailors and held them still while 'Amphitrite' shaved their heads, then tied them up and ducked them over the side. Neptune turned on the crowd of girls and bowed deeply.

'Ah, most beautiful ladies, come away with me to where the rocks of coral grow and you will all be my princesses and live like queens with my fair wife in our palace beneath the sea, and I'll deck you in pearls and all the jewels of the oceans.'

'I'll come,' called Biddy, laughing cheekily and reaching out her hands to him.

Neptune winked at her as a matron slapped Biddy's hands back down, then he disappeared behind the poop-deck. A moment later, a blazing tar barrel was cast overboard. The girls rushed to the side to watch the barrel disappear as the ship sailed swiftly away.

'I've read that he's meant to have a conch shell, drawn

by sea-horses, and trumpeting Tritons beside him as he wheels across the waves,' said Caitlin.

'What's wrong with you, girl!' said Biddy Ryan, turning on Caitlin. 'Do you have to spoil everything with your stupid book-learning?'

'I didn't mean it like that.'

'Well, have some sense, woman. You're always spoiling the fun.'

'At least I have common sense, while you've no sense at all,' said Caitlin.

'I've heard about your "sense". The sense to leave your sister lying half-dead in a ditch while you made yourself cosy.'

Caitlin flinched but it was Bridie who struck out in response, pushing Biddy onto the deck. She wrapped a hank of Biddy's hair in her fist and yanked on it, hard, and then bit fiercely on Biddy's shoulder until she could taste blood. Biddy screamed and scratched back, a whirling mass of skirts and hair. Bridie could hear Caitlin shouting for her to stop and then the matrons were tearing them apart, taking each girl roughly by the arm and hauling them below decks. Biddy and Bridie sat sweaty and breathless on the edge of their bunks, glaring at each other.

Suddenly, Biddy grinned and smoothed her hands across her chestnut hair. 'You fight like a vixen, never mind how you play the good girl with that whore Cait Moriarty.'

'She's no whore,' said Bridie, resting her fingers against the bruise that was swelling on her cheekbone.

'You may be a little one, Bridie O'Connor, but there's none on this ship that's so dainty that they haven't lied and stolen to be here. Sure, but there must be something black inside each of us to keep us strong while all our kin are buried deep.'

'Maybe you and I are cut from the same cloth, Biddy Ryan, but Caitlin Moriarty's made of finer stuff,' snapped Bridie. 'I wish they hadn't stopped me before I could belt the priest's share out of you for slagging off at an angel.'

'*Oanshagh*, you fool, you'll scrab my eyes out 'cause I tell the truth, will you? Every girl from Kerry knows the story of how Caitlin Moriarty left her sister at the workhouse gate where she died that night while Caitlin herself nestled up warm and safe in the straw. I'll not damn her, but I'll not suffer her airs either. She's no better than any one of us.'

Bridie wanted to pummel the foul-mouthed girl until Biddy cried out that everything she said was a lie, but she tucked her clenched fists under her arms to stop herself from swinging another blow and turned her back instead.

14

Winds of freedom

Now that they were sailing through warmer climates, there seemed so much more to do. Every morning just after dawn, a tent was set up on the deck, and inside it, behind folds of calico, was a large bath full of seawater. Bridie loved the way the cold water made her gasp and her flesh tingle. When she scrubbed her skin, it was as if she was scrubbing away all the vestiges of her old life. It seemed as if all the pain and hurt and squalor of the workhouse had happened to someone else. The sounds of the ship's bell ringing, the lapping of the waves, the creaking of the timbers: everything about being at sea seemed to add to her sense of happiness, and she sang to herself quietly as she washed. High above in the patch of blue sky between the folds of canvas, an albatross floated, watching over her, turning in graceful curves as it soared above the ship.

On a fine hot day as they sailed through the tropics, the Superintendent ordered the girls' boxes hoisted out of the hold. The sailors hated the whole ritual of airing the girls' possessions and grumbled as they flung the trunks onto the deck.

The deck was soon covered with boxes and girls

shrieking with excitement as they pulled out their frocks for airing and took out special objects that had been packed away these past months. Some of the girls had managed to cling to small treasures from their homes and Bridie watched as they lovingly fondled the familiar ornaments. The chore wasn't of much interest to her. She looked into her box of possessions and was amazed at the number of things inside, but she felt no connection to any of them. They were new and crisp and smelt unfamiliar. There was nothing of her family, no memento from her own home, not one thing that made her soul yearn for her old life. Perhaps if they'd let her keep her wooden spoon, or if she'd thought to cut a lock of Brandon's hair, then the box would stir some feeling.

Margaret O'Shea sat holding a locket from her mother, with tears in her eyes.

'Ah, but it's a harsh thing to be sent away from your own loved country and all your own folk,' she cried. At first her lament was just in a sing-song voice, but soon it turned into a howl and a moment later other girls had joined her, each wringing her hands and wailing at her fate.

Bridie watched them but she couldn't make herself feel their sharp grief. She glanced across and saw that Caitlin too was sitting quietly, her hands folded over her skirts, staring out to sea. Bridie tried to push away the fears she'd harboured since the fight with Biddy. Maybe it was true; maybe there was something dark inside herself and Caitlin. Why couldn't they grieve like the other girls? Was it because they were so black-hearted? It was only when the shrieks of the wailing girls began to echo the length of the ship that a vision of the women of Dunquin around her father's body came to Bridie, and she felt a wave of grief break over her so powerful that a cry rose up in her throat for all the things she had lost.

The Surgeon-Superintendent stormed on deck and ordered all the boxes to be shut and put away. In a loud voice, he ordered the girls to be quiet. Bridie wiped away her tears with the back of her hand and began repacking her trunk. When they were lined up to go below again, she glanced into Caitlin's face and saw it was as still and calm as ever. The fear that everything Biddy had said was true gripped her and wouldn't let go.

Eighty-four days after leaving Plymouth they came in sight of Van Diemen's Land. A ripple of excitement swelled through the decks but it quickly turned to fear as a wild gale blew up from the north-east. During the night, Bridie heard something snap, timber cracking like gunshot fire, and then a shuddering crash as something heavy hit the deck. Sailors shouted and screamed above the roar of the storm and the girls below decks shrieked in alarm. Bridie snuggled closer to Caitlin.

As the seas grew rougher, a girl cried out that they were being locked below deck and they all heard the sound of the hatches being fastened tight. The ship pitched back and forward and Bridie fought back the image of the ship sinking with all the girls drowning between decks. Some of the girls were crying. Biddy Ryan was sick in her bunk.

Suddenly, Caitlin's voice rose up above the creaking timbers and the roar of the sea as she read from her Bible. Even though the lantern swung wildly, making the shadows rush back and forward, Caitlin read steadily. Bridie lay close beside her and focused on Caitlin's voice, trying to shut out the sound of the bilgewater churning beneath them. 'Behold, I show you a mystery; We shall not all sleep, but we shall all be changed, in a moment, in the twinkling of an eye, at the last trump: for the trumpet shall sound, and the dead shall be raised incorruptible, and we shall be changed.' An image came to Bridie, bright and clear, of her family and all her friends at Dunquin, rising out of the ocean; brightest of all was an image of Brandon, walking through the wild sea towards her. With a rush of guilt, Bridie realised she hadn't thought of him for days. Perhaps more frightening than the storm that raged around them was Bridie's sudden fear that she had been changed, that as her life became better, her heart was becoming blacker. Then Caitlin slipped an arm around her and hugged her as she read, and Bridie felt the darkness lift.

The next day when the girls came up for air, they found that the big brown-and-white albatross that had been following them was lying, half-drowned, on the deck. Its long brown wings, large enough to carry a man, and each one longer than the tallest sailor on board, were stretched taut. At first Bridie thought the storm had rendered the albatross flightless, but then a sailor pulled a baited hook from its beak and she realised the bird had been caught. The sailor lashed its beak shut with a piece of string, handling it with rough disregard. The bird struggled to its feet and walked about the deck in distress, no longer the beautiful sky creature Bridie had admired for the whole voyage, but a clumsy, pathetic beast, unable to take to the air. Some of the girls laughed, and a sailor in the rigging looked down and called out that it looked just like the second mate. Bridie leapt forward, tore the string from around the bird's beak and, using all her strength, heaved the great creature over the side of the ship. The sailor grabbed her by the arm. 'You brat, it was naught but a bit of fun I was having.'

Bridie's cheeks burned in the flush of her rage. 'The curse of St Martin upon you,' she shouted, drawing her leg back and kicking the sailor in the shins as hard as she could.

Later, sent to her bunk again in disgrace by the Surgeon-Superintendent, she seethed at the injustice of being punished for rescuing the albatross. Caitlin came down below deck and sat beside her. She reached over and took Bridie's hand in hers.

'I know you felt you were doing right, Bridie, but you've got to mind that temper of yours. It won't serve us well in the Colony.'

'But he was doing wrong, Caitlin! That bird never did him any harm.'

'It's not the point, girl. It's the same as when you set upon Biddy Ryan. I know you meant to help me, but you have to learn to rein in your feelings. You and I, we've talked about how we're going to make good, how we're going to get ahead. But if you go losing your temper, getting in the way of other people's business, then it's going to be harder. Harder for us to be together.'

'Did your sister have a foul temper? Is that why you left her outside the gate?' said Bridie, feeling the sting of her words even as they escaped her.

Caitlin recoiled.

'Bridie, your own sweet mother died in a ditch,' said

Caitlin so softly that Bridie had to lean closer to hear the bitter words.

In the long silence, Bridie heard all the sounds of the ship about her, the creaking of the timbers, the wash of the sea, the voices of the other girls above deck and the cries of the sailors. And she heard her own breath coming fast and sharp and her heart pounding. Gently, Caitlin reached out and put her arm around Bridie.

'Darlin' girl, I want you to promise me you'll try harder to mind your temper.'

Bridie sighed, and leaned her head against Caitlin's shoulder.

'When my dad died, staying angry was what kept me and Brandon alive, like it fed the fire inside me. And then when we were at the workhouse, I felt like all the fire had gone out in me. But the sea breeze, it's like the wind of freedom, Cait, blowing off the new world and making me feel like the spark in me is alive again. Don't make me promise a lie.'

'I don't want you to promise for my sake, girl,' said Caitlin, taking Bridie's face in her hands and staring hard into her eyes. 'It's for your own sake, Bridie O'Connor. How are you going to serve your new master if you let your temper make you battle-mad?'

'I'll be a good servant to an honest master,' said Bridie. 'I can promise that.'

Now, it was Caitlin who sighed. 'Let's pray that the new world is full of honest men.'

15

The New World

It was a bright January day when they sailed into Port Phillip Bay. The country on either side was grey-green, stark and stripped dry in the harsh sunlight. Bridie hung over the side of the ship and stared hungrily at the foreign shore. After all those months at sea, it would be strange and delicious to feel earth beneath her feet.

Even though the land was only a stone's throw from them, the girls weren't to be taken ashore until the following day. Bridie stood on the deck beside Caitlin and stared at the docks of Williamstown.

'They're taking us to a depot tomorrow. Then folk will come and sign for us, take us to be indentured in their homes and in their businesses,' said Caitlin.

'Let's pray that we go together,' said Bridie, full of hope. Caitlin didn't reply as she bent over the side and stared down into the green water.

The docks were teeming with men. Margaret O'Shea stood on her tiptoes and stared into the crowds, searching for the cousin she swore was coming to meet her. Bridie heard Margaret squeal with pleasure as a tall man with a red beard approached the dock. Several other girls were met right there on the waterfront, and Bridie pushed down her feelings of envy. One day, she'd be waiting on the docks for Brandon. One day, she told herself.

The air was sour with the smell of fish and tar. Bridie looked down at her heavy boots flashing out from beneath her long skirt, sidestepping brackish puddles of seawater. It was peculiar to be able to take so many steps in a straight line, to not have to take into account the swaying of the timbers beneath her feet. It made her feel unbalanced.

The girls were marched to a jetty where some small boats were waiting to take them up the yellow river to Melbourne. Bridie sat quietly in the boat, her hands folded in her lap, but she stared out across the salt marshes in wide-eyed amazement. The whole landscape was drenched with a harsh, raw light. The foliage of the gnarled shrubs was silver and grey and blue-green, nothing like the exotic lush jungle she'd imagined. Further along the river, they passed a strange, tangled clump of trees with leaves that all seemed to hang limply and point down in a way she'd never seen before.

The river widened and then narrowed as they travelled upstream. As they approached the wharf Bridie caught sight of a jumble of buildings on the north shore, and further up the river, on the south bank, was a crowd of canvas tents – a small town in itself.

The girls were marched up from the wharf and along a busy street. Bridie had imagined Melbourne as a village no bigger than Dingle, but here was a town as grand as Tralee, with wide streets and tall bluestone buildings, even though it was only a few years older than she was. People stared at the girls as they walked in line up King Street, and Bridie moved a little closer towards Caitlin so their arms touched. Caitlin looked down at her and smiled.

Halfway up a small hill was the immigration barracks, the depot that was to be their home until they were assigned an indenture. A cloud of dust and flies rose up from the square yard at the centre as the girls shuffled around the carts that had brought their trunks from the wharf. They were instructed to assemble in the yard and their names were checked off the ship's list. A small group of girls from an earlier shipload of orphans stood on the verandah of the bunkhouses and watched as the new arrivals were sorted into groups. Bridie was taken aback by their sulky, angry expressions.

Inside the bunkhouse, each of the girl's boxes sat at the end of a single bed. Bridie looked at her own narrow bunk and felt a wave of loneliness. It would be the first time in her life that she'd had a bed to herself, and she wasn't sure she liked the idea.

'Why are those other girls still here?' whispered Bridie to Caitlin as they knelt before their trunks, folding their cloaks away. 'Their boat must have come weeks ago.'

'Maybe no one wants them. Maybe they're wicked girls like Biddy Ryan.'

Bridie felt a ripple of unease. 'They don't look wicked to me. They just look like ordinary girls,' she said. 'How can you make up your mind so quickly about whether a girl is good or bad?'

'Lucky for you, Bridie O'Connor, that I do make up my mind that quick. I knew the first time I clapped eyes on you outside the workhouse that your heart was good, and I've seen nothing to prove me wrong yet. And I knew the first time I saw Biddy Ryan that she was a slattern, and you know her as well as I do now and what do you think?'

Bridie didn't reply.

They took the bunks nearest the door and set their trunks down at the end of the beds. Bridie noticed the name of the smallest girl in the bunkhouse, 'Honor Gauran', painted on her box. It looked battered compared to Bridie's. Bridie smiled at her but she turned away. That night, all the *Diadem* girls whispered to each other, the rise and fall of their voices like the swelling sea.

Bridie woke to the sound of shouting. Honor Gauran was cowering in her nightgown before the Matron.

'You filthy brute. We offer you our charity, and you show us your respect with this disgusting behaviour. No wonder your mistress sent you back.'

Honor hung her head. 'I'm sorry, ma'am. I'll clean it up, ma'am,' she said in a small voice.

Then Bridie saw it: a big puddle on the floor beside Honor's bed. After the Matron left, Honor turned to the other girls, her eyes brimming with tears.

'I was dreaming of the master. It was the master's fault I come back. The mistress was out one night and I was in my little bed and the master come in and took off his trousers and climbed into my bed with me. I had to hit him to get away and then I ran into the street in my nightgown but he came out the door shouting at me and threw my box into the street. That's how it got the lid broke. All my things strewn across the cobbles.' She sniffed deeply and wiped her eyes with the back of her hands. 'I knows I should have gone to the water closet last night. But I'm too scared to walk about in the dark. I feel scared all the time now.'

Bridie and Caitlin looked at each other and felt answering stabs of alarm.

'It's all right, Bridie,' whispered Caitlin. 'It won't be like that for us.'

Everyone grew restless, waiting for their new lives to begin. There was nothing to do in the depot, and the girls hung about idly. Biddy Ryan liked to lean over the fence of the depot and call out to passers-by until the Matron hurried out and shooed her back into the barracks.

One day a whole family of black natives walked past the fence. Their clothes were ragged, as Bridie's and her family's had been when they lived in the hut on the edge of Dingle, and they had a lean and hungry look about them. Bridie had never seen such ebony skin. Their big, dark eyes and the sharp angle of their bones reminded her of the hungriest time in her life. When they looked back at her staring at them through the fence, she turned away.

Every day, some of the girls would leave with their indenture certificates signed and their bonnets tied beneath their chins, but still Bridie waited. There were rumours that the citizens were angry at the presence of the orphan girls, that no one really wanted them and that the newspapers were describing them as ignorant and useless.

At the end of the second week, Caitlin came to tell Bridie she had a place. A draper from Flinders Lane wanted a girl to work in his shop, but only one.

'Can't you wait until there's somewhere we can both go?'

'Bridie, sure you're like a sister to me, but no, I can't wait. I'll come and visit you if my new master will let me, and if not, then I'll write to you care of the depot, so you can write back to me, like I taught you.'

Bridie frowned. She'd made small progress at learning her letters. The thought of having to read a whole page of writing made her feel sick, but she couldn't admit that to Caitlin.

'But why can't you ask the draper to take me on as well?'

'There's evil talk, saying the orphan girls are a bad and lazy lot and always arguing for their own way. I've heard the Irishmen and the Bishop have called meetings to say we're the best of Ireland, so we have to hold to that and show them it's true and not make trouble. Someone will come and give you a place soon. And then you'll work hard and mind your temper and save your money, just as I will do. How else will we have enough to make our own little home? Don't forget that. You have to hold to that, how we'll take in sewing and have our own place together. I promise we won't lose each other.'

The first night without Caitlin, Bridie lay in bed listening to Honor Gauran crying. After what seemed hours, Honor finally drifted off into restless sleep but Bridie lay awake, staring into the darkness. For a long moment before sleep took her, the new world seemed to be the loneliest place on earth.

16

Beaumanoir

Heat lay in shimmering waves across the depot yard. Bridie sat on the verandah of the bunkhouse with the other girls, fanning herself with her bonnet.

'Hell couldn't be any hotter than this!' exclaimed Biddy Ryan, shaking her skirts out to cool her legs. 'This heat's draining every morsel of life from my poor body.'

'Wishta!' said Honor, darting a glance in the direction of Matron. 'You're not to be complaining. If they hear you, they'll send you to some terrible master or mistress. They'll tell you it's for your own good, to knock some sense into you.'

'Then I'll run away, like you did, girl,' said Biddy defiantly.

Bridie was just about to ask Biddy where she'd run away to when Matron stepped out onto the verandah and called Bridie into the Supervisor's office. A big, plump woman dressed in dark clothes was chatting to the Supervisor when Bridie walked into the room. The Supervisor didn't look up from the papers he was signing. Bridie knew instantly they were her papers of indenture.

'You are a most fortunate girl, Bridie O'Connor,' said

the Supervisor. 'You are to be apprenticed to the household of one of the finest families in Port Phillip. This is Mrs Fairlea, the housekeeper of Sir William and Lady Adeline De Quincey, who will act on behalf of Sir William as your guardian from this day forward.'

Bridie glanced at the dour-looking woman and made a small curtsey.

'You will learn all the skills needed to be a useful servant, and if you apply yourself and work hard, you will never be without employment and will one day make a fine wife for any man.'

'Begging your pardon, sir. I don't want to be a domestic. I want to be a seamstress, sir.'

The Supervisor glared at her and coughed, and went on as if she hadn't spoken. He looked down at the indenture papers and spoke in a loud and insistent tone.

'You are to be paid eight pounds for each year of indenture. At the end of a period of two years, your indenture may be reviewed and the terms of your indenture may vary, but otherwise you are to remain in the house of the De Quinceys until you are nineteen years of age, or until such time that you marry. You will be trained in the domestic arts by the De Quinceys' housekeeper, Mrs Fairlea, commencing your duties as a scullery maid. Your new mistress will be the gracious Lady De Quincey, and you will serve your new mistress faithfully and at all times behave yourself with respect and decorum towards the family during the term of your indenture. The Board, for its charity, expects you to serve your new mistress honestly and obediently, and to be a faithful apprentice in every way. You will be provided with lodging, meat and drink, medicine when required, and all other things but for your clothing. You will be allowed to attend Divine Service of your religion, if practicable, once on Sunday.'

The Supervisor continued to drone on, but Bridie had stopped listening. Seven years before she would be free! Seven years before she would be her own mistress and able to send for Brandon.

'Please, sir, I'd rather go to a draper's, like Caitlin Moriarty. I've a fine hand with a needle.'

The Supervisor went bright red in the face and leaned across his desk, scowling.

'Listen to me, young lady. You are extremely fortunate to find someone willing to take you at all,' he said in a harsh whisper, his voice full of suppressed rage. 'There's not much favour for you Irish girls in Port Phillip. The whole town's crying out against you, so consider yourself lucky for whatever you get and be grateful, my girl.'

In a daze, Bridie put all her things in her box and followed the Matron out into the yard of the depot where a cart and driver stood waiting. Mrs Fairlea climbed up beside the driver, while Bridie sat in the back of the cart on top of her small trunk. They drove straight to Market Street, where Bridie followed her new mistress through crowds of fat, red-faced men, shouting out their wares. When Mrs Fairlea had finished her shopping, they climbed back onto the cart, now loaded with boxes of produce and sacks of flour and grain. Bridie sat among the purchases, feeling like an item on Mrs Fairlea's shopping list. They passed by grand houses in East Melbourne and the big, empty government paddock that stretched down to the muddy river. Eventually the cart turned and trundled down a long, dusty road to the banks of the Yarra.

There was a small house, built right on the water's edge, which belonged to the punt-keeper. He was halfway across the river, ferrying a load of cattle. The sun was bright on the water as they waited for his return and Bridie wondered why everything was so harsh and difficult to look at in this country. And where did all the swarms of flies come from?

It was late afternoon by the time they turned onto a gravel drive leading to a big white stone house with wide verandahs running all around it and a balcony on the second floor.

'This is Beaumanoir, the home of the De Quinceys,' announced Mrs Fairlea, speaking to Bridie for the first time since they'd left the depot.

The cart trundled along the driveway around the side of the building, and into a big coach-house. Inside were two coaches, one small and one grand, with a family emblem embossed on the door.

'Come along, Bridie,' she said. 'Pip will bring your trunk.'

Bridie followed her out of the dark coach-house and into the sunshine. The servants' entrance was around the back of the building. They passed into a long kitchen where a woman was working at a big, black stove. Her face was red, and little beads of perspiration stood out on her forehead as she leaned over a cast-iron pot.

'Mrs Arbuckle, this is the new kitchen skivvy, the Irish girl.'

Mrs Arbuckle glanced across and grunted in reply. Even though she seemed surly, Bridie felt a rush of pleasure at the thought of working in the kitchen, surrounded by food. The room was long and wide with two huge work tables in the middle and pots and pans stacked along deep shelves all around the walls. There was even a big pantry opening onto the kitchen, with shelves from floor to ceiling full of supplies.

'I'll show you your quarters and then you can start work with Mrs Arbuckle straight away. You're to do as she directs you and make yourself useful.'

Mrs Fairlea led Bridie down a narrow, dark hallway with stone floors. They went up a flight of rickety wooden stairs to a bedroom not much bigger than a cupboard. There was barely enough room to stand between the two narrow beds. A small window looked out over an orchard of young fruit trees and a kitchen garden. Bridie's box was already waiting at the foot of one of the beds.

'You're to share with Dora, the parlourmaid. You can have five minutes to make yourself ready. Hang up your bonnet and cloak on these pegs on the back of the door, and be back down in the kitchen as quick as you can.'

Mrs Fairlea shut the door behind her. Bridie turned and looked out the window. In the dappled light of the orchard, three boys were chasing each other between the trees. The smallest of them had thick yellow curls that caught the afternoon sunlight as he ran. The two bigger boys grabbed at his coat and pulled him to the ground, where the three of them rolled over and over in the grass, laughing. Bridie could hardly remember what it was like to be like that any more, to simply run around for the sake of a game. She turned away and undid the ribbon of her bonnet. For a few minutes, she sat on the narrow bed, holding her cloak and bonnet, wishing she was out in that orchard with Brandon, playing a game, laughing like a child. She was eleven years old.

17

Gilbert Clarence Arthur Bloomfield De Quincey

'Bri-dee,' called Mrs Arbuckle, her voice booming out across the cobbled yard. 'Where is that wretched child?'

Bridie scowled and wiped her hands on her apron as she trudged back into the kitchen. She'd never known people to use so many dishes just to make one meal. And so many different plates for all the different things they ate! And so many things that they pushed to one side and didn't eat. She scraped the good food into a bucket in the wash-house to be fed to the pigs, but the sheer waste of it made her feel hot with disgust. She looked over her shoulder to check no one was near, picked one of the roast potatoes off a plate and crammed it into her mouth.

'What are you doing, you filthy girl?' asked Dora, coming in through the scullery door with another tray of dishes. 'That's for the pigs!'

'It's a sin to waste it when there's a Christian to eat it,' said Bridie, not meeting Dora's eyes.

Suddenly Dora's hand caught her hard across the cheek.

'A Christian indeed! You're a papist! What would you know about being a Christian!' said Dora.

Bridie shut her eyes and fought down her rage. She thought of her promise to Caitlin and tried to make a picture of the moment when she and Caitlin would be together in their own home. If she held that image clear and bright in her mind she could keep from belting the lard out of Dora.

That night, Bridie crawled into bed, exhausted. Dora came into the room and poured some cold water into the washbasin.

'Aren't you going to wash yourself before bed?' asked Dora.

Bridie's hands were red raw, and the last thing she felt like doing was having to wash them again. 'I'm too weary,' said Bridie, pulling the blanket up to her chin and turning her face to the wall.

'Bog Irish. That's what they call you and now I know why. They said you girls were a useless, slovenly lot, and it looks to be true,' said Dora. 'I don't know what Lady Adeline was thinking when she sent Mrs Fairlea to fetch you.'

Bridie gritted her teeth and even though she was exhausted, a spark of anger flared inside her. 'Perhaps she heard the news from the minister and took pity on a Catholic girl,' she said.

'What news are you talking about?'

'That the bottom dropped out of Purgatory and all the papists fell straight into Hell.'

Dora snorted with disgust. 'What a stupid story. Besides, if they did fall into Hell, it's only where they belong.'

'Maybe,' said Bridie. 'But it was a terrible crushing for the Protestants, to have all those Catholics landing on their heads.'

It took a moment for the barb to sink in. Bridie braced

herself for a slap but Dora simply flushed red with rage and confusion then reached out and snuffed the candle.

Bridie spent most of the first few weeks at Beaumanoir in a haze of exhaustion. There was so much to learn, so many mysterious rules and methods for doing everything. Each day merged into the next, a blur of scrubbing, cleaning and dishwashing. Sometimes it made her gnash her teeth with frustration that there could be so many fernickety parts to a house, so many little chores that made no sense to any mortal soul, and so many strict rules. She tried to learn quickly, but it was never fast enough to satisfy Dora. All day Dora flew back and forward through the green baize door that led into the main part of the house. Bridie wasn't allowed beyond the kitchen and Dora made sure that Bridie knew where she fitted in the hierarchy of the servants – at the very bottom of the heap.

Early one morning, when Bridie came into the kitchen to fetch the first round of breakfast dishes, Mrs Arbuckle stopped her. 'The little master's sick. You can take a tray up to the nursery for him,' she said, slopping some gruel into a bowl. 'Dora's too busy with the breakfast table.'

'Dora won't like it, ma'am,' said Bridie, as she loaded the breakfast tray.

'Never you mind what Dora likes. She's not in charge of my kitchen.'

Bridie often heard the voices of the three De Quincey boys, Thomas, Henry and Gilbert, as they played in the grounds, and some days they would canter past the open door of the scullery, riding back to the stables after an excursion on their ponies, but she had never been to the nursery. She followed the directions Mrs Arbuckle had given her until she found the room at the end of the upstairs hallway.

When she pushed open the door to the nursery, the yellow-haired boy was sitting up in bed. The other beds were empty. He didn't look particularly sick to Bridie, though one of his eyes was bruised and swollen.

'Your breakfast, sir,' she said. It seemed ridiculous having to call a boy smaller than herself 'sir'. He was younger than Brandon. The boy looked up and smiled.

'Thank you,' he said, politely. 'You must be the new girl. The Irish one.'

'Bridie O'Connor, sir.' Bridie felt a small rush of pleasure. No one had thanked her for anything since she'd begun work at Beaumanoir, and the boy's smile was like a ray of sunshine in the gloom of her morning's work.

'My proper name is Gilbert Clarence Arthur Bloomfield De Quincey, but you may call me Master Gilbert.'

'Well, I hope you'll be feeling better shortly, Master Gilbert,' she said, setting the tray on the bedside table.

'I'm not sick at all,' he said perkily. 'It's just I had a fight with my brother Henry this morning and he gave me this black eye and knocked out a tooth, so Mama says I should stay in bed.' He grinned at her and pulled his mouth wide to show where the missing baby tooth had been.

'He's a bully, that brother of yours. I saw him and the other lad pelting you with fruit the day I arrived.'

'Oh, that was all right,' said Gilbert, shrugging. He blushed a little as he spoke and looked away from Bridie. 'I can't say I didn't deserve a trouncing this time. Last night, while he was sleeping, I poured treacle on Henry's pillow so it oozed down and stuck to his hair.'

Bridie burst out laughing. 'So it was you! I heard Cook in a temper about the treacle gone missing!'

Gilbert grinned. 'Henry always loses his temper when I best him, but I didn't care. Now I get to spend the morning reading and I don't have to do my lessons.'

'Bible stories are a fine way to pass a glum morning.'

'Oh, it's not the Bible that I'm reading,' said Gilbert, laughing. 'It's all about Odysseus, the Greek hero. It has marvellous stories in it. You should read them. I'll lend it to you if you like.'

Bridie shrugged. 'I'd never have the time for reading. I have to work.'

'That must be terrible,' said Gilbert. 'So you don't even know any stories?'

Bridie put her hands on her hips and stared at Gilbert with defiant amusement. 'I know more stories than you'd find between the covers of a hundred books.'

Gilbert raised one eyebrow.

'How can you know any stories if you never read?'

'My dad was the finest storyteller from Slea Head to Tralee.'

'I mean exciting ones about heroes and adventures. That's what a real story is. Not village gossip.'

Bridie marched over to the bedroom door and put her head out into the hall, glancing either way. There was no one out there but she shut the door, just to be safe. She knew she should hurry back to the kitchen but here was an opportunity she couldn't pass up.

'I'll tell you a grand tale, Gilbert De Quincey. Have you ever heard of the great Irish hero Cú Culainn?'

Gilbert shook his head and leaned back on one elbow, set for judgement.

'There was a king,' began Bridie, 'the high king of Ulster, which is up in the north of Ireland, and this king's name was *Conchobhar*. In English you call him Connor.'

'Like your name, O'Connor?'

'Yes,' said Bridie, 'the very same. Well, one day, a famous smith called Culann invited the king and all his finest warriors to a feast.' She frowned for a moment, trying to think how best to tell the story in English.

'So this King Connor, he puts on his travelling clothes and goes to say farewell to his boys. And when he comes out onto the green, he sees a most amazing vision. One hundred and fifty boys are playing at the ball, and a single little boy is thrashing them. When it was the boy's turn to keep goal, he could catch one hundred and fifty balls and none would get past him, and when it was his turn to hurl, he never missed a shot. So the king is full of wonder for the child and he asks the boy to come to the feast. But the boy doesn't want to leave his friends because they are still a-playing, so he says, "Go on and I'll follow the tracks of the chariots and catch up with you by and by."

'So off go King Connor and his men, and when they're all in the stronghold of Culann the Smith, Culann asks the King if it's time to be locking the keep for the night. Now the King forgets all about the boy, so the stronghold is made fast and a great ugly bloodhound set to guard the place. It was a mighty savage beast, this bloodhound. Like a giant wolf he was, guarding the ramparts and staring out over the land, ready to rip into pieces any traveller who dared to come near.

'So when the bloodhound sees the little boy carrying his ball up to Culann the Smith's house, he's all ready to bite the child in two, and his roar is heard all over the land. The beast leaps over the ramparts and comes charging at the little boy, set to swallow him in one gulp.'

Gilbert was leaning forward now, his eyes bright with interest.

'So what did the boy do?' he asked.

'Well, he's no means of defending himself, has he? So when the giant bloodhound comes lunging at him, the boy he throws his ball so hard that it goes straight down the monster's throat and rips all the guts in the beast out through the back way! And then the boy, he seizes the giant bloodhound by its two back legs and smashes its skull wide open against a standing stone, and so the beast falls in pieces on the ground.

'And it's then that Connor and all his men come rushing out, because they've heard the hound and remembered the boy and think he must have been eaten alive. And amazed and relieved they are at what they find, but Culann the Smith is angry to see his great hound in bloody pieces and he sets up a mighty wail.

'"Don't be angry," says the little boy, "I will make all right again. Until you find another, I will be the hound to protect your lands." And so he did. And that's how he got the name of Cú Culainn, because he was like the mighty bloodhound and guarded Culann's lands for years after.'

Gilbert lay back on his pillows and smiled.

'That is a very fine story. I like it when the guts get ripped out of the monster dog. Do you know another story about that hound boy? Did he become a great warrior?'

Bridie grinned. 'The greatest warrior in all Ireland, and I know a hundred stories about warriors and all the magic folk and the saints and the druids of Ireland.'

By this time Gilbert had finished his breakfast. Bridie gathered up the dishes and turned to go.

'Don't leave yet,' said Gilbert.

'I'm in trouble enough, thanks to you, boyo. Cook will be fuming that I've taken so long.'

In the kitchen, Mrs Arbuckle was slamming a big slab of pastry down, pummelling it hard with her hands. When Bridie walked past, she reached out with a floury fist and boxed her on both ears, so that a cloud of white flour dusted Bridie's black hair. Bridie only just managed to keep a grip on the breakfast tray.

'That'll serve you for taking so long at a simple task,' said Cook.

'I told you Master Gilbert could have waited until *I* could take him his breakfast,' said Dora sulkily.

Mrs Arbuckle's floury hand lashed out at Dora as well, clipping her across the back of the head.

'That's enough from you, Dora. Weren't you listening when I read you St Paul's words this morning, child? *Servants, obey in all things your masters,* and *Rebuke not an elder.* Who in this kitchen is mistress and your elder, may I ask?'

Dora hung her head and mumbled an apology. Bridie didn't linger to hear it. She carried the tray out to the scullery, whistling as she walked across the cobbled yard, thinking with pleasure of the next story she would tell Gilbert Clarence Arthur Bloomfield De Quincey.

18

By the waters and the wild

A dry autumn settled on the District, and then the first frost on the grass appeared. Bridie had imagined it would be hot all the year around, so the bitter mornings were like a gift. Some mornings her breath came in a misty stream as she crossed the yard to the scullery, and the icy water from the pump bit into her skin.

Bridie spent most of the working day in the scullery, a little stone room on the other side of the kitchen yard. That was where Gilbert would come looking for her. Sometimes she'd turn to find him standing in the doorway of the hut, leaning against the door frame, grinning at her. And then he'd turn a bucket upside down and sit upon it and beg her for a story, and she would tell him all the old stories: of Cú Culainn; of the Fenians, mighty warriors of Ireland; or of the magic folk she'd once imagined lived at Dunquin. Bridie began to listen for his footsteps in the yard, hoping he would come and make the long day pass more quickly.

In the kitchen, she watched everything Mrs Arbuckle did, and whenever she could learn something, she quickly offered to help. The only dish she hated helping with was the soup Mrs Arbuckle made from the pippies that the boys occasionally brought back from their trips down to the seaside; the scent of them cooking reminded her strongly of Dunquin. They smelt of the soup kitchen at Ventry and of her father's death. The new world was full of strange new smells: the sharp scent of the lemons that she gathered from the tree that grew by the scullery; the warm tang of the eucalypt leaves when she walked past the stand of ghost gums by the gate.

On Saturday afternoons she had a half-day holiday, but there was nowhere for her to go. There was little for Bridie to do at Beaumanoir except work. She was meant to be allowed to attend Mass on Sunday morning as well, but there was no chapel nearby and no one offered her any help in finding a priest, though they were keen to take her to their own churches. When she asked Mrs Arbuckle if the priest might come to Beaumanoir, the old woman frowned disapprovingly. 'We'll not have an agent of the devil in this good place.'

Bridie suppressed a snort of annoyance, but Mrs Arbuckle smiled with the first flash of affection Bridie had seen in her face.

'Now, Bridie, you can't be knowing this, raised in ignorance as you were, but Hell is waiting for you, my girl. That devil in Rome, he's not interested in your eternal soul. If you need to hear counsel from a man of God, you can accompany Albert and Dora and I to church any time you like. Our Reverend Tilly, he'll set you on the path of righteousness.'

'Reverend Tilly says the finger of God is in everything,' chimed in Dora. 'He says the reason the Irish had a famine is God willed it so that they could see the error of their ways, and the reason why England will always be victorious is that God wills that too.'

Bridie could barely contain her disgust, but Mrs Arbuckle smiled and nodded. 'Aye, the finger of God is in everything. Dora has seen the light and been baptised in the true faith.' She leaned forward and spoke with fierce enthusiasm. 'What a happy kitchen we'd have if you would come over to the truth too, Bridie.'

Bridie looked at the floor, afraid her angry eyes would betray her. 'At home, ma'am, we call that taking the soup. My mam always said she'd sooner die than take the soup. And I'm truly my blessed dead mother's true daughter and a member of the Holy Catholic Church.'

Mrs Arbuckle reached out and rested one hand on Bridie's shoulder.

'Your mother is burning in hellfire, child,' she said, pityingly. 'But you could be saved.'

Bridie shut her eyes, and for a moment she could picture her mother as she was on the last day they'd seen each other, her face pale and drawn, her thin hands stroking Bridie's cheek. She opened her eyes and stared at Mrs Arbuckle.

'If my mother is burning in Hell, then it's Hell I'm bound for, 'cause I'd rather burn with them I love than bask in Heaven with the likes of you and Dora!' shouted Bridie, shaking herself free.

The smile drained away from Mrs Arbuckle's face. 'If you're determined to have the flesh seared from your skin, to live knowing that damnation awaits you, I can't force you to the baptism, but your sins are before us every day, child. Every day.'

So on Sunday morning, while the servants and masters

hurried to and from their churches, Bridie would sit in her room, looking out the window and flicking through the prayer book the Board of Guardians had given her. She'd pick out words she knew and puzzle over the longer ones, and dream of the day when she and Caitlin would be together again and Caitlin would read the pages to her.

One Sunday, she asked permission to go for a walk outside the gates of Beaumanoir.

'Don't you be walking too far, and keep out of the long grass. There's snakes everywhere this time of the year. I don't want to have to send Pip out to search for you when you're lying dead in the grass,' said Mrs Arbuckle crossly.

Bridie was just turning out of the front gate when Gilbert came riding past with his brothers, returning from Sunday school. All the other riders ignored Bridie, but Gilbert turned around in the saddle and waved. Henry reached out and punched him in the shoulder as they turned towards the stables. Gilbert simply laughed.

Bridie was only a short way from Beaumanoir when she heard someone running. She turned to find Gilbert racing towards her.

'Where are you going?' he asked breathlessly.

'Just a-walking,' she said.

'Would you like me to show you where the river is?' he asked.

'That would be fine,' said Bridie, pleased.

As they drew closer to the riverbank, the scrub grew thicker. Gilbert picked up a stick and beat the long grass around them.

'To let the snakes know we're coming,' he said, over his shoulder.

'There are no snakes in Ireland,' said Bridie. 'St Patrick drove them out when he brought the word of God. For all the churches you have in the Colony, this is a strange godless land.' She stopped for a moment to listen to the sharp, whipping cry of the bellbirds.

Bridie raked the mud on the riverbank until she found a flat stone and then stood up, aiming carefully. The stone skipped seven times across the river, flecking the water silver each time it bounced across the surface.

'That's very good,' said Gilbert, surprised. 'My best is only six.'

Bridie smiled. 'It's much easier on a smooth, flat river. Sure, if it was the ocean I'd only manage half as many. My brother was the only boy I knew that could send the stones skipping across the waves on the beach for a count of seven.'

'Where's your brother now?' asked Gilbert.

Bridie sat down again beside him and took a stick to draw patterns in the mud. 'In Ireland. In the workhouse, unless they've sent him out.' She felt her heart twist at the thought. If he left the workhouse, she might never find him again.

'Hasn't he written to you yet? My big brother William, he writes a letter every week from England, though they do take a long while to reach us.'

'How can my brother be writing to me if he doesn't know where I am?' snapped Bridie.

'Why don't you write to him and tell him where you are?'

Bridie blushed angrily. 'And how would I be doing that when I can neither read nor write!'

Gilbert frowned and looked out over the muddy river. 'Don't they have any schools in Ireland?' he asked.

Bridie wanted to slap him.

'Oh, there were schools for some where they beat the Irish from you and taught you nothing, but my father would never see us suffer that. Then there were hedge schools which the priests and scholars took wherever they could hide. My brother Brandon went for a while, but the hunger took everything away from us.'

'Well, if your brother could read it, I could pen a letter to him,' said Gilbert.

'You'd do that for me?' said Bridie.

'My sister Charity says I have the finest hand of all us boys,' he said.

Bridie laughed out loud and skipped another stone down the length of the brown river.

The following Saturday afternoon, Bridie and Gilbert met outside the gates of Beaumanoir and walked down to the river again. Bridie wanted to skip all the way there, so sweet was the excitement of their secret project.

At the bend in the river, Gilbert drew a leather writing case from the inside of his shirt, opened it out on a flat stone and set a small bottle of ink in the dirt so it wouldn't tip over.

'Here, in this corner, I'll write "Beaumanoir, Near Toorak Village, Melbourne, The District of Port Phillip, Australia". And then your brother's name and the name of the workhouse here. Now, what is it you want to say?' said Gilbert, his pen poised.

Bridie wanted to weep. There was so much to tell

Brandon. Everything, from the voyage across the sea, to the terrible wait in the depot, the strangeness of this world, how she and Caitlin would have a house and send for him if he could only wait, and how much she missed him.

'I can't make the words for it,' she said glumly, after minutes of silence. 'And his English isn't good. He won't understand it. And you can't write in the Irish.'

'Well, you could write him something simple. That you're here and well and hope that he's well. That's how letters usually start out. Surely he could ask someone to read it to him and explain.'

Gilbert dipped the pen into the little bottle of ink and scratched words onto the white paper. When he'd penned a few lines, he sat back beaming.

'How's this, then?' he asked.

'My dear Brother,

I avail myself of the opportunity of writing you these few lines with the aid of a kind young gentleman. I am hoping this letter finds you well. I have found employment in Melbourne town at the residence of a most excellent gentleman and his family.'

'That sounds very fine, don't you think?' asked Gilbert, looking pleased with himself. Bridie nodded. Haltingly, she dictated the rest of the letter, twisting the hem of her skirt in her hands as she spoke.

'Could you read the words back to me, please, Master Gilbert?'

Gilbert smoothed the paper out. *'It is a world of separation between us but there is one consolation and that is that one day, dear brother, you and I will be together again. If you can find help to do so, write to me and tell me how you are getting on so that we shall not altogether lose each other.*

Your loving sister, Brigid.'

'That's a grand letter,' said Bridie, grinning.

'I'll tell you what I'll do,' said Gilbert. 'I'll keep it with me until Father takes us into town, and then I'll post it with my letter for my own brother. Do you think your brother will find someone to help him write back?'

'To be sure. Or perhaps he's learnt his letters in English now and can write to me himself,' said Bridie, full of an optimism that she'd forgotten she could feel.

The idea of the letter was like casting a line into the wild turbulent sea of her past. The notion that Brandon might take hold of the other end sent a shiver of pleasure coursing through her.

19

Silken threads and golden needles

In the spring of 1850, Gilbert's sister, Miss Charity, was married. Bridie woke up early on the morning of the wedding and looked out the tiny bedroom window. The orchard behind the house was a mass of blossom in the moonlight, with a cloud of white on the ground beneath. She couldn't believe another season was unfolding already.

Bridie and Dora got up in the dark and set to work in the kitchen, polishing the silver and glassware so everything shone. Mrs Arbuckle had been cooking for days, preparing a feast for the wedding reception.

'I saw Miss Charity's fiancé this morning outside in the driveway with Sir William, and he's the handsomest man I've ever set eyes upon,' said Dora to Mrs Arbuckle. 'And such a gentleman you never did see. They say he's a gentleman through and through. The nephew of the Earl of Warwick himself, they say.'

Mrs Arbuckle's hand flicked back and forward across the pastries she was glazing and she looked up with a satisfied smile.

'And Miss Charity,' enthused Dora. 'She's like a princess and she let me help spread her things out. You've never seen a dress like it. I don't think there's been as fine a dress made in the Colony ever before. And she says there's never been as many people invited to a Colony wedding, with Superintendent La Trobe himself in attendance and all the most important families in Port Phillip.'

Bridie wished more than anything that she, too, could have helped with the dress. As Dora described it in detail, Bridie imagined how satisfying it would be to have actually made such a gown herself, to have sewed each of the seed pearls into place with her finest, smallest stitches.

Before the guests arrived, all the staff were lined up and looked over by Mrs Fairlea to ensure they were presentable. They heard some of the carriages moving down the driveway, wheels crunching on the gravel, as the family returned from church and the guests began to arrive. There was still so much to do. Bridie was sent back to her room to comb her wild black hair into place beneath her cap. She scowled as she leapt up the stairs to the back servants' quarters and wondered why Mrs Fairlea cared for how she looked. No one would be seeing much of her during the party. There was so much work to do in the kitchen and the scullery she'd be sweating out there until darkness fell.

She flung the door open to the bedroom to find Dora, clutching at her bloodied petticoat. All the colour had drained from her face.

'What's the matter?' asked Bridie. 'Have you cut yourself?'

Dora just looked at Bridie, then turned to lie face down on the bed, moaning.

'Dora?' said Bridie, leaning over the other girl, alarmed. 'They'll be wanting you downstairs. Are you ill?

'I'm dying,' said Dora, half-mumbling into the pillow. 'My mam died like this. I'll bleed to death just like she did.' She was trembling.

Bridie ran from the room and into the hall, calling for Mrs Arbuckle, but when she reached the kitchen, the old cook had disappeared and all the servants had gone in different directions. Bridie turned and ran back through the house. On the landing of the second floor she almost collided with Miss Charity. For a split second, her hand brushed against the beautiful thick white silk of Miss Charity's bridal gown and she leapt back, staring with a mixture of awe and embarrassment.

'Sorry, miss,' said Bridie, breathlessly.

'What is it? Is everything all right?'

'I have to find Mrs Fairlea or Mrs Arbuckle. It's Dora, she says she's dying.' Even as she spoke, Bridie wondered what exactly could have happened to Dora.

Miss Charity frowned with concern.

'Where is she?'

Dora was still lying on the bed weeping when Bridie returned. Miss Charity's bridal gown filled the small bedroom, the fabric rustling gently as she leaned over Dora and spoke to her softly.

'Oh, Miss Charity, I'm dying and here it is your wedding day,' moaned Dora. 'Bridie, what have you done, bringing Miss Charity to a servant's deathbed?'

'Hush now, Dora. Bridie,' said Miss Charity, 'I think you'll find Mrs Fairlea on the front lawns. Run and fetch her. I'll tend to Dora until you come back.'

By the time Bridie returned with Mrs Fairlea, Dora's mood had changed completely. She was dressed in clean clothes, and her cheeks were flushed with colour. When she saw Bridie, she scowled, and Bridie knew that somehow she had recovered from her life-threatening illness. There was a quick, muted conversation between Mrs Fairlea and Miss Charity that Bridie couldn't quite catch; then Miss Charity turned and hurried down the dim hallway. As she passed a corner of the balustrade, there was a loud ripping sound and a little gasp of distress. Bridie darted down the passageway to her side.

Miss Charity tried to smile through her exasperation. 'If it's not one thing, it's another. They'll be wondering what's become of me.'

'Don't worry, miss. I can mend it. I'm a fine swift seamstress. Let me show you.'

'Follow me to my room, quickly,' said Miss Charity, gathering up the folds of her dress and hurrying away.

A moment later, Bridie was kneeling before Miss Charity, with the beautiful fabric spread across her lap like dreamlike folds of snowy cloud. Bridie's needle flew through the silk, binding the tear together with tiny invisible stiches as Miss Charity's sisters fussed around her, straightening her veil and listening to her explanation of where she had disappeared to. Bridie had often heard stories from Gilbert about his sisters, and she could easily pick which was which from his descriptions. Alice was the youngest, and her golden hair reached down her back like fairy princess tresses. Emily had mousey-coloured hair and big pale blue eyes that made her look like a china doll. And then there was Constance, plump and cheerful, who was the closest in age to Charity.

'Ma'am, please, is Dora all right?' asked Bridie.

'You mustn't worry about Dora, Bridie. She had a fright

but she's not ill. She's become a woman, that's all it was.'

'Ma'am?'

Miss Charity smiled a small, secretive sort of smile. 'It's something that happens to all females,' she said awkwardly 'as we grow into women.'

Alice suppressed a giggle.

Suddenly, Bridie realised what they meant. The girls on the ship had told her about what it was like to bleed each month. Bridie hoped it would never happen to her. But there was something else Dora had said, something about her mother dying, that made Bridie feel uneasy about the way everyone seemed amused at Dora's distress. She lowered her head and concentrated on making her stiches perfect.

'Gilbert's told me about you,' said Charity. 'He says you tell good stories. How lucky for me that you have other talents as well.'

Bridie blushed shyly, smoothing the fabric out, the job completed. In that moment, she felt something so unfamiliar that she was surprised by it: a fleeting sense of her own happiness. To be useful, to be appreciated, to share in the excitement of the day, felt like balm after the endless drab cycle of washing and cleaning.

The reception was held in the big front drawing room. The guests spilled out through the long doors that opened onto the front lawn, where tables laden with the best silverware shone in the afternoon sunlight.

Late in the day, Bridie was sent to clear the tables. She came around the side of the big house and saw Sir William's mother sitting in her wicker chair with one of Gilbert's baby cousins on her knee. Miss Charity was glowing as she farewelled her guests, one hand hooked around the arm of her new husband, Martin Degraves. He was just as tall and handsome as Dora had described him, with straight dark hair and a wide moustache, and every now and then Miss Charity would gaze up at him and smile. They looked like a prince and princess as they stood together with Sir William and Lady Adeline beside them. Gilbert was there too, standing by one of the tables, eating the last of the tarts with his brothers and laughing. He didn't seem like the bullied youngest brother today. Bridie felt something hard and tight growing in her chest, as if she was standing far away, outside the richness of their world.

'What are you gawking at?' asked Dora crossly as she passed Bridie carrying a tray loaded with teacups. 'You expecting me to do all the work? Don't dawdle!'

Later that day, when the last of the guests had left and Bridie was back in the scullery with her hands deep in greasy water, she thought of what she'd seen. She tried to make a picture in her mind of her own family all together again, but it was like a gathering of ghosts. Hot tears coursed down her face and dripped into the tepid washing-up water. She forced the ghosts away and tried to conjure a brighter vision. She thought of the little house she and Caitlin would have. There'd be a room for Brandon, ready for him when he came across the sea. And there would be a room where ladies as grand as Miss Charity would come to have their gowns made, and then Bridie would measure and sew and have finest silk between her fingers every day. She saw the needle slip through the fabric, trailing threads of spun silver and gold as she made a dress fit for a princess, and Caitlin and Brandon sitting by the fire of their new home. She pushed the thoughts away and hoisted a heavy black pot into the tub.

20

The fate of girls

'Now, girls, no dilly-dallying tomorrow,' said Mrs Arbuckle. She laid out the baskets they would need for the morning on the kitchen table. 'I want to be at the market bright and early so we can get to Beaumer in good time. Miss Charity is going to need all our help. Imagine expecting a young thing like her to have all her sisters and Master Gilbert to stay and no servants of her own yet! Just as well Sir William and Lady Adeline and the older boys are going away elsewhere so there won't be no call for us here.'

Bridie went to bed tight with excitement. She lay awake long after Dora's heavy breathing signalled sleep. Tomorrow would be the first time that Bridie had been back to Melbourne Town since leaving the depot. Sometimes Dora was taken along on shopping trips to help, but up to now, Bridie had always been kept busy in the scullery or the kitchen. Bridie knew Dora was jealous that this time Bridie was coming along too. It had taken her a while to realise that most of Dora's nastiness grew out of jealousy. She was jealous of how fast Bridie learnt everything that Mrs Arbuckle taught them, and jealous when any of her jobs were given to Bridie. And it incensed Dora that Mrs

Arbuckle continued to spend so much time trying to 'save' Bridie.

When they reached town the next morning, Mrs Arbuckle led the girls into Flinders Lane and past the pubs where the heady scent of beer flooded into the lane, and then on to her favourite draper's. Bridie followed Mrs Arbuckle into the shop, where the swish of fabric and the smell of new cloth made her shiver with pleasure. There were jars full of buttons and pieces of card with lace and finery stacked along the counters. In a small glass cabinet was a display of silver thimbles and she gazed at them with wonder and longing. Spools of thread were stacked on long sticks and rolls of cloth were piled up high to the ceiling. Bridie ran one hand over a bolt of heavy red velvet and her whole body tingled. She could just see the outline of a group of girls at work in the back room with great folds of cloth lying across their laps as they sewed, and she sighed with envy.

The marketplace was teeming with people, and their shouts and the sheer noise of the place made Bridie feel giddy with excitement. Mrs Arbuckle forced her way through the crowds with the big basket over her arm. Bridie followed Dora, pushing a small wheeled contraption while Mrs Arbuckle ordered stallholders to fill it with bags of potatoes, onions, carrots and cabbages. Bridie drank in the whole spectacle of the place, her eye roving from one thing to the next. Suddenly, over to one side, she spotted Biddy Ryan standing by a stall. As soon as Dora's back was turned, Bridie raced over to talk to Biddy.

'God be with you, Biddy Ryan,' she exclaimed, but Biddy stared straight past her. 'It's me, Bridie O'Connor,' she added. 'Don't look away like that. Tell me what's been happening! Did you find a position or were you sent back to the depot, or have they found you a new place since then?'

Biddy made a little gesture with her head, and hurried away into a narrow laneway. Bridie followed her.

'You mustn't recognise me. I'm not going back there. They sent me to another situation and I hated it. I've hated all of them. I ran away again this last week past.'

'But how are you getting by, Biddy? Have you saved any money?'

'There's gentlemen who'll help a girl out, if she does them a little favour,' said Biddy, smiling archly.

'Biddy Ryan! They had a rally to defend us. Did you hear of that? A thousand Irishmen and the Bishop were in the Town Hall to let it be known that we're decent girls. Girls like you give us all a bad name.'

'Girls like me!' snorted Biddy. 'So it's better to be a girl like Honor Gauran?'

'Honor Gauran? The little one that wet her bed?' asked Bridie, confused.

'You know Honor Gauran. You remember her story. She ran away again. Ran away and drowned herself in that filthy river.'

'Drowned?' Bridie swallowed hard.

'Aye, drowned, and her belly all swollen with the baby she never birthed. You wait, Bridie O'Connor. You're such a skinny runt of a girl, seems none of them want you yet, but when you're a woman and the master lays a hand on you, we'll see which way you jump.'

Bridie thought of Sir William and then of Gilbert and

his brothers and shook her head disbelievingly. She almost laughed. And then she remembered Honor Gauran weeping at the depot.

'Someone should hang that master, or flog him, or punish him somehows; but not all masters are like that.'

Biddy looked her up and down. 'That may well be, but I like being my own mistress and that's what I am, not a little skivvy that jumps when she's shouted at. I used to think you had a bit of spark in you, Bridie O'Connor, but I suppose I was mistaken.'

Bridie clenched her fists and turned her back on Biddy. She pushed her way through the bustling crowd, past the fish merchants and the fruiterers, but couldn't see Mrs Arbuckle or Dora anywhere. She hurried up Flinders Lane. Surely, if she waited by the punts that took passengers across to St Kilda Road, she'd see Mrs Arbuckle pass. She was in such a hurry that she didn't recognise the woman stepping out of a narrow shop entrance until they were right in front of each other.

'Caitlin!' she cried.

'Well, if it isn't Bridie O'Connor herself!' said Caitlin. She looked plumper than last time Bridie had seen her at the depot, and well content.

'So this is the draper's shop where you work,' said Bridie, forgetting all her urgency. She peered into the shop enviously.

'Not for long,' said Caitlin, smiling. 'I'm to be married this very morning. I got the judge to sign a paper that lets me break my indenture. My husband's from a town called Hamilton, far down along the coast, and this afternoon we'll be setting out to his cabin there.'

Bridie stared at her blankly. 'But you're not fifteen,

Caitlin,' said Bridie. 'You can't be marrying yet.'

'You're the only one who knows my true age and you mustn't tell anyone, Bridie. They think I'm all of seventeen. And he's a lovely man.'

'Have you known him long then?' said Bridie, fighting down her swelling disappointment.

'A week or so,' answered Caitlin.

'You can't know he's lovely if you've only known him a week!'

'He's been into the shop half a dozen times and seems honest enough. Bridie, this is what I've always wished for: my own home. And Daniel can give it to me. This is why you and I came here, remember, to have our own homes.'

'To have a home together. To be our own mistresses, that's what we planned. So I could send for Brandon.'

Caitlin sighed. 'When you've finished your indenture, you can come and visit with us. I'll write to you and then you can come.'

'You said before that you'd find out where I was and write to me. Six months now I've been at Beaumanoir and not a word from you. Wouldn't the depot tell you where they'd sent me? Why didn't you write me?'

Caitlin blushed and stumbled to make an excuse. 'Well, the days were so busy. There was not time to find you, girl, and besides, you never wrote me either.'

Bridie felt she was looking at a stranger. 'But you can't be marrying, Caitlin. You can't. There'll be nothing for me to hope for if you leave Melbourne,' said Bridie miserably. She felt her eyes prickling with tears.

Caitlin's face grew hard and angry. 'Well, now, you have to make the best of it, Bridie. A few more years, you'll meet a lovely man like my Daniel and then you'll have your home too.'

Bridie scowled. 'I want it for myself, and I'll have it for myself and not because I've given myself to some filthy stranger.'

Caitlin slapped Bridie hard across the face.

'My Daniel's no filthy stranger, and who are you to be talking like that to me?'

Bridie pressed one hand against her burning cheek. She could feel the sting of the blow vibrating through her long scar. She turned away from Caitlin and ran. She could hear Caitlin calling after her as she pushed her way into the crowd, but she didn't look back.

When she finally reached the riverside, she wandered down to where the punts were crossing over the river to St Kilda Road. The sky above was a deep blue, the river beneath yellow as clay. A long thin streak of whitish smoke stretched up into the air above the brickworks on the other side of the river. Bridie stared into the eddying waters and thought of Honor Gauran, floating face down in that water, and she shuddered.

When Mrs Arbuckle finally arrived, with her basket overflowing and Dora scowling behind her, Bridie knew she was in trouble. How could a day that started so well end so badly?

'That's the first and last time we're taking you to town, my girl,' scolded Mrs Arbuckle as she pushed Bridie ahead of her and onto the punt. When they reached the south side of the river, Dora leaned close to Bridie and pinched her hard on the arm.

'Oww! What was that for?' hissed Bridie.

'For making me be the one to do all the carrying, you lazy brat.'

Bridie was made to sit right up the back of the cart crammed between sacks of potatoes and baskets of vegetables. No one spoke a word to her all the way to Beaumer but she was glad of the silence. She stared down at the road as it passed away beneath the wheels of the cart and wished she was travelling far away. For the first time in weeks, she thought of Ireland with such longing that she had to press her hands against her chest, as if to stop her heart from breaking.

21

Sea change

They drove along the Brighton Road, the afternoon sun flickering through the gum trees, and passed through the tiny seaside village of St Kilda before turning onto the beach road. Bridie looked out over the sea and was suddenly filled with longing. The smooth still waters of the bay shone blue and gold in the late afternoon sun. Far away, on the edge of the horizon, she could see the outline of land. She knew it was only the heads of the bay that she had sailed between all those months ago, yet part of her wanted to imagine that the hazy blue peninsula was Ireland – that she could simply cross that body of shimmering water and be home again. All those months since she'd had her last glimpse of Ireland seemed to disappear, as if it was only yesterday that she'd sailed across the tumbling grey Irish sea.

They turned onto the last stretch of road that led to Beaumer and Dora started squealing excitedly as they came in view of Miss Charity's house. Bridie thought it looked like a doll's house. It had whitewashed walls, high gables and bright blue fretwork along all the eaves.

'Isn't it lovely?' said Mrs Arbuckle. 'Sir William, he's

had it built specially for Miss Charity for her wedding present and part of her dowry.'

Miss Charity looked flushed as she showed them the kitchen and the little room behind it that they would share for the next few days. Bridie and Dora immediately set to work, unloading the shopping, peeling vegetables and kneading pastry for the evening meal, while Charity sat down with Mrs Arbuckle and discussed what food was to be prepared for the week.

As Bridie worked a lump of pastry into shape, her knife slipped and the blade nicked her finger. Red blood splattered across the smooth white dough.

Dora looked up and saw the ruined pastry. 'You clumsy idiot!' she shouted, snatching the knife away from Bridie.

Bridie stood absolutely still, holding her hand, watching the blood run down her fingers and drip onto the floured board. She stared blankly at the spreading bloodstain but her mind was full of much darker visions. She saw Honor Gauran floating in the murky river, her body swollen with child and with grief. She saw Biddy Ryan and Caitlin Moriarty each choosing to lie with strange men. She thought of her mother lying in the ditch on the other side of Dingle, and all the events that had brought her across the ocean to this doll's house by the sea. There was no sense in any of it. What had any of them done to deserve their fates? The injustice of it all made her want to shout with rage.

'Are you listening to me, you stupid Irish dolt!' yelled Dora.

'The Devil blister your hide for you,' said Bridie in a low, angry voice, like the growl of a cornered dog.

'Don't you talk to me about the Devil, you Papist

slattern. Mrs Arbuckle offered to show you the light and you're so stubborn, you don't know what's good for you. Your whole family are burning in the hellfires and that's where you're bound yourself, because not even God himself cares what happens to you!' Dora turned her back and resumed her task.

Blind rage and grief whirled inside Bridie. The next moment, she leapt on Dora's back, tore off her white cap and pulled a hank of mousey hair out by the roots. Dora screamed and turned on Bridie, slapping her hard across the face. A cloud of flour rose above them as Bridie fought back, scratching and biting like a creature possessed, but Dora was too strong for her. She dragged Bridie across the kitchen and threw her against the wall, then bashed her head against the chimney stone.

'Dora! Bridie! What's possessed the pair of you!' shouted Mrs Arbuckle, forcing them apart. Blood was streaming down Bridie's lip and her head ached, but she noticed with some satisfaction that Dora already had one eye starting to swell and a trickle of blood seeped out from her hairline.

That night Bridie lay in bed listening to Mrs Arbuckle snoring and the heavy breathing of Dora. She'd endured a long lecture from Mrs Arbuckle while Dora sat opposite her, weeping so loudly that Bridie almost felt sorry for her. Bridie heard little of what the old cook said to her. Her mind wouldn't stop whirling, full of voices and images, of Honor Gauran floating face down in the Yarra River, of Biddy Ryan in the market square; but mostly, it was the angry words with Caitlin that echoed in her head, and she ached with a sickening sense of betrayal. Was this how she had betrayed Brandon – leaving him to find a better life while he had nothing ahead of him but years of enduring the drudgery of the workhouse? All these months, Bridie had tried to keep her mind fixed on the future, on what lay ahead when she and Brandon and Caitlin would be together under the same roof. And now the dream had come crashing down, as if the lintel had been pulled clean out of her dreamhouse. She thought of the little cottage that had once been her family home, high on the hill above Dunquin, looking out over the sea. Suddenly, Bridie had a deep craving for the ocean, a hunger just to touch salt water and know that on the other side of the world it washed against the rocks of Slea Head.

Leaving her shoes beneath her bed, she tiptoed out of the kitchen in bare feet and ran across the front garden in the dark. A few lights still shone from the windows of the second floor but Bridie kept to the shadows of the trees. It didn't take her long to find a path through the scrub and down onto the beach.

The water lapped around her ankles, sharp and cool. She only walked a short distance before she found a boat. It was tied with a weathered rope to a pole that stuck up out of the sand. In the moonlight, it looked like a small currach, like the ones her father had taken her in as a small child. Almost before she could understand her own actions, she was dragging the boat along the beach and down to the water's edge. Small waves kissed the timbers of the craft and it glided into the water smoothly. She guided it with her body, one hand holding up her skirts, until the water lapped about her knees. Then she jumped in and pushed the boat further away from the beach with the oar. Her heart surged with happiness, to be out on the water, to be away from her bondage, to be free with no one to tell her what to do and what not to do. She felt wild and strong as she took both oars in her hands and began to row, pulling hard against the tide.

The shore became a pale bright strip, and then suddenly, the boat began to sway and rock, as if some sea creature had wrapped its tentacles around the prow.

'What are you doing?' panted Gilbert, as he pulled himself up over the side. 'This is stealing, this is our boat. I saw you from my bedroom window, running through the garden, so I followed you. I never dreamed you were going to do something stupid like this.'

'Get out,' said Bridie, furious. 'It's my boat now – I'm going away from here. I'm going home.'

'But you can't row all the way back to Ireland! You're mad!'

He tried to pull himself into the boat, but Bridie swung an oar and knocked him back into the black water. He sank under the waves, his pale golden hair swirling down into darkness.

Bridie leaned over the side of the rowboat and plunged her hand into the sea, grasping a handful of hair.

'Let go!' he shouted as he broke the surface. 'I can swim perfectly well. I don't need you to save me.'

Bridie sat back and let him climb on board, seawater running off his clothes.

'Bridie, you can't row back to Ireland,' he said, wiping the water from his eyes. 'You know you can't. You'd be exhausted before you even made it across the bay. You're being stupid.'

Bridie stared at him. She knew he was right. All her

resolution flooded out of her and she crumpled as she grasped the mad impossibility of her instinct, the hopelessness of her situation. She slumped in her seat and let the oars slide from her hands. Gilbert leaned forward and grasped them.

'Bridie, here, move over,' he said. 'We'll row back in together. I can't quite manage this boat all by myself.'

Bridie didn't respond. All the rage and fire was draining out of her, sucked into the big black bay. She shut her eyes and let hot tears course down her cheeks.

'Two years,' she said despairingly. 'Two years of Mrs Arbuckle trying to "save" me and dopey Dora telling me what to do, and then maybe longer – maybe until I'm nineteen, until I'm a grown woman! How will I endure it? I'll never be able to bring Brandon to me. Caitlin and I, we were going to save all our wages and have a home together. Caitlin, she was like my sister, but she's lost too. And I promised Brandon I'd make a home that he could come to one day, but I'll never have one, never. And Brandon will forget me and nothing will ever change.'

Gilbert looked out across the dark waters. 'Everything changes, even if you don't want it to. Two years isn't so long. It takes four months to get home to England. I tell you what, we could write to him again. If I was your brother, I'd never forget you. I'd wait, however long it took.'

Bridie brushed her hand across her face, wiping away the tears.

'You'd do that?'

'Of course I would, and Brandon will too. Don't tell my brothers I said that.'

Bridie laughed, a little hiccuping sound that echoed with the trace of a sob.

They pulled the rowboat back up onto the beach and Gilbert tied it firmly to the post. Then they trudged up through the tangle of ti-trees. The driveway shone brilliant white in the moonlight and the air seemed suddenly warm against their damp skin. Bridie looked up at the night sky.

'Sometimes I think I'm in a dream and tomorrow I'll wake up and be in my home above Dunquin. Or now, that we'll turn this corner up ahead and there'll be the path from the beach up to my house. I don't know where I am or where I belong any more.'

'Look up,' said Gilbert. 'At the stars. Then you'll always know where you are. See those stars there? That's the Southern Cross. Those are the stars you're under now. You never saw them from your Dunquin, did you?'

Bridie stopped and turned her face up to look at the huge night sky. For a moment, until she fixed on the stars, she could imagine she was on the beach with Brandon and not with this white-gold English boy. She reached up with one hand to trace the outline of the Southern Cross with her fingertips.

'I'm glad you didn't go,' said Gilbert. 'Glad you didn't get away.'

Bridie glanced across at him. His eyes were bright in the dark night.

'And I'm sorry I swiped you with the oar,' she said. 'It's just as well your head's as thick as your hide.' Then the grin came and she couldn't stifle it, and the next moment they were both laughing, a wild night-sky laugh beneath the Southern Cross.

22

Hearts of fire

Bridie knew that Gilbert must have spoken to his sister. When Miss Charity asked if Bridie could stay on as her kitchen maid, Mrs Arbuckle tried to argue that Bridie was too unskilled to be anyone's servant, but Miss Charity simply smiled and insisted on having her way. No one ever contradicted Miss Charity when she made her wishes clear. Bridie watched with growing admiration as Miss Charity stated her case in the kitchen on that warm October afternoon. Charity looked exactly like Gilbert when she was sure of her course, wearing down her opposition with a sharp, determined smile.

Once the decision was made, Mrs Arbuckle set about teaching Bridie as much as possible in the course of the next few days. Dora sullenly stood at the trough washing pots and pans while Bridie followed Mrs Arbuckle around the kitchen, committing all her instructions to memory. A daily would be coming in from St Kilda village to do most of the cooking, but Bridie would be the person responsible for all the day-to-day chores in the kitchen. Mrs Arbuckle warned her that she'd be working harder than she ever worked at Beaumanoir, but Bridie's heart sang at the thought of being so independent.

Bridie felt at home in the little kitchen at Beaumer. Even though the cook from the village took control of it much of the day, Bridie loved the quiet nights and early mornings when she had it to herself and could pretend it was her very own. She slept in the small lean-to that was built onto the back wall of the kitchen and she loved the way the scent of firewood and food drifted into her tiny room. Some nights, she'd drag her little pallet bed outside and sleep beneath the stars; if it was cooler, she could pull it closer to the stove.

Every morning, Bridie got up before dawn. It was her favourite time of day. After stoking the fire, she'd cook breakfast for Miss Charity and Mr Degraves. They would eat in the small breakfast room at the side of the house. Bridie would make sure that everything was laid out just as Mr Degraves liked it, carefully arranging all the small jars of marmalade, honey and jam, making sure that the silverware was shiny and his favourite breakfast cup was in place. She fried slices of soft bread in pork fat, and cooked kidneys and creamy scrambled eggs with lots of butter and sherry, just the way he liked them.

Martin Degraves was very particular about what he would and wouldn't eat. He never spoke to Bridie as she moved in and out of the room, freshening the tea and bringing extra butter and toast, but after the meal, as she was washing the breakfast dishes, Miss Charity would come out to the kitchen and discuss whether the eggs had enough cream mixed in with them or whether the tea was brewed exactly as the Master liked it.

The only times Martin Degraves spoke directly to Bridie was when he'd come in late from a night in town. On the nights he was not at home, Bridie slept in her clothes so that when she woke to the sound of his heavy footfall in the kitchen, she could leap up and set to work, cooking his favourite late-night snack of pig's trotters. If he'd had a pleasant evening, he'd smile as she served him, but sometimes he'd be in a dark and angry mood and not even notice her as she crept in with the tray. On those nights, he would sit alone in the front parlour for hours, cradling a glass of brandy in his hand, while Miss Charity slept on overhead.

Bridie remembered how her father used to come home late after sharing a few whiskeys with Mick O'Farrell, singing, and fall laughing into bed beside her mother. But drink didn't seem to bring Martin Degraves much happiness, and when his mood was dark, Bridie's heart ached for her gentle mistress. She knew how much Miss Charity wanted him to be happy.

Bridie knew she should think of Miss Charity as Mrs Degraves now but it seemed impossible that someone so young and kind could be a mistress. Miss Charity was so easy to work for. Like Gilbert, she seemed pleased with and interested in everyone and everything around her. And there was no one she was as passionate about as her new husband. She watched him constantly, looking for ways to please him. Bridie discovered there was no surer way to cheer-up her mistress than to take good care of all Mr Degraves' needs. Looking after Martin Degraves became a passion for both of them. Bridie made sure that his boots were clean and shiny, his white shirts perfectly starched and pressed, and his meals inviting and satisfying. Even though Bridie had so much housework to do, she longed to be allowed to cook all their meals. Mrs Smythe, the cook from the village, was a big, silent woman who set about her work with a firm hand and small conversation. But Bridie watched everything she did, learning more recipes and ways to please her master and mistress with each passing day.

Gilbert regularly came to stay at his sister's cottage by the sea. Whenever he fought too much with his brothers, he was sent to Beaumer. Bridie knew he baited his brothers even more often than before, just for the chance to come and stay. As long as his other brothers and sisters weren't with him, Gilbert could spend most of his stay in the kitchen with Bridie. She would cook up fudge and marzipan and treacle pudding with hot custard when he was staying. And then there was always the chance to swap stories. If Martin Degraves was in town on business, Miss Charity would join them in the kitchen, eating fudge at the kitchen table and licking her fingers like a child herself.

One bright November morning, Gilbert came into the kitchen with a strange and beautiful fish on the end of his line. He laid it on the table, grinning with pride.

'It's a fine creature you've hooked there,' said Bridie. 'As beautiful as Fionn MacCumhaill's salmon.'

Gilbert drew up a stool and watched the shimmering scales fly off the fish as she cleaned and filleted it.

'Does that mean I get a story in exchange for my fish?' he asked hopefully.

'Perhaps,' said Bridie teasingly. 'I don't know that a boy who puts penny bungers under his brothers' beds is deserving of stories.'

'That was only a joke! Did Charity tell you that's why I'm here again? I don't care. I like coming here. It's not a punishment! Though perhaps you've run out of good stories and I'll have to start behaving myself,' said Gilbert in reply.

'Oh, so you think insulting me will get the story out? There are more ways of killing a dog than by choking him with butter, Gilbert De Quincey. Can't you see I've got work to do?'

Gilbert put his hands together in a mock gesture of pleading and Bridie laughed.

'Quickly then, I'll tell you how Fionn mac Cumhaill was the fairest boy in Ireland. And when he was not much older than yourself, the boy met a soothsayer called Fionn the Seer living beside a deep pool. Now this old Fionn, he'd heard a prophecy that someone named Fionn would catch one of the salmons of knowledge, magic fish that in their flesh had all the wisdom of the world.'

'So did this Fionn mac Cumhaill catch one of these fish like me?'

'Oh no. Not young Fionn, but the old soothsayer did. He caught the fish and gave it to young Fionn to prepare. But here's the rub. See, Fionn's other name was Deimne, and the old Fionn only knew him by that name. So young Fionn was cooking the fish for his master, and a big blister came up on the skin of the salmon and the boy went to push it down with his finger and the blister broke and the hot sweet juice of the salmon scalded the boy's finger, and straight to his mouth it went. And he sucked it hard to soothe the burnt flesh. And then he took the fish to his master but the seer knew something was amiss and he said to the boy, "You've not eaten any piece of it, have you, boy?" and Fionn answered truthfully, and told how he'd sucked the sweet juice from his finger. So then the old seer knew that fate had tricked him and he asked the boy if he had another name. Hearing it, the old man shrugged. "Eat the salmon yourself," he said. "Seven years I've waited for this fish, but I'm not the one to fulfil the prophecy for all my waiting." So Fionn ate the salmon of knowledge and afterwards he had only to put his thumb under his tooth and he had the gift of prophecy and magic counsel in all things.'

By the time the story was told, Bridie had cleaned and gutted the fish and put it in a pan to poach. She cut two thick slices of bread, one for her and one for Gilbert, and then set the fresh cooked fish between them.

'That Fionn mac Cumhaill is like you, not me,' said Gilbert, sounding a little cheated as he crammed in mouthfuls of bread and fish.

'And what makes you think that, then?' asked Bridie.

'Well, you cooked the fish, like Fionn! And sometimes I feel afraid that Fate might trick me, like that old man. I wish we could know what's going to happen to us next, when we grow up.'

'Maybe it's better not to know,' said Bridie darkly.

'You can say that, because you're so brave.'

'Me? Brave?'

'Anyone who even thinks of trying to best Dora in a fight has to be either brave or completely barmy!'

Bridie laughed, but Gilbert put his elbows on the table and rested his face in his hands. 'It's true, Bridie. You're like that young Fionn, not me. I think you must be the one with the gift of magic counsel. So tell me another story, but one about your Cú, I like the stories about him best.'

And so they cleared the table together, and Bridie told him another story of Cú Culainn that sated him more than fish and bread.

The next morning, Charity asked Bridie to pack a picnic lunch, for the whole household was going into town to celebrate the opening of the new bridge across the Yarra. News had arrived that Port Phillip was to become a colony in its own right, with a full government in Melbourne, rather than being ruled from Sydney. Bridie couldn't see that it made a lot of difference, but Gilbert was as excited as Charity. He paced restlessly up and down the driveway, waiting for Martin Degraves to return in the carriage so they could all go into town. At midday, they heard the distant roar of cannons being fired and Gilbert came storming back into the house.

'Where is he, Charity? We'll miss everything!'

Charity sat in the front parlour by the window, wearing her blue silk polonaise and bonnet, her hands folded in her lap. She'd been sitting there for over an hour, waiting patiently for Martin.

'I'm sure that whatever has happened, Martin will explain it when he arrives. Perhaps he has had important business. You know, Gilbert, he's hopeful of a position in the new government. We must be patient.'

At two o'clock, Bridie laid out the picnic lunch on a rug on the front lawn. Gilbert slumped down angrily on the grass and picked at the little pies she had prepared.

'Superintendent La Trobe will have cut the ribbon hours ago,' he said sulkily. 'And then he was going to give out buns, two thousand of them, to all the children. We've missed the soldiers parading from the barracks. We've missed everything! I should have walked into town. Someone would have given me a ride on their cart or carriage. Hundreds of people drove and walked past the gate this morning. Everyone in the whole of Port Phillip is at the bridge except us!'

'Never mind, Gil, we'll be there in time for the fireworks,' said Charity quietly.

But Martin didn't come home. When the shadows lay long across the garden, Charity took off her bonnet and hung it on the hallstand before going upstairs to her bedroom. When Bridie brought her a pot of tea in the early evening, she noticed that the pages of the book on Charity's lap were unturned and her gaze was fixed on the road.

Gilbert thumped around downstairs until Bridie persuaded him to come to the beach with her in the hope they'd see some of the fireworks displays at a distance. The sand was still warm, and small waves lapped against the shore as they sat and watched bonfires being lit all along the bay.

'I'm sorry for you, Bert,' said Bridie.

'Oh, I suppose it's all right. Henry and Thomas didn't see it either.'

'And why's that?'

'They've been sent away to school. Home, to England. They both begged Father to let them stay until after Christmas, but he said that they should have gone home when they were seven and that they'd never be gentlemen if they didn't get a proper British education.'

'Does that mean they'll send you too?' asked Bridie, alarmed.

Gilbert laughed. 'Mama has promised me I won't have to go. She says she has to keep one of her boys close by. And besides, Martin Degraves had a proper British education and I can't see it made him much of a gentleman.'

'But he must be a good man in his heart, for your sister loves him.'

'Oh, I suppose there's some good in him, but he's a blaggard for not keeping his promise.'

Bridie looked out over the dark water to the bright lights of the bonfires and found she was thinking of Caitlin, wondering if her husband left her alone at night, if he treated her well, if she had found happiness in her new home.

'It's a hard thing to forgive a broken promise,' she said.

The summer was long and hot. Bridie had hoped that Gilbert would spend a lot of time at Beaumer, but as the months wore on, fewer visitors came to stay. The little doll's house by the sea grew stifling in the heat. For reasons she couldn't fathom, Bridie had a sense of impending disaster. It was almost as Gilbert had said, that she had been given the gift of prophecy. She pushed the idea away from her like a poisoned cup.

On a Thursday morning in February of 1851, Bridie woke to the smell of smoke. For a moment, as she struggled to consciousness, she imagined Beaumer was on fire, but when she checked the kitchen, all was still and as she'd left it the night before. She ran to the baize door and put her head around into the main part of the house but it smelt sweetly there. The smoke was coming from somewhere else. She dressed quickly and went out into the yard. Smoke lay like a mist across the garden. She hurried down the gravel drive to the gates and slipped across the road to the beach. Even though it was early morning, the air was heavy with heat and the sun itself was a dark red ball in a mahogany-coloured sky. A thick fog of smoke lay across the flat waters of the bay. The strangeness of the Antipodes struck her anew. It was as if here, at the bottom of the world, everyone was closer to the gates of Hell. The thought made her shudder and turn to run back up to the house.

She quickly prepared breakfast for Miss Charity, with the strange sense of foreboding hanging over her like a pall. Mr Degraves had been away for days, so the breakfast preparations were simple, but the heat made everything difficult. The water from the pump came out too scorching hot to drink, the butter in the butter dish turned to oil within moments of setting it on the table, and the bread dried to a rusk as soon as it was cut. But the worst of it was Miss Charity's misery. When Bridie came to clear away the tray in the breakfast room, Miss Charity looked up with eyes that were red from crying. Later in the morning, Bridie saw her sitting in the bay window of the front drawing room pretending to read, but tears were coursing down her cheeks again.

All through the day, little flecks of soot and cinder drifted down from the smoky sky and settled on everything. Bridie hung a line in the wash-house so the sheets could dry out of harm's way, but even so they were flecked with black, and every surface in the kitchen was covered with a film of ash.

That night, Bridie asked Miss Charity if she could go down to the foreshore and watch the bushfires that were raging on the far side of the bay.

'Why don't you come and see too, ma'am? You've not been out of the house all the long day.'

They followed the path through the twisted ti-trees down to the beach. People from all across St Kilda were standing on the shore, watching in awe as the whole of the coast opposite glowed red. Huge flocks of birds, black against the red-brown sky, wheeled overhead, fleeing from the firestorms.

'It's like the end of the world,' said Miss Charity. 'Everything in ashes.'

'At home, we used to build the new fire on the ashes of the old,' said Bridie. 'My mam used to talk about the fire as a holy thing, but here it's not like that. I suppose that's why they call it the New World. Everything's just beginning.'

'Do you think so?' asked Miss Charity wearily. 'Sometimes, Bridie, I feel this world is so ancient that we don't fit in it at all. I hardly remember England, but I feel I carry it in my heart in a way I'll never carry this place. That's what it's like for Martin. It's so hard for him. He doesn't belong here, he's too fine for this country.'

'Do you and Mr Degraves want to go back to England?' asked Bridie, dreading the reply.

'No, Bridie,' said Miss Charity, resting a hand on Bridie's shoulder. 'Don't you concern yourself with that. We'll probably all live happily at Beaumer for many years to come, and if Mr Degraves and I have to move to a smaller house, I'm sure there'll be a place for you there too. We've been very happy with your work.'

Bridie looked at her pale, elegant profile in the dusky light and felt a rush of love for her. She was so like Gilbert, even in the way she could guess Bridie's thoughts.

That night, Bridie lay awake for a long while, listening to the hot north wind turn with a roar and the cool southerly bring rain to the burning landscape. She knew Miss Charity was lying awake listening for the sound of Mr Degraves' horse on the gravel drive. Bridie found she listened for him too, praying that he would come home and make Miss Charity happy.

23

Ember prayer

Bridie prepared the recipe Miss Charity had given her with care. She took the stopper off a bottle of rosewater and tipped some of it into the small pot on thc stove, adding witch-hazel and three tablespoons of honey and stirring. When the potion was ready, she transferred it to a china bowl and then carried it on a tray up to the main bedroom.

Miss Charity was sitting at her dresser. Her three younger sisters lay stretched out on the big lacy bed. Alice, the youngest, was bouncing up and down on the bed with her long hair swinging, but Constance and Emily seemed subdued. Normally there was lots of excited chatter and laughter when they got together like this. Bridie set the tray down on the dresser and waited for instruction.

Miss Charity looked pale, as if she'd already masked her face with creamy lotion. Her hands moved about the dresser in a distracted fashion, picking things up and setting them down again. Bridie crushed dried rose petals with a mortar and pestle while the sisters took turns experimenting with the potion she had brought them. Usually Miss Charity loved this sort of play; she would lead the game with her sisters, braiding their hair, letting them borrow her jewellery. But today her jewellery box lay closed and her mouth was down-turned.

Bridie noticed a small envelope with Martin Degraves' looping handwriting across it. Mr Degraves had been away for more than two weeks and Mrs Smythe didn't come to the house any more. Bridie knew there was nothing to pay her with. It was more than a month since she had been paid herself.

Later that afternoon, when Lady De Quincey called by to collect her younger daughters, Miss Charity took her mother aside into the front parlour and shut the door while her sisters waited in the carriage. Bridie stood in the hall outside the parlour, longing to press her ear to the door to discover what it was that had stricken her mistress. She could hear Miss Charity crying and the low murmur of Lady De Quincey's voice as she tried to offer some comfort.

That night, Bridie knelt before the fire and smothered the flames with ash to stop them sending up sparks. The house was still and dark as she knelt on the hearth and sprinkled the ashes, whispering the prayer for the embers: '*Coiglim an tine seo mar choigleann Criost cáidh; Muire ar mullach an tí, agu Brid ina lár—*'

'What's that you're saying?' came a voice from behind. Bridie started and turned to see Martin Degraves, leaning at the door of the kitchen.

'It's a prayer.'

'What's it mean?'

Bridie was careful not to look at him when she replied. 'At home we say it to save the house. In English, it means

"I save this fire as noble Christ saves; Mary on the top of the house and Brigid in its centre; the eight strongest angels in Heaven preserve this house and keep its people safe." But I didn't finish.'

'Bridie in its centre, you say.'

Bridie looked down, her face burning. 'Saint Brigid.' She leaned forward, sprinkling another handful of ash over the embers. Martin Degraves strolled across the room and picked up a loose strand of her long black hair, tucking it behind her ear.

'Little Bridie O'Connor,' he said. 'You've changed. I remember thinking what ugly runts you Irish girls were, but the Colony's been good to you.' He grabbed Bridie by the arm, pulling her to her feet. Bridie kept her gaze fixed on the floor.

'You're fleshing out nicely. Soon we'll be having to keep the baker boy from the door. I've heard you Irish orphan girls make wild brides for the lucky brutes that get you.'

Martin Degraves was such a big man. Bridie's head was level with his chest. She stood as if frozen, her gaze fixed on the chain of his fob watch, with hot anger burning in her.

'What's the matter with you?' said Martin. 'Look at your master when he pays you a compliment.'

'The Devil bless you, sir, I didn't know it was a compliment you were paying me,' said Bridie in a hissing, angry whisper, her fists clenched.

He swept one arm behind her and lifted her off her feet, pushing her hard against the chimney. She could feel the warm bricks at her back and the hot scent of his brandy-laced breath. Her heart pounded. She thought to call out, but her horror of Miss Charity finding her like this was almost as great as her fear of the Master.

Degraves grasped her face in his hand and forced it close to his. Mustering all her strength she spat a huge gob of spit at him, and wrenched one of her hands free to rake his face with her nails. Bright drops of blood spouted on his bloated cheek, and with a roar of outrage he let her go. Bridie bolted across the kitchen as fast as she could. She slammed the door of her lean-to bedroom, pushed her cot against it, and wedged the brooms hard between the wall and the door to brace it. She stood on the bed, trembling, and then realised there was another voice in the kitchen.

'Martin,' she heard Charity cry, 'Martin, what have you done?'

'Shut up, woman,' growled Martin. 'I've done nothing. Besides, I'm the master of this house and I'll do . . .' He didn't finish. Bridie heard a cry of distress from Charity, then a door slammed and footsteps receded into the distance.

Slowly, Bridie edged the door open a crack and looked out. Charity stood in the middle of the kitchen in her nightgown, her long golden hair hanging loose around her shoulders, gasping as she wept. Bridie pulled the door open wide and Charity looked up, with a quick, pained glance, as if Bridie was a small, repugnant animal. Then she fled from the room.

Bridie stepped out into the still kitchen. She swept the ash from the hearth and glanced around the kitchen to reassure herself that all was as it should be. In her bedroom, she lay in the flickering candlelight, listening to the sharp, angry voices of Martin and Charity echoing above. She drifted in and out of sleep, startled by the smallest sounds.

Just before dawn, she woke from a dream where Charity stood on the beach at night in her wedding gown and the folds of white silk were burning. In the dream, it was Bridie's skin that felt the searing pain of the flames. She sat up in bed and burst into tears.

24

Gold dust

Mrs Fairlea arrived on the doorstep to arrange the packing-up of Beaumer. Bridie filled Miss Charity's trunks, carefully folding up the lace and cotton garments that she knew so well. Bridie was to return to Beaumanoir when the work of closing up the house was finished. Mrs Fairlea went from room to room, inspecting everything, making arrangements with the carriers and dealing with the tradespeople and shopkeepers who came to have their final accounts settled. Everyone knew that Martin Degraves had brought financial ruin on his home and then disappeared to the Bathurst goldfields in New South Wales.

Miss Charity had left Beaumer with her mother the evening before. She'd barely spoken to Bridie since the night that her husband had left.

When Bridie took her cape and bonnet off at Beaumanoir and hung them in the little room that she had shared with Dora a year ago, it was as if the walls closed in around her. She pressed her face against the small window, looking out at the orchard. The last of the autumn harvest still hung on the trees, and windfall fruit lay rotting in the long grass.

Downstairs in the kitchen, Mrs Arbuckle was rolling

out pastry. Bridie put her apron on and set to work, peeling the mountain of potatoes required for the evening meal.

'Ma'am,' she asked, 'why hasn't the fruit been gathered in from the orchard?'

'It will be us three who'll be left to do that chore, my girl. There aren't enough men to care for the grounds any more. Even the gardeners have left for the goldfields. You've heard they've struck gold right here in Victoria now?'

'The gold fever even came upon Pip during the night,' added Dora. Think of that, a stupid stable boy, lying there in the dark, imagining he'll be the lucky one. But I still don't understand why a wise and honourable man like Mr Alfred should take himself off like that.'

Mrs Arbuckle looked stricken at the mention of Alfred, the butler. 'It's a terrible time for us women. One by one they've gone – the gardeners, the stable hands and then finally our Alfred. Who'd have thought the gold fever would take him too? A God-fearing, upright man like him! Took him during the night like it did young Pip.'

Dora and Mrs Arbuckle shook their heads but Bridie felt a rush of excitement. If only she was a man, or even a boy. Gold! It made her skin tingle to think about it, that the world could so easily be turned on its head by a stroke of good fortune.

She met Gilbert behind the stables later that afternoon, when she could use the excuse of feeding scraps to the chickens to make an escape from the kitchen. Gilbert looked miserable.

'What's the matter with you, boyo?' asked Bridie.

'Charity says I shouldn't come and talk with you any more.'

Bridie felt her chest grow tight.

'And why's that?' she asked, her heart beating faster.

'She says we're both getting too old. That's it's not proper for the son of the master to be hanging about with the serving girls,' he said, blushing and looking away. Bridie knew Charity wouldn't have told him about the incident in the kitchen at Beaumer.

'And what do you think?' asked Bridie.

'I think it's bloody,' said Gilbert angrily. 'And that Martin Degraves is a damned bolter and a bludger!'

She'd never heard Gilbert swear before. She watched him stride up and down in the shadow of the stable, punching his fist into his hand and muttering oaths against Martin Degraves, and suddenly she laughed out loud.

'Strong words, boyo,' she said.

'Not bloody strong enough,' said Gilbert. 'Charity had £500 a year from Father, and Degraves spent all of it and then borrowed more and nearly lost Beaumer as well! He couldn't keep his place with Governor La Trobe because he couldn't stop getting drunk. And worst of all, Charity is still in love with the blighter! I hope a bushranger shoots him!'

'And I hope that bushranger blows the guts right out of the bastard!' said Bridie fiercely.

Gilbert looked shocked at Bridie's language. Then suddenly he laughed. For a moment, Bridie was glad to be back at Beaumanoir.

The feeling didn't last long. With fewer servants to maintain the huge house, Bridie was on the run from early dark until long after Gilbert was in bed. They had small chance to speak to each other, and Bridie started to feel bleak with exhaustion. It wasn't like working at Beaumer, where Bridie had been able to cook and order the kitchen as she pleased. Even if Mrs Arbuckle let her help with the food preparation, it also meant she had to endure the old cook's renewed attempts to convert her. No matter how hard she tried, Bridie would never feel at home at Beaumanoir.

On a cold September morning, Gilbert helped Bridie hitch up the cart for a trip to the markets in town. Not enough shops were left open in the Toorak Village to supply the manor house. Mrs Fairlea had to drive the cart the long way up the St Kilda Road because even the punt-keeper had shut his door and taken to the goldfields.

The town was the busiest Bridie had ever seen it. New arrivals were pouring into Melbourne by the boatload as news of the latest goldrush spread. Bridie stopped at the end of Elizabeth Street and watched the parade of carts and a long, snaking line of people heading out of town.

Turning into Collins Street, Bridie saw two women climbing into a carriage, and a ruddy-faced man in a top hat reaching down to help them. The women's clothes were of velvet and silk trimmed with lace, and they laughed loudly as the man waved his silver-topped cane at the driver, shouting for him to move off. His voice was coarse and his accent thick London cockney.

Mrs Arbuckle scowled. 'What a spectacle! Trollops and shysters, the lot of them! The whole world's turned on its head when rabble like them can pretend to be fine ladies and gentleman. Why, anyone can become a master overnight, even if they're putrid with sin! What is the world coming to?'

Bridie stared at the women in the carriage. One of them looked strangely familiar. When her eyes met Bridie's, she smiled knowingly and raised one hand in the air, pointing to the gold rings on her third finger. It was Biddy Ryan. As soon as Mrs Arbuckle's back was turned, Bridie waved to Biddy. 'Good luck to ye, girl,' she muttered to herself as she followed after Dora and Mrs Arbuckle.

The 'spectacle' had obviously given Dora something to think about. She leaned towards Bridie and whispered, almost conspiratorially, 'Lieutenant-Governor La Trobe said he'd seen a team of five men dig 136 ounces of gold in a single day and then 120 ounces the next! Ordinary blokes! A servant would have to work for years and years to earn as much in currency!'

'Do you think there's any women that go to the goldfields?' asked Bridie. 'Do you think a girl could go and make her fortune?'

'Don't be stupid! Of course a girl couldn't go! But I've heard that the maid at the Excelsior made a fortune, simply shaking the gold dust from the clothing of the miners that stayed. She shook it out of the rugs and the sheets, and now she's bought herself a fine little house in Fitzroy.'

Bridie couldn't imagine how much gold you'd have to shake out to buy a house, but the thought that a maid could become a mistress almost overnight made her laugh out loud. She had eight pounds – a year's wages – tucked away in the bottom of her trunk, but it made her giddy to think that an ounce of gold was worth all of that – and men were picking up nuggets as big as their fists on the goldfields.

When they reached the marketplace, it was packed with

new arrivals, all buying up supplies for the journey to the diggings. 'I'll have a penny loaf,' said Bridie to the grubby baker's boy, pointing to his full basket of loaves.

'You'll pay sixpence for it,' said the baker's boy, turning away.

Bridie had to go back to Mrs Arbuckle and report that there wasn't a loaf to be had for under sixpence. The old cook snorted with disgust and disbelief.

Mrs Arbuckle did nothing but exclaim at both the prices and the raggle-taggle crowd of goldseekers. When they finally met up with Mrs Fairlea and the cart headed back towards Princes Bridge, Mrs Arbuckle folded her hands in her lap, shut her eyes and began to pray. Loud, brassy miners spilled out of the pubs along Swanston Street and called out to the two girls, but Mrs Fairlea quickly guided the horse and cart onto the bridge and back down St Kilda Road.

'They've found gold in Lonsdale Street,' said Mrs Fairlea with grim wonder.

'Here, in Melbourne?' exclaimed Dora.

'Aye, there'll be no end to the madness that will bring,' scowled Mrs Fairlea. But Dora swivelled around in her seat and looked wistfully back at the town.

Bridie was the one who had to stable the horse, as no one else was there to do it. As she was waiting for the other women to climb down from the carriage, a ragged man walked in through the gates of Beaumanoir. At first Bridie thought he must be looking for work, but Mrs Arbuckle cried out in surprise, 'He's come back! Back from the goldfields, the poor gentleman.' Dappled sunlight fell across the man's face, and for a moment, Bridie thought

Albert had returned, but then the man looked up and Dora called, 'It's Mister Degraves!'

Bridie shook the reins and drove the horse around the back to the stables, her heart pounding. How could he be back? Surely Miss Charity wouldn't welcome him home? But then Bridie remembered how Charity had ignored or forgiven every wrong Martin Degraves had ever done, and she knew, deep in her soul, that Charity would talk her parents into taking him back into the family.

Bridie was hanging up the harness when she heard a sigh from behind her. Sitting in a corner of his black pony's stall was Gilbert, his knees drawn up against his chest, his expression troubled.

'What is it, Gilbert? What's the matter?' asked Bridie, sitting down in the straw beside him.

'They're sending me home, to England,' said Gilbert flatly. 'Mr Hassledon has run away to the goldfields, so I've no tutor. Papa says the schools here aren't suitable and I'm to go to his old school in Essex and join Henry. He says I'm sterling, even if I was born currency, and he won't have me being a colonial. And Mama has given in. But I don't want to go. I know Mama and Papa say I'm going home, but Beaumanoir is my home. Henry has sent us letters and he says it always rains in England and it's cold all the time and I won't be able to have a pony and they cane you whenever you do anything wrong. I don't want to go there. I've never wanted to go there. I'll have to be months on the boat and then years and years in school, and then I'll be a man before they let me come home and nothing will be the same.'

He slumped lower in the straw and the black pony bent

her head and nuzzled him. Gilbert's lip trembled. 'Besides, how can I ever leave Sugar?' he said, reaching up to stroke her.

'There's nothing for it, then,' said Bridie, suddenly determined. 'We'll have to run away, the both of us.'

25

Billy Dare

Bridie took out a long length of muslin and wound it tightly round and round her chest. Then she pulled a coarse cotton singlet over it and a top shirt over that. She examined her reflection in the nursery mirror and smiled. Even though she felt too hot in these thick trousers, it felt good to be someone else. Not Bridie the scullery maid but Billy Dare, a boy adventurer, off to the goldfields to make his fortune.

'Do I look like a boy?' asked Bridie, putting her hands on her hips and striking a pose.

Gilbert sat on the end of his bed in the nursery and frowned. 'I wish you hadn't cut your hair.'

'Only tiny little boys have long hair. I had to cut it,' she said, taking off her cap and running one hand over the thick crop of curly black hair. It made her face look sharper and her green eyes even bigger.

'You don't look like you any more,' said Gilbert, uneasily.

'Good. I don't want to look like me any more. I want to look like a lad.'

Gilbert's clothes fitted her well enough, even though she was two years older. The only disadvantage was that his legs were a little shorter than hers, leaving an unsightly gap between the bottom of her trousers and the tops of her boots.

'So we'll go down to Sandridge and see if we can get a boat to Geelong,' said Gilbert, pulling open his dresser drawer and fishing around for his moneybox.

'We can't spend all our money on passage,' said Bridie.

'We're not spending any money on passage,' said Gilbert. 'We'll stow away. I've read lots of stories about boys doing that. Besides, it's not as if it's very far to Geelong.'

'But if we go by sea, then we'll have to walk all the way to Ballarat. If we take Sugar, we could ride together some of the way and then take turns and she could carry supplies for us.'

Bridie loved Gilbert's little black horse. Sugar reminded her of the wild black pony she and Brandon had ridden through the surf. But more than anything, they needed the horse to carry their stores. Bridie knew the journey would be long and hard without Sugar.

'I hadn't thought about taking Sugar,' said Gilbert, frowning.

'I thought you said you didn't want to be parted from her? Who'll look after her when you're gone? Maybe they'll get Martin Degraves to take care of her,' said Bridie, baiting him.

Gilbert blanched. 'No,' he said sharply. 'I won't allow it.'

'Tonight, then?' she said, looking at him fiercely. 'You don't have to come, but if you are coming, it has to be tonight. As soon as Cook sees I've cut my hair off, she'll be angry, and I'm not taking a beating for nothing.'

'Tonight,' he agreed.

They waited until all the lamps were out and then scrambled over the wall of the stables. Bridie had filled two calico bags with supplies – bread, flour, salt pork, onions, apples and currants. She'd been gathering them together for the past few days, hoping that Dora wouldn't discover what she was up to and that Mrs Arbuckle wouldn't notice the odd missing onion. She needn't have worried. Mrs Arbuckle was so stricken at the loss of Albert that she seemed to have lost interest in most of the workings of the kitchen and spent every spare moment on her knees in prayer before the hob.

Bridie watched as Gilbert saddled up Sugar and filled her saddlebags with supplies. All of a sudden she wished Gilbert wasn't coming with her. What if something happened to Sugar? Or worse, Gilbert himself? She tapped him on the shoulder to speak to him, to tell him he shouldn't leave his home, but he put his finger to his lips and led the pony out of the stables. Her hooves clopped sharply in the cobbled yard, and Bridie felt the hair stand up on the back of her neck. Once they were through the gates of Beaumanoir, there was no turning back.

Moonlight fell in dappled patterns along the road. There was not a soul in sight as they rode through Toorak towards St Kilda Road. Bridie rode behind Gilbert, her arms around his waist, feeling the slow, steady rhythm of Sugar's gait. An hour later, when they'd reached Princes Bridge, she glanced back over her shoulder down the long stretch of St Kilda Road, checking that no one was following them. Elizabeth Street was still and empty as they passed through the city.

'We'll have a good head start by dawn. They'll never

think we've gone so far,' said Bridie, pleased.

'Yes, but we have to get off her now,' said Gilbert. 'I don't want her to get worn out, we're too heavy for her. We still have to make the Keilor Plains by daylight. We can take turns, one riding Sugar and sleeping in the saddle while the other walks.'

The sun came up behind them as they headed west along the track to Bacchus Marsh. Gilbert was the first to take the sleeping shift while Bridie led Sugar through the salt flats on the edge of the town. When it was her turn, she leaned forward in the saddle and rested her face in Sugar's thick, black mane. The rolling gait of the little pony quickly lulled her to sleep.

By dawn the road was crowded with other goldseekers. They came out of the bush and joined the track, like ants drawn to honey. Most of them were men with broad, battered straw hats, wild beards, and trousers thick with clay and mud. Some were on horseback, some on foot, and a lucky few had carts loaded with supplies. Bridie and Gilbert led Sugar to a drinking trough and stood looking at the procession of people streaming past.

'Do you think everyone will find their fortune?' asked Gilbert, frowning.

'Probably not,' said Bridie. 'But we will.'

'How many days do you think we'll need to get to Ballarat?'

'As many as it takes,' said Bridie.

The first night out of Melbourne, they led Sugar off the road and made a fire of sticks they'd collected along the way. There were campfires all over the flat plains on either side of the road. Bridie set a snare in the yellow grass at the edge of the camp, hoping to catch a rabbit, while Gilbert unsaddled Sugar and set her to graze.

'What are you doing?' asked Gilbert, wandering over.

'What does it look like? I'm setting a snare to catch us a rabbit.'

Gilbert laughed.

'And what might you be laughing at?' snapped Bridie.

'You'll not catch a rabbit with that snare.'

'I've caught rabbits all my life. My father caught rabbits. There's nothing wrong with my snares.'

'Bridie, it's not your snare. There are no rabbits in this country. Maybe you'll catch something else, but whatever it is, it won't be a rabbit, and I don't know that I'll want to eat some sort of ratty-looking thing.'

Bridie looked out over the flat, salty landscape. 'Well, before too long we'll have to eat whatever I catch. We can't be buying all our whack, and I can't make you broth from thin air.'

'You don't need to get short with me,' said Gilbert. 'It's not my fault that there are no rabbits. I dare say someone should bring some out from home. But until they do, there's not much point setting snares for them. I've heard that some settlers eat possum, but they live in trees.'

Bridie didn't speak much as they sat by the fire and ate the stew she'd made from their supplies.

'Don't be cross, Bridie. We're meant to be chums. Tell me a story. About gold, about finding gold or treasure.'

Bridie looked across the fire at Gilbert. He was right. It was a long way to Ballarat and they couldn't afford to be at each other's throats.

'Well, they say at home that if you dream of finding gold, you like as not will find it. I heard of a man, he dreamed one night that there was a bridge in the next county and beside the bridge was a blacksmith's and beneath the bridge was a crock of pure gold. So the man crossed the county and then strode out onto the bridge and all day he searched, under the bridge and beside it, and the smith working at his forge watched him and called out, "Now why is it you've been walking back and forth across the bridge all day?" So the dreamer told the smith about how he'd dreamed of gold beneath the bridge, and so the smith, he laughed and said, "Well, I had such a dream myself. But I dreamed the gold was in a garden," and as he described the garden, the man realised that it was his very own garden at home in Dunquin, so he hurried home and sure enough, there was gold in his own garden, and the dreamer had no end of riches. But I never heard that the smith found gold under the bridge by the forge.'

'So do you think if I dream there was gold beneath Beaumanoir, I should go straight home?' Gilbert asked, teasingly.

Bridie shrugged and took his empty plate, wiping it clean with a handful of grass.

'I suppose you must follow your dream, as I'm following my own.' Indeed she was afraid that when the going got rough, Gilbert would find himself yearning for the garden at Beaumanoir. Bridie knew how the past could reach its tentacles towards you and tear at your heart.

They stretched out on a blanket beside the fire and watched the stars come out. Bridie recalled the cold nights huddled in the ruined village with Brandon, that gnawing knot of hunger in their bellies, the way the world seemed to be folding in around them with only the sky offering hope. For the first time since she'd left Ireland, she felt as if those bleak times had happened to someone else. The memory of Brandon was the only thing that bound her to her past.

'Bert,' said Bridie softly, 'do you ever wonder about the stars on the other side of the world?'

'No, I know I like being under these stars. Under that cross,' he said pointing at the Southern Cross. In the firelight, his curls spilled out from under his cap and lay like rings of gold on the saddle he used as a pillow.

'Miss Charity told me that she thinks of that sky all the time, that she carries it inside her.'

Gilbert wriggled uncomfortably. 'Charity's real sterling. She was born at home in England. I'm currency. It makes me different.'

Bridie looked up at the swirling stars and realised she felt different too, even though she was born under another set of stars. It was as if the sky and the whole world was opening up before her. She hadn't felt like this since she'd disembarked from the *Diadem*. In her rough boy's clothes, she wasn't Bridie O'Connor, an Irish waif from Dunquin. She wasn't an orphan girl at sea, an unwelcome newcomer to a new land. She wasn't even a servant of the De Quinceys any more. She had money in her leather pouch, a swag full of food and a stalwart companion. She could be a whole new Bridie. It was a feeling that made her feel dizzy with pleasure. She shut her eyes, but the stars still whirled in her imagination as sleep took hold.

26

Leap of faith

By mid-morning, the track was swarming with goldseekers again – men pushing barrows, men in carts, and Chinamen with bundles balanced on long poles across their shoulders. Gilbert kept close to Sugar's head so the pony wouldn't be frightened by the press of men and horses. The noise of carts and barrows was so loud that Bridie and Gilbert couldn't hear each other speak. There were hardly any women, and Bridie was glad of her boy's clothing. No one paid any attention to them, just two lads in the crowd of men and boys.

In the late morning, it started to rain and the yellow earth turned to mud. Sugar struggled on, her flanks spattered with mire, her mane wet and bedraggled. By midday, they were all soaked through. Gilbert tethered Sugar to a slender gum tree and he and Bridie sat down on the side of the road, using Gilbert's coat to shelter them from the rain. Bridie pulled a loaf of bread from inside her shirt and broke the end from it.

Gilbert picked at the soft, doughy centre of the loaf and stared out into the rain. Bridie wondered if he was thinking about his warm bed in the nursery at Beaumanoir. Then his face lit up in a smile as a small dog trotted towards them, its curly tail erect. It sniffed at Gilbert's boots and looked at the two wet children with curious brown eyes. Bridie broke her bread and offered the pup a piece. It took the morsel daintily between its teeth and then it was gone, scampering off into the rain, weaving its way between the parade of legs.

Bridie and Gilbert got to their feet again and followed the long, yellow mud road. By late afternoon, they were in dense bush and Bridie was starting to feel uneasy. She'd heard stories of bushrangers and wild natives that murdered unwary goldseekers. She was relieved when they rounded a bend and saw the flickering lights of a fire where dozens of diggers had set up camp in an open clearing.

Gilbert and Bridie trudged into the ring of bright campfires. Suddenly, there was a flurry of dust, and scampering across the clearing towards them was the dog they had fed earlier in the day. He stood up on his hind legs, doing a little dance. Gilbert dropped on one knee to pat him, laughing.

A man in a battered top hat with tufts of silver hair sticking out sauntered towards them, swinging a walking stick.

'Hello, my lovelies, I see my Marmalade's taken to you.' He swung his cane and the dog leapt over it playfully. Then man and dog began a series of circus-like manoeuvres, the dog leaping and twisting as the man swished his cane in looping figures of eight. When he finished, the man caught Bridie's eye and winked, tipping the edge of his crumpled top hat. His plaid suit was flecked with mud and the colours in the fabric were dulled by a heavy layer of dust.

'Why did you call the pup Marmalade?' asked Gilbert, scooping the dog into his arms and offering him back to the old man. 'Isn't that a cat's name?'

'Ahh, but he's the sweetest thing, especially in the morning, wakes me up and makes the day worth living through, that one does. Little Marmalade in the morning with a nice cup of tea and a piece of toast – there's not a better way to start the day.'

Gilbert laughed and then looked away when he realised Bridie was hanging back, frowning.

'Aloysius Alphonse Jacobus,' said the man, taking his hat off and bowing.

'I'm Gilbert De—'

But Bridie intervened. 'Bert, that's my brother Bert, and I'm Billy Dare.'

'Bert and Billy,' said Mister Jacobus. 'Well, I can see you're a fine young gent, Gilbert,' he said, ignoring Bridie and smiling at Gilbert. 'But what are you doing taking off to the goldfields? A fine lad like yourself, and from a good home, shouldn't be taking such risks.'

Jacobus turned to Bridie and eyed her with a calculating look, reaching out to tweak a lock of her black hair.

'Now, young Paddy here, I can see why he's on the run.'

'My name's not Paddy,' she said crossly, pushing the man's hand away from her.

'Well, it's not Lord Alfred, either, I'll wager you that,' said Jacobus, grinning.

Bridie swallowed hard and looked across at Gilbert. They didn't look much alike. He was so tall and straight-limbed and handsome. His face had an open look about it, a look that showed he'd lived well and been much loved. He'd become dirty and more ordinary-looking in the last days of travelling, but his clear blue eyes and intelligent expression belied the dirt and grime. She wouldn't claim him as her brother again.

'Why don't you come and join me and Marmalade by our campfire and tell me how you've found the road? I've got a pannikin of water on the boil to make ourselves a nice cup of tea. Would you young gents care to join me?'

'Mister Jacobus,' Bridie began, 'I don't reckon . . .'

'You can call me Alf, most folks do.'

'Mister Jacobus, we appreciate your hospitality but Bert and me, we'd planned to get closer to Ballarat before setting up camp today. We have to move along.'

'What's the matter?' hissed Gilbert, leaning closer to her.

Bridie rolled her eyes and dragged him away.

'Why can't we camp with him?' complained Gilbert.

'I don't trust him,' said Bridie, glancing back over her shoulder to make sure they'd got well ahead of Jacobus and his dog.

'You don't trust anyone, Bridie,' said Gilbert grumpily.

'I trust you,' she said.

'Then maybe you should trust my judgement too. I don't want to have to gather a lot of wet firewood and pitch camp in the mud. He seems nice enough to me, and he's got a good dry spot under that big gum tree.'

Bridie sighed. She loved the way Gilbert was so willing to like people. That was why the two of them were friends – he hadn't cared that she was just an Irish serving-girl. But there was something about the old man that made

Bridie's thumbs prick. Reluctantly, she crossed the muddy clearing with Gilbert to join the old man squatting by his campfire.

'We'd like to take you up on your offer, thank you kindly, sir,' said Gilbert, flashing his wide, white smile.

Gilbert tended Sugar first, taking off her saddle and rubbing the weary pony down with a small cloth and then covering her with a horse-blanket that he kept rolled tight in the saddlebag.

'Fine-looking animal you have there, Bert,' said the old man, offering Gilbert a tin mug of tea.

'She's the best pony a boy could wish for. We've come all the way from Melbourne and passed many a bigger, stronger horse, but Sugar hasn't faltered once.'

'Aye, did ye see the big draughthorse caught in the mud a few miles back, sunk to his haunches. His owner shot him rather than leave him to die there.'

Gilbert and Bridie both shuddered. Bridie couldn't bear to think how Gilbert would cope if anything should happen to Sugar.

'So what do your parents think of the pair of you, heading off to seek your fortunes?' asked Jacobus, his eyes flashing.

Bridie said nothing, scowling into the fire. 'Well, you see, sir, Mr Jacobus, my brother Billy and I, we're orphans,' said Gilbert, folding his hands and smiling earnestly. 'So there are no parents to worry about us. We've lost our parents and it's only each other that we've got for company now.' Bridie groaned inwardly at Gilbert's cheerful tone. He'd never make a good liar.

'You two are no more brothers than I'm a blackfella.'

Bridie narrowed her eyes. 'Looks can be deceiving, Mr Jacobus. You could have a black heart and Bert here could be my soul's own kin. There's no accounting for the mysteries of this world.'

Jacobus laughed and reached into his pocket for a small metal flask which he took a swig from. 'That's the truth, my boy. That's surely the truth.'

'And what were you before you came for the gold?' she asked, pointedly.

'Ah, before I sought the sacred trail to El Dorado, I was both a thespian and a magician. But I still am a thespian, will always, in my black heart, be a thespian. Of late I have been plying my wizardly skills. Always a sure way to secure some coinage for the adventuring man.'

'How do you do that?' asked Gilbert, leaning forward, his face lit by the campfire.

Jacobus leaned over, brushed his hand past Gilbert's ear and as if by magic withdrew a card, the Ace of Diamonds. He gave it to Gilbert. 'A symbol of what lies ahead for you, my boy,' he said. Gilbert turned and grinned at Bridie. Then Jacobus leaned towards her and she flinched as his hand brushed past her face. He held up another card, a Queen of Spades. 'I'm sorry, young Billy Dare, it seems you have the luck of the Irish.' And he cackled.

From the folds of his coat he produced a dog-eared deck of cards and did some tricks with them, fanning them out, selecting cards at will from the thick fold and making them appear and disappear. Then he brought out a small concertina and played a little tune. Marmalade came close to the fire then and rose up on his hind legs, dancing a spinning jig.

After the music finished, Gilbert tried to persuade Jacobus to show him how to do the card tricks.

'I can't wait until I can pull that trick on Constance. She won't believe I can do it,' he whispered to Bridie.

Bridie drew further away from the circle of light, watching man and boy together. Marmalade came and sat by her, nuzzling her hand in the hope of a scrap, but she pushed the dog away. Finally, Jacobus grew tired of instructing Gilbert and made moves to settle for the night.

'When you've struck your gold, you mustn't forget your old wayside chum, my lovelies,' said Mister Jacobus, shaking his blanket out and covering himself up. 'Goodnight, boyos. Let's all of us dream of the treasures that lie ahead.'

Bridie could have sworn that he winked at her as he said it. She turned her back to the campfire and lay very still, listening to the gentle patter of the rain on the canopy of leaves above them.

27

Midnight

Gilbert's shout woke her. He was standing on the edge of the clearing, calling for Sugar, his voice sharp with desperation. The rain was still coming down in a light but steady fall. Bridie sat up and looked around. The campfire was a smouldering pile of ashes. She scrambled across the campsite to the place where Jacobus had slept the night before, and put her hand on the ground. It was long cold. Bridie knew, without even looking further, that the man was probably hours away, on the road to Ballarat.

'How could he! How could he do that to us!' Gilbert shouted, his fists clenched, his face red with fury.

Bridie shrugged and resisted the urge to say, 'I told you so.'

'There's only one place he's gone to with Sugar, and it's the same place we're headed. We'll get her back, Gilbert.'

All around the clearing, the other goldseekers were breaking camp, loading their animals or barrows and heading down along the rutted track. Luckily, Bridie had unloaded all the food from Sugar's saddlebags and piled them up close to her beneath a square of canvas, but Gilbert had left Sugar's saddle beneath the tree that she had been tethered to, and the old wizard had taken it as well.

Wearily, Bridie and Gilbert set off, following the trail of a big dray. It was slow going, stumbling over the ruts and jostling for space with all the other goldseekers. When the sun broke through mid-morning, steam rose up from the forest all around them and from their backs as their shirts dried.

All the spark had gone out of Gilbert. He talked wildly about going back to Geelong to fetch the police to pursue Jacobus, about finding the old man's camp and murdering him in his sleep, and then he grew silent and tears welled at the corners of his eyes. Bridie felt guilty at having persuaded him to join her and especially for encouraging him to bring Sugar along. She was going to have to think up something fast to stop him sinking deeper into despair. The grief of losing Sugar was settling on him like a cairn of stones, crushing his spirit.

They walked in silence for a while. 'You have to look at it like what happened to that hero of yours, Odysseus,' Bridie said, casting around for something to fire his imagination. 'He had lots of things to try him. This is sent to try us. An evil sorcerer has crossed our path and stolen your steed. You can't turn back. You have to pursue him and set things to right and bring home the Golden Fleece. That's your story.'

'That was Jason, not Odysseus. Anyway, I think I'd rather be like your hero in your story, like Cú Culainn, and just take the evil druid's head off. We should tell the troopers as soon as we get to the goldfields. We could have him arrested and then they'd hang him as a horse thief.'

'But he's the evil sorcerer,' insisted Bridie. 'We have to

outwit him. The police can't help us. Besides, the police will make you go home and I'd probably be arrested for breaking my indenture.'

That night, they tagged behind a big dray that had overtaken them as the evening shadows grew long across the track. The driver glanced down at them as he steered past, his long gun across his lap. When the dray finally pulled in between a stand of tall gums, Bridie and Gilbert stopped too, camping a little distance away from the reassuring bulk of the dray and its passengers. Bridie didn't like the feel of the dark and brooding bush around them. She couldn't explain why, but as soon as Gilbert had fallen asleep, she stamped out their fire and dragged some fallen branches over their swags to disguise where they lay. Perhaps being robbed by Jacobus was making her uneasy, but it was more than that, something in the eerie stillness of the bush around them.

She woke with a start. It was still dark but she could hear the sound of horses and men's voices quite close to where she lay. In the faint starlight, she could just make out the outline of three men. They came so close that she could smell the heat from their horses and the sour scent of the men's sweat. Silhouetted against the night sky, she saw a long gun lying across the pommel of a rider's saddle. She knew the whole encampment was in danger. Leaving Gilbert where he lay, she moved stealthily through the darkness to where she'd seen the big driver of the dray crawl under his cart to sleep.

'Mister, mister,' she said whispering hoarsely, close to the driver's ear. 'Mister, there's bushrangers on the edge of the camp. Wake up, they'll kill you in your sleep. Wake up.'

She shook his arm and the man sat up abruptly, hitting his head on the cart.

'What the divil!' he said, rubbing his head.

'You got your gun, mister?' asked Bridie. ''Cause I think it's time to use it.'

The man turned and looked out into the dark bush. 'How many?' he asked as he groped to one side for his gun.

'Three.'

It was awkward for the dray driver to load both the shotgun and his pistol beneath the cart. Bridie could smell the sharp tang of the gunpowder as he opened a little leather pouch. 'What do you think they're waiting for?' asked Bridie, peering out into the darkness. Shadows flickered all along the edge of the campground but it could have been trees moving in the breeze.

'Likely they're scouting the camp, figuring how they'll take us. But we'll take them first. Put the fear of God in them and send them back into the bush. Here, boy, hold this while I load up my pistol as well.' Bridie took the musket from him and felt the cool, hard weight of the barrel in her hands. 'Now, boy, you'll needs be my right hand. No time to wake my mate George. You hands me the pistol soon as I've fired the musket. Follow me.'

The driver scrambled out from under the cart and quickly raised the musket to his shoulder, scanning the dark edge of the bush. Bridie could just make out the shadowy outline of a man on horseback, edging through the gums.

'There,' she said, pointing.

The musket went off with a deafening roar. There was a loud curse and the bushranger appeared, his horse rearing up over the embers of the central campfire. Shouts came from all directions as other miners woke, and another gun went off. Something cut through the air near Bridie's head.

'Bloody oath!' cursed the driver, dropping to his knees and clutching his shoulder. 'I'm hit, boy. Fire the pistol, fire straight at the bugger before he kills us both.'

Bridie stepped forward past the wounded driver and pointed the pistol straight at the rider who was struggling to control his terrified horse. The darkness whirled around her as she squeezed the trigger hard.

The force of the pistol going off threw her back onto the ground. The horse bolted into the black bush, and out in the darkness she could hear someone screaming in pain.

'Sweet Jesus, forgive me,' muttered Bridie as she kicked the hot pistol away from her.

Figures were running in all directions. A torch flared nearby and a man stirred up the dying embers of the fire. Someone caught a riderless horse that bolted into camp. Voices were calling out in the darkness, and the receding sound of horses' hooves reverberated in the air. The driver was on his feet and striding towards the circle of light cast from the fire, holding his right arm with one hand.

'It's all right, people. It's all right. George, light some more torches.'

'Are you hurt, Big Bill?' asked the man called George.

'Just a nick. Reckon the bloody bushranger's bleeding a damn sight worse than me! Where's the lad that fired my pistol?'

'Oi, I caught one of them bushrangers,' said a bearded miner, wrestling a struggling figure into the firelight.

'If that's a bushranger, he's a young 'un,' called someone

else, laughing, as Gilbert was dragged into the light.

'That's my chum,' said Bridie, stepping forward and standing close to Gilbert.

'And that's the boy that fired the pistol,' said Big Bill, striding over to Bridie and gesturing for Gilbert to be released. 'This lad saved us from having our throats cut in our sleep. Why set on decent folk heading out for the fields? Lazy bludgers, can't find their own tucker.'

One by one the other goldseekers came and slapped Bridie on the back or shook her hand. She wanted to feel proud but the screams of the wounded man still echoed in her head.

'Now then,' said Big Bill. 'You lads, you've had a fine old night of it. I reckon you should sleep under my cart, safe and sound. Me and George are going to keep watch for a bit, make sure those buggers don't come back and cause more trouble.'

Bridie and Gilbert crawled under the cart and lay side by side. It was so much warmer and drier there. Looking out through the spokes of the wheels, they could see the reassuring sight of the two big men, their guns across their laps, talking quietly.

'Why didn't you wake me?' asked Gilbert, his voice small and disappointed in the dark.

'I couldn't, Bert. The bushrangers would have heard me. I had to move like a cat to get to the driver and raise the alarm. I wanted you to be safe.'

Gilbert sighed. 'But you got to shoot one of them, didn't you?'

'Yes, God help me,' said Bridie, wearily.

They lay silent beside each other and as Gilbert drifted

off to sleep, Bridie clasped her hands tightly together and prayed for forgiveness.

The next morning, Big Bill the dray driver laughed at the two bedraggled children that crawled out from beneath his cart. 'Well, you're a skinny enough pair. If you don't make any trouble, you can sit up back for the ride to the goldfields. I owe young Billy Dare for raising the alarm last night.'

'And for shooting a bushranger,' added Gilbert, beaming with pride.

Bridie shrugged. She wasn't proud to have anyone's blood upon her hands.

It was a relief to watch the track pass beneath their feet. The big cart made good progress and they overtook many people. Coming over the rise and catching her first glimpse of Ballarat, Bridie felt her heart leap with excitement. In the valley below lay a sea of tents, white and gold in the glowing afternoon light, with thousands of people swarming over the yellow hillside. Bridie turned to Gilbert and knew he felt the same. The moment was so sweet, the rush of excited happiness so complete, that she could almost believe it was a sign, a promise of things to come.

28

The choice

Bridie rolled over and opened one eye. Beside her, Gilbert was curled up like a kitten under a thin blanket. The sun was just peeking over the horizon but already the hill was alive with noise and movement.

Bridie stretched her aching limbs. She set the fire and walked down to the creek to catch a cupful of muddy water for the damper.

As she mixed a handful of flour with the water and set to kneading, a knot of worry formed in her mind. Their supplies were almost gone. The evening before, it had cost her a whole shilling to buy half a pound of flour and a few potatoes. If they didn't find gold soon, they'd starve.

They'd spent most of the last few days wandering along the edge of the creek with a pannikin, being shouted at by the other miners for encroaching on their territory. They'd swilled handfuls of grit around in the pan, hoping for a glimmer of precious gold. All day, the goldfields resounded with the sound of pistols being fired into the air as miners announced their good luck, but Bridie and Gilbert found nothing to celebrate. At night, they'd go and watch the men play cards at Big Bill's camp with well-thumbed, greasy decks.

Gilbert awoke and joined her by the campfire. Bridie grinned at him.

'Today's going to be our lucky day,' she said, handing him a cup of muddy, sweet black tea. 'I feel it in my bones.'

Gilbert smiled sleepily and rubbed the dirt from his cheek where it had been pressed hard against the ground.

'I didn't know luck could make your bones hurt so much,' said Gilbert. 'I thought that was rheumatism.'

After their meagre breakfast, Gilbert set off, as he had every morning since they had arrived, to search for Jacobus and Sugar. It wasn't easy to pick the miners apart with their filthy clothes and their wide hats, they all merged into an army of identical bodies. The horses, tethered or grazing, were easier to find.

Bridie bound up the last of their supplies and belongings and took them over to Big Bill's. George was standing outside the tent, his long thick red beard dusted with yellow clay.

'Just come to store our things, George,' said Bridie, slinging their bundle inside the flap of the big canvas tent, an A-frame with yellowing canvas stretched across solid logs of eucalypt. George and Big Bill had come down from the New South Wales goldfields and they seemed to know everything about setting up a diggers' camp. They also knew how to keep thieves from their gear. There were never enough troopers on the goldfields but George and Big Bill were happy to take the law into their own hands.

On the day they had arrived, a small, wily-looking man had tried to steal a sack of potatoes that Bill had unloaded from his dray. Big Bill had tied the thief to the nearest tree and flayed him with a length of rope while other miners looked on approvingly. It made Bridie shudder just to think of it, the way the thief had screamed and the blood had streaked his tattered shirt. She knew too well how hunger could drive a soul to theft.

Gilbert caught up with Bridie as she headed down to the creek, looking for a place to pan for gold. Swarms of black flies settled on their backs and buzzed around their faces as they squatted down by the muddy water. The sun rose higher in the sky and Bridie pulled the collar of her shirt up to shield her neck from the burning rays as she watched yellow water swirl over the dirt and quartz. She longed to unwrap the bandages that kept her chest flat. Suddenly, Gilbert let out a yelp and Bridie turned to him.

'Billy, look,' he exclaimed. Lying in the palm of his outstretched hand was a small, dirty nugget of gold. Bridie sat back in the mud, laughing in astonishment.

'I can't wait to tell Henry and Thomas! They'll be sick with jealousy.'

'We can sell it right now,' said Bridie. 'Let's take it down to the trader's and see how much it's worth!'

They were halfway across the diggings when Bridie spotted two horsemen at the crest of the road, silhouetted against the burning blue sky. Bridie thought nothing of it until the first rider took off his hat and wiped the sweat from his brow. A chill ran through her body. It was Gilbert's father, Sir William De Quincey.

'Gilbert—,' she said. She stopped. If she could distract Gilbert now, before he saw his father, they could go and spend the afternoon in the bush behind Golden Point and Sir William might never find them.

She looked at Gilbert, studying his grubby, sunburnt

face. If she pointed out the riders to Gilbert at this moment, what would he do? Would he run to them with open arms, or would he run away with her? If she gave him the choice, which way would he turn?

'What's wrong?' he asked.

Bridie drew a deep breath. 'Look,' she said, pointing. Gilbert squinted into the sun.

'Father!' he cried, running down the hill, shouting an excited welcome.

Bridie followed with dragging footsteps and a leaden heart.

Sir William leapt off his horse and gripped Gilbert by the shoulders.

'Gilbert, Gilbert,' he said, his voice choked with emotion.

'I'm sorry, Father, but I had to go. I had to! Please don't send me away to England. I want to come home, but I can't bear the thought of going away from you and Mama for years and years.'

'These aren't decisions you can understand, Gilbert. This country will be the ruin of you. Look at what it's done to you already – look at yourself, child.'

The other rider joined them, pulling off his hat as he did so. Bridie felt sick with revulsion. It was Martin Degraves.

He looked her up and down, and Bridie pulled her cap lower over her face.

'What the blazes—,' he said. 'Good lord. Sir William, it's that little Irish tramp.'

Bridie stepped back, but he was too quick for her. He dismounted from his horse and grabbed her by the arm, pinching the muscle till it hurt.

'What is the meaning of this, Gilbert?' said Sir William.

'Did you really run off with this girl? I hadn't believed it possible! Explain yourself!'

'Let go,' said Bridie, furious and terrified in the same instant. 'You've no rights over me.' She struggled to free herself from Martin's grip.

'Oh yes we do, you filthy little slut, it's back to the scullery for you,' he said, twisting her arm until she cried out in pain. Bridie looked at Gilbert, her eyes wild.

'Father!' cried Gilbert. 'Make him stop!' He launched himself at Martin and sank his teeth into the man's wrist.

'She's turned the boy into a damned animal,' said Martin, shaking Gilbert off and losing his grip on Bridie in the same instant.

'Run, Bridie!' called Gilbert. They raced between the tents, leaping over camp ovens, ducking and weaving between the miners' tents and claims.

Bridie didn't dare look back as they ran through the creek, pushing past the crowds of prospectors that lined the water's edge and then up the side of Golden Hill, until they were lost in the maze of tents beyond.

When they reached the edge of the forest, they crouched down in the shade of a gum and stared down over the field. They could see the two horsemen weaving their way between the tents. Bridie sat back against the tree trunk, feeling sweat run down her face and neck. She wrapped her arms tight around her knees to stop herself trembling. Gilbert put his head in his hands, and then he began to shake, his breath coming in heaving sobs as if his heart was breaking.

When he looked up, his face was streaked with dirt and tears.

'I have to go home, Bridie,' he said, as if the words were being dragged out of him.

'It's all right, Bert. I know.' She fought down a swell of bitterness and grief that threatened to drown her sympathy. He reached out and took her hand.

'Here,' he said forcefully, 'I want you to have this.'

Bridie stared at the nugget.

'But it's the only good thing you've got out of this. You have to show it to your father, to your brothers, you can't be giving it to me.'

'No, it's yours, Bridie.'

The afternoon sunlight cut across Gilbert's face and made his blue eyes as bright as the summer sky. Bridie smiled sadly and slipped the piece of gold into the leather pouch that hung about her neck. It clinked dully as it fell against the last of her coins.

Half an hour later, from the shelter of the forest fringe, Bridie watched as Gilbert swung up into the saddle in front of his father and Sir William put his arms around him. The two horses climbed the southern hill and turned onto the track that led back east towards Melbourne. As they disappeared from view, a bank of cloud moved down the hillside and Bridie felt as if her whole world was about to be submerged in darkness.

29

Alone

It was fine pretending to be a boy when there was another boy to act alongside. But now there was no one to share her secret, Bridie became wary of the other miners. Everyone had liked Gilbert. Big Bill and George had taken to him straight away, and he could talk to all the men with such ease that it had made Bridie easy with them too. But now she felt awkward in their company, constantly aware of the bandages that bound her chest and chafed against her skin.

The night that Gilbert left Ballarat, Bridie crept up close to George and Bill's camp but didn't join them. She slept under their cart and woke, startled and disoriented, to the early-morning sounds of George setting the billy to boil. She felt stiff and sore and filthy. She looked down towards the creek, where hundreds of men were already at work, and sighed.

Crawling out from under the cart, she set off across the hill towards the forest. She followed the creek far into the bush, scrambling over rocks, scratching her hands on sharp twigs, pushing back the prickly, matted undergrowth, until finally she came to a place where the creek widened to form a shallow pool among the rocks. She stripped off her clothes, shook the dirt from them and then laid them across the top of a shrub before slipping into the cool creek water. Even though it was still early, the morning air was hot and it rippled with the buzz of insects. She shut her eyes. It was good to have the wrappings off – they were so hot, and had grown scratchy with grit and dirt. She put a hand over the leather wallet around her neck feeling the solid shape of the nugget that Gilbert had given her the day before. Suddenly, her eyes filled with hot, stinging tears at the memory. She gasped and plunged her head under water, as if to drive away her painful feelings.

When she lifted her head from the surface again, she found she wasn't alone.

'Good morning to you, young Billy Dare,' said a familiar voice, followed by a low laugh. Standing on a rock on the edge of the creek, his arms full of her clothing, was Jacobus. Marmalade was there too, wagging his tail and watching Bridie with bright brown eyes.

Bridie gasped and folded her arms across her chest. She smacked the surface of the creek awkwardly with one hand, sending a spray of water over man and dog.

'You devil! You thief!' she shouted. 'Put my clothes down and get away!'

'A fine how-do-you-do from a damsel in distress,' said Jacobus, chortling as he flung her clothes into the creek. Bridie tried to stay low in the water as she waded towards them. She pulled her shirt out of the creek and slipped it back on. Gathering the rest of the soaking wet rags, she crawled out on the opposite bank and hid behind a bush while she struggled into them. She had to walk back through the water fully clothed to retrieve her boots, and all the while Jacobus stood watching her, a crooked smile on his face.

'And where's his young lordship?' he asked.

'Where's Sugar?' countered Bridie, angrily.

'Touché, my lovely. I'll be honest with you. Though I liberated Sugar from your young friend with good intentions of returning the pony to him later, I in turn lost possession of the steed. I can only hope the bushrangers who took her from me intended to ride her and not eat her. There are many hungry and unscrupulous men in the hills around here.'

'You're a devil to talk about scruples, liar and thief that you are.'

'Then you and I make a fine pair. For like me, you're not what you seem, young Billy Dare.'

Bridie blushed and sat down to pull her boots back on. 'I've a mind to report you to the troopers,' she said.

'And I have a mind to do the same of you,' said Jacobus sharply. 'A young girl, alone on the goldfields – how long did you think you'd last before some brute took you as his woman?'

'I'm only a girl. I'm not fourteen years old yet.'

'Not a girl for much longer, my dear, judging from what I've just seen.'

Bridie blushed angrily and felt her scar blaze.

'How much longer do you think you can keep your little secret?' asked Jacobus.

Bridie couldn't answer. She wanted to fly at him and scratch his eyes out, but she couldn't bear the thought of him touching her, so she crouched low in the grass and glared at him mutely.

Jacobus turned and headed back towards Golden Hill, whistling as he slashed at the undergrowth with his cane to clear a path. Bridie waited until he was out of view and then set off for the goldfield, dripping wet, furious and lonely, lonely in a way she'd never known.

Later that morning, as she squatted by the creek, watching the water swirl hypnotically in her pan, she thought about Jacobus' taunts. She had to find more gold. If Gilbert could find a nugget, she could too. If she could only gather enough gold to buy a new life for herself, then this nightmare could come to an end. Little beads of perspiration ran down her neck and were soaked up by the muslin wrappings that she had carefully put back on, damp and itchy and heavy as they were. She longed for a simple shift and a clean skirt. She thought of her box of clothes back at Beaumanoir and how she would never be able to return and claim them, and she fought back the sob that was forming in her throat.

In the late afternoon, Bridie trudged back to Big Bill and George's camp. Everything was in turmoil. The tents were torn down, the cart had been dragged out into the roadway. Tools and timber lay scattered all over the site.

'Hey there, young Billy!' called George. 'You and Bert had better be finding yourself another place to doss down. We're sinking a shaft directly over where you boys were sleeping. Big Bill found a nugget, right here in camp!'

All Bridie's possessions were piled up alongside Gilbert's. She bound the two swags together and heaved them onto her back. The men were so busy sinking the shaft that they didn't say a word to her as she turned and walked away. She found a place at the far end of the creek among the new arrivals, keeping her distance from everyone so that nobody would draw her into conversation.

The next day was Sunday and the smell of roasting mutton wafted across the hillside. Miners sat in groups, smoking their pipes and drinking sweet black tea. Somewhere up on the hill, men were singing hymns, and their voices resounded through the gully. A man sat in the shade of a gum tree playing a bagpipe while a group of other miners stood around, listening, their eyes half closed. In some camps, men knelt before tubs of water and scrubbed their clothes. Makeshift lines were strung up everywhere, with shirts and worn trousers stirring gently in the morning breeze. Along the creek, men were rinsing out their sluices, but few were panning for gold on the Sabbath.

Bridie heard that a priest was conducting Mass in a tent somewhere in the goldfields, and she thought if she could get down on her knees and pray, if she could confess herself to a priest, maybe she would discover what she was meant to do next. She packed up her swag and set off in search of him, but when she finally found the priest's tent, Mass was over and she couldn't bring herself to talk to him. Mrs Arbuckle was probably right. She probably was putrid with sin. The acts of contrition that she'd have to perform would be endless. She turned away from the priest's camp and stumbled back along the road. At least if she was alone, she was her own master.

She walked the full length of the gully, wrestling with her unhappiness. A strange musky odour, like flowers and spice mixed in with the smell of exotic foods, made her realise she had strayed into the Chinese area. Sunday made no difference here. Chinamen with long black plaits and golden skin were hard at work with their cradles or digging their claims. She couldn't decide whether she was shocked by the fact that they were working on a Sunday, or relieved that there were worse sinners in the world than herself.

At the end of the Chinese camp, she came across the Chinese doctor. He was sitting at a small table outside his tent, grinding something in a mortar and pestle. He looked very calm and peaceful, reaching out to add a pinch of something from a bowl and add it to the mortar as he worked. He looked up at Bridie, and nodded as she passed.

Beyond the Chinese camps, at the far fringe of the fields, was a small group of Aborigines sitting under a lean-to of branches. Two of the men were selling big sheets of bark to the miners for building huts. Some naked children were playing nearby, and they watched Bridie walking past and laughed at her. Bridie kicked up a cloud of dust and walked on, to the very edge of the forest. A flicker of movement caught her eye and she screamed as a big black snake slithered towards her. One of the black girls leapt forward and grabbed the snake by its tail. She swung it through the air like a whip, bringing it down so swiftly that its head smashed hard onto a rock and split open. The other children ran up and talked at Bridie in a rapid tangle of sounds. Bridie couldn't understand, but something drew her to follow them.

Back at their camp, the girl flung the snake straight onto the embers of the fire. At first Bridie thought this was just to dispose of the body, but once the skin began to smoke, the girl pulled it from the flame and peeled off the charred skin, picking out pieces of white meat. She offered some to Bridie, and when Bridie refused she laughed and put the piece of snake in her own mouth.

Mrs Arbuckle had once told Bridie that the blacks were worse than the Irish and not even baptism would save such heathens from hellfire, but as Bridie watched the girl and her family, she felt a swell of longing. The girl knew Bridie was still watching and she came back again with a second offering of snake meat. This time, Bridie ate it. The meat was sweet and tender, and Bridie was surprised at how good it tasted.

When the family walked into the bush, Bridie hid her swag near the edge of the scrub and followed. One of the women turned and shouted something, gesturing Bridie to go away, but the girl who had killed the snake looked back and smiled. Bridie followed at a distance as the girl and her family moved deeper into the bush, until they came to a deep, still pool of water, the colour of black tea. Some of the adults took off the remnants of clothing or possum-skin that they wore but the children were already naked and they leapt into the water with shouts of pleasure. Bridie felt hot and miserable as she watched the family in the water together. She turned and ran back the way she had come, following the trail through the low shrubs and long grasses.

She sat staring out over the diggings as evening settled over the landscape. She could hear a woman singing over her family's evening meal. Everyone seemed to have a mate to work alongside, or they were part of a team or a family or group of miners. Everywhere she turned, people seemed to be connected to each other in some way. Everyone, except Bridie.

30

The night fossicker

Bridie strode up to the store where Mrs Anmonie was sitting under a stretch of canvas, sucking on a cigar and weighing the nuggets that miners brought to her for sale. Mrs Anmonie carried a pistol in the waistband of her dress and everyone was afraid of her. As well as buying gold, Mrs Anmonie ran a sly grog shop. Alcohol was illegal on the goldfields but there were never enough troopers to enforce the law, and often as not the troopers were among her best customers. When trade was slow, Mrs Anmonie would wander around the diggings with big bottles of whiskey strapped under her voluminous skirts, and the miners would pay her to fill their tin mugs.

Bridie opened the pouch that she wore around her neck and took out Gilbert's nugget. She'd spent the last of her coins that morning and there was almost no food left in her swag. The nugget had looked so big when Gilbert found it, but as Bridie offered it up to the buyer, it seemed tiny. She stared disbelievingly at the coins the woman offered in exchange.

'I'd heard eight pounds an ounce was fair,' said Bridie.

'Show us your licence then, boy,' said Mrs Anmonie, shifting the cigar to the other side of her mouth.

Bridie eyed her coldly and put her hands on her hips.

'You think I'm a *duine le Dia*?' she asked angrily. 'Women and children don't need no miner's right,' she said, holding her ground.

'Four pounds,' said Mrs Anmonie, throwing more coins onto the pile.

Bridie scraped the money off the table, her face expressionless.

'Oi, you have to sign here,' said the dealer.

Self-consciously, Bridie dipped the pen into the inkwell and placed her mark on the contract of sale.

Every day, new miners arrived at the fields, and with them more troopers sent by Governor La Trobe to gather up the licence fees from the miners. Bridie kept her distance. If anyone discovered she was a runaway servant, she'd be sent straight back to Melbourne. Servants who broke their indentures were the only people not allowed on the goldfields.

Bridie wandered aimlessly through the fields with no clear ambition. Each night she found a different place to roll out her swag, never stopping two nights in the one place. It was strange to have no occupation, no master to answer to, no chores to do. Every day the little pile of coins in her pouch grew lighter.

On a burning hot Saturday afternoon, she found herself a spot in the shade of a gum tree and sat thinking of everything that had led her to this place. She was so wrapped up in her own thoughts that she didn't notice a small dog approaching until its wet nose was nuzzling her hand. It was Marmalade. She looked beyond him, expecting to see Jacobus, but there was no one else in sight. She tried to push the small dog away, but when he climbed into her lap and settled there she couldn't resist the comfort of his warm little body. She rubbed his soft, velvety ears between her fingers.

Marmalade's yelp woke her. A ragged man was running up the winding, dusty road and Marmalade was lying in the long shadows, completely still. A thin trickle of blood oozed out of his mouth and into the dust. Bridie joined the crowd of diggers gathered around his body.

'What happened?' asked Bridie.

'A night fossicker, I reckon,' said one of the miners. 'You was lying there and a gent was watching you. I saw 'im reach down and go for that wallet you got round your neck.'

Bridie's hand flew to the leather pouch and she cursed herself for letting it slip outside her clothes. She tucked it down inside the folds of her shirt.

'But he didn't take it,' she said.

'He would have if the pup hadn't set on him. Probably thought you couldn't give him much grief, so you was a likely target. Your little chum here, he went for him, drew blood, I reckon. The fossicker got your pup by the throat and booted him into the road. Poor little blighter.'

'Stealing from a small lad. Someone oughta catch that bugger and string him up.'

'Aye,' said another.

The men took off in a group, following the trail of the runaway thief. Only one stayed behind with Bridie and Marmalade. He knelt down and felt for a pulse in the dog's throat.

'I reckon it would be a kindness to put the creature out of his misery, boy.'

'No,' gasped Bridie. She scooped the tiny dog into her

arms and set out along the road clutching him against her chest. She had no idea where Jacobus' camp was, but she was determined to find him. All through the long evening, she carried the limp body of Marmalade through the diggings, asking everyone if they'd seen the magician in the battered top hat. Finally, when night was settling, someone pointed her in the direction of his tent. It was a single tattered sheet of canvas slung over the low branch of a slender gum and pegged to the ground.

'Mr Jacobus?' she said nervously, standing outside the opening. There was no reply.

Holding Marmalade with one hand, she raised the flap of thc tent with the other. Inside, in the muted light beneath the canvas, Jacobus lay flat on his back. The tent reeked of alcohol. The old magician's limbs lay at an odd angle to his body, and his mouth was open; a trickle of saliva was visible on his chin. Crouching down, Bridie gently laid Marmalade on the ground beside his master.

'Mr Jacobus,' she said, shaking him slightly to waken him. But the old man simply shuddered and drew his limbs in closer to his body. Up close, Bridie could see his brow was beaded with perspiration. Fever had a grip on the man, she knew it.

Bridie felt a flush of panic as she crawled backwards out of the tent. All around were the sounds of a Saturday night – men making music and laughing, guns being fired off into the night sky – but inside that tent, a man and his dog lay dying.

It took her only a moment to decide. She eased her calico swag from her back and put it just inside the flap of Jacobus' tent.

It was a long night. Bridie lit a tallow candle she found among Jacobus' possessions and sat by him, sponging his brow and moistening his lips with water she'd fetched from the forest. Big Bill had warned her not to drink the water on the diggings any more, so fouled was it by human waste and poisons from the mining process. Bridie used Gilbert's blanket to make a pillow for the old man's head and folded up her own to make a bed for Marmalade. She dripped water into the pup's mouth from a rag, but there was not much else she could do for him. It was his master that drew her energies and attention.

At dawn, Jacobus seemed no better. If anything, he seemed to be racked with even worse pain. Bridie felt hollow inside, thinking about her mother alone, burning with fever in the roadside ditch near Dingle.

By ten o'clock in the morning, the tent had grown stifling hot. She raised the flaps at the front to let some fresh air in and the fetid stench of the dying man out into the morning.

All day, she kept vigil. She cleaned and tidied inside the tent, and set a small pile of green gum leaves to smoke near the entrance, to discourage the flies. She stripped the old man's fouled clothes from him and washed them in the creek, beating them against stones to drive away the putrid smells. The hardest part of the day was just after midday when the heat was so intense and Jacobus' fever raging so wildly that she wondered if he'd live through another hour.

'Amy,' he cried, his voice thin in the shimmering heat. He struggled to raise himself on one elbow.

'Lie still, old man, and rest yourself,' said Bridie. 'It's Bridie O'Connor taking care of you here.'

'O'Connor,' he muttered. 'From my own sweet home. Don't let me die here, child. Don't let my bones be buried in this cursed land.' He slumped back, his mouth twisted in pain, as he struggled to speak.

'My soul, pray for my soul, darling child, pray for its return to Ireland, like a gull, like mist. Away from this burning hell. Blessed St Columcille, take me home,' he wept and then lapsed into incoherent fever again.

Bridie took her leather pouch from around her neck and tipped out all the coins she had left. There were nineteen shillings. She'd heard there was doctor, a big bluff Englishman that some of the miners sought out to cure their sufferings. She left the tent, raising a flap so Jacobus' soul could escape if he should die while she was gone, and set off in search of the English doctor.

She found Doctor Halibut sitting at a table outside Mrs Anmonie's sly grog tent with another, younger man. The doctor had a round, fat, red face and thick fingers like sausages which were curled around a tin cup full of whiskey. Each time he raised the cup to his lips, his hands trembled.

'Sir,' she said, holding her cap in hand as she approached him. 'Sir, my grandfather's took the fever.'

He looked hard at Bridie, taking in her ragged clothes and dirty face, and then he looked away. 'Ah, the fever, well, there's not much to do but pray for him then, child.'

'But maybe, sir, if you came and saw him, you could help him.'

'I can't give charity to every sick old blighter whose greed drives him to over-extend himself on these wretched fields.'

'I can pay,' said Bridie insistently. 'I wasn't asking for charity.'

The doctor watched as Bridie tipped the contents of her pouch into the palm of her hand and thrust it towards him. For a moment, he leaned forward to glance at the money and then, laughing, he turned back to his drink.

'A pound, child. I'll not trouble myself for less than a pound.'

'It's nearly a pound, sir. It's all I have.'

The younger man sitting beside the doctor looked at Bridie and smiled sympathetically. He was clean-shaven, and his yellow hair was combed neatly away from his face. He wore a pale blue cravat with a silver pin in it and his smooth white hands showed he'd not spent that day, nor any day, sinking a shaft or panning for gold. Just under his waistcoat, tucked neatly into his belt, was a beautiful silver pistol. Everyone on the goldfields carried a gun, but Bridie had never seen such an elegant one.

'C'mon, old Halibut, show a bit of Christian charity,' said the elegant gentleman. 'You can at least take a look at the child's grandfather.'

'Keep out of it, Bones,' said Dr Halibut, banging his mug down on the table. 'Christian charity indeed. You don't know this place as I do. I'd be an even poorer man than I am if I tried to cure every patient hereabouts. It'll just be another case of dysentery. They're dying like flies all across the field. What's a man to do? They live on tea and damper and think their strength will hold out until they strike it lucky. The young and the old should keep clear of the goldfields, they are only for the bluff and hardy.'

The dapper Mr Bones shrugged and took a long

draught of ale from his cup, but he watched Bridie with a curious, sympathetic gaze.

'Go and say a prayer for your grandfather, boy. He's more hope of help from Heaven than from me!' said the drunken doctor, laughing.

'It won't be Heaven that the old man is heading for,' said Bridie, angrily. 'But wherever he goes, I hope he lays a curse on you and all like you who'd let a soul burn in Hell before you'd raise a finger to help them. He's a magician and a wizard, is my grandfather, and I'll make sure he casts a hex on you before he goes.'

The doctor waved her away with one of his blotchy hands, but the other gentleman looked at her with renewed interest.

'A wizard you say, child?' he asked. 'And what might his name be?'

'The great wizard Jacobus,' said Bridie, her voice brimming with venom as she turned away.

31

Eddie Bones

Bridie was halfway back to the tent when she realised the man that Doctor Halibut had called 'Bones' was following her. His cane swung lightly beside him, sending up small flurries of dust as he walked.

'Boy, I think I know your grandfather,' he called out as he approached. 'Old Alf Jacobus used to go by that name.'

'That's his proper name, sir,' said Bridie. 'But he won't know you. He doesn't know his own mind, the fever's got such a grip on him.'

They went on to Jacobus' tent. Mr Bones shook his head when he saw the frail old man lying on filthy blankets. He turned to Bridie and held out two coins.

'Here's two guineas. But don't give it to Halibut, he's a quack and a charlatan. Get the Chinese physician to tend the old man. A celestial may be of more use in a case like this. The money should cover whatever supplies you need as well.'

'Thank you, sir,' she said, astonished by the stranger's generosity. 'Should I fetch you when he comes to consciousness? Are you a friend of his?'

The stranger laughed and coughed into his hand, as if embarrassed.

'No, I'm not his friend, but I'd like to know how he fares. My wife and I are camped up on the rise, where the road turns towards Melbourne. Ask for Mr Edward Bones, Esquire.'

Bridie ran all the way to the Chinamen's camp. The Chinese doctor listened to her quietly and then gestured to his servant to gather up his bag of medicines and instruments while he put up a parasol to shade his head from the sun.

That night Bridie brewed the herbs and powder the Chinese doctor had given her, carefully following his instructions. She had to hold Jacobus' head up with one hand and gently spoon the dark tea into his mouth with the other. All through the night she tended the old man, and the tent was pungent with the scent of Chinese medicines. Near dawn, Bridie lapsed into a fitful sleep, curled up between the man and his dog.

The next morning, she woke knowing something had changed while she slept. At first she thought maybe the old man had died, he was so still, but when she sat up she realised he had rolled onto his side and was sound asleep, his breath even and his lined face at peace. Even Marmalade seemed to have improved a little. Bridie held the pup gently and offered him water and a tiny morsel of food. All that day, at regular intervals, she spooned the Chinese doctor's potion into Jacobus and water into the loyal Marmalade. The old man didn't speak at all, until late in the afternoon when he opened his eyes and looked at her with a flash of recognition.

'You may not be a boy, Billy Dare, but you're an angel of mercy,' he said in a hoarse whisper.

'I just did my Christian duty,' she said, scowling to mask her relief.

'You're a fine girl. You owed me nothing but your scorn. I'm indebted to you.'

'A gentleman who said he knew you, a Mr Bones, he gave me money to pay the Chinese doctor. It's him you have to thank.'

'Eddie Bones? He's here?' asked Jacobus, his eyes wide with surprise. And then he laughed and his laugh turned into a jagged cough that left him weak and depleted. 'Ah, this life is full of mystery, ain't it?' He lay back and closed his eyes again.

Bridie watched him, her heart full of mixed emotions. Now that his face had regained some of its natural cunning, she liked him much less. Suddenly she was astounded at what she had done. She slipped out of the tent and squatted down in front of the campfire, poking at the embers with a stick.

That night, Bridie slept by the fire. She needed to put a distance between herself and Jacobus. The next morning, when she had made sure everything was in order in the tent and Jacobus and Marmalade were sleeping, she set off for the Ballarat Road, in search of Eddie Bones. She had just reached the bend in the wide road and was looking about for someone to give her directions when she heard screams of fury. She saw Eddie Bones backing out of a long white tent, with one arm raised to shield his face. A teacup flew past his head, smashing on the ground in front of the tent. This was followed by battered tins, bowls, and lastly a hatbox. Eddie Bones stood a short distance from the tent, sighing.

When he turned and saw Bridie standing with her mouth open, staring, he quickly smoothed his hair and approached her. The screaming had stopped but the sides of the tent billowed angrily, as though someone was whirling around inside it.

'My dear boy,' said Mister Bones. 'You bring good news of your grandfather, I hope.'

'Yes sir,' said Bridie, glancing at him uncertainly and continuing to stare at the strange swelling of the tent canvas.

Eddie Bones laughed. 'Don't pay attention to that, my boy. Just Mrs Bones in a temper. We've only been here a week and the goldfields are a less convivial place than she had anticipated. She's not pleased with our new arrangements. She'll settle down shortly. Tell me your news.'

'He's much improved, thank you, sir,' said Bridie. 'And I wanted to tell you the truth. Mr Jacobus isn't my grandfather. I just took to caring for him when he was at his worst. But now that he's recovering, I don't think I'll be staying on and . . .' She trailed off, her attention completely taken by the sight of the tent flap opening and a woman stepping out into the afternoon sunlight.

There were a few women on the goldfields, hardy women who worked as tirelessly as their men, but Eddie Bones' wife was nothing like any of them. The woman emerging from the tent was dressed in dark green silk. Her skin was smooth and white except for the faintest flush of pink in her cheeks, and her long, thick black hair was loose around her shoulders. She was like a princess from a fairy story.

Bridie felt herself blushing. Mrs Bones gazed intently at Bridie and smiled, a rich, kind and knowing smile.

'Good morning,' she said. 'I'm Amaranta El'Orado, also known as Mrs Edward Bones.'

'Also known as El Ave Chant D'Oro,' said Eddie proudly. 'Or the songbird with a voice of gold. My wife has sung for kings and princes all around the world. The most celebrated performer of the London stage.'

Amaranta touched her husband lightly on the cheek and laughed, and then she held out a small hand to Bridie. Bridie looked at her smooth white skin and graceful fingers and felt ashamed to touch it with her grubby, work-worn hand. She looked shyly at the ground and suddenly blurted out, 'Bridie O'Connor, ma'am. I'm not a boy at all.'

Eddie Bones looked startled, but Amaranta laughed again. Eddie stroked his chin with one hand and looked at Bridie with renewed interest. 'So you're Mr Jacobus' granddaughter?'

'No, sir,' she said. 'I told you before, we're not kin. I'm near fourteen years old, sir, and have earned my living these past two years as a maid in a gentleman's home in Melbourne. I can cook and wash and keep camp as well as any grown woman, and I was thinking, if Mrs Bones needs someone to help with the camp, well, I could make myself useful.'

Amaranta looked at her husband and her eyes were bright and laughing.

'Well Eddie, it looks as if your prayers may be answered.'

32

Songbird of the South

Bridie took the lengths of calico that had bound her swag and Gilbert's and sewed them together to make a tent. It looked tiny beside the one that Eddie Bones and Amaranta shared. The Boneses' tent was longer than almost any that Bridie had seen.

'Bought from a gentleman whose luck had failed him. Surprising what you can buy for a trifle from a retreating prospector,' said Eddie Bones, laughing. 'You wait and see! In no time at all, for the price of a song, I'll have the best outfit a man could dream of.'

Bridie watched Eddie Bones sceptically. She still couldn't understand how he never seemed to have a speck of dust on his exquisite suit. She couldn't imagine him working a claim, and yet he spoke as if he would strike it lucky any moment.

That evening, when Bridie entered the Boneses' tent to discuss her new position with Amaranta El'Orado, she was surprised to discover the volume of things they had brought with them to the goldfields. In the middle of the tent was a big brass bed with a shiny, red satin coverlet. A makeshift bark table was cluttered with bottles and brushes, combs and a large carved wooden jewellery box. Beside it was a long mirror with a crack running the length of the glass and scarves draped across its frame. All around the edges of the tent were trunks and a huge assortment of miners' equipment.

Amaranta was rummaging through one of the big trunks, pulling out gowns and garments of all colours and flinging them onto the bed.

'Ah, you've come at last,' she said. She stood with her hands on her hips, looking Bridie up and down with an amused expression.

'Don't you think it's time you changed out of your costume?' she asked. 'I can hardly have you as my lady's maid, dressed like that!'

Reluctantly, Bridie undressed, folding up her old shirt and jacket and making a neat pile of them on the dirt floor of the tent. Amaranta laughed when she saw the thick binding. She reached out and took a corner of the muslin, slowly unwinding it from around Bridie's chest, and when all the cloth was unravelled, Bridie stood before Amaranta in nothing but her ragged pants. Instinctively, she folded her arms across her breasts.

'How old are you?' asked Amaranta, staring at her intently.

'Fourteen years this month, ma'am,' answered Bridie, unable to meet the woman's gaze.

'I remember exactly what it was like to be your age. Betwixt and between, neither woman nor child. You remind me of myself, girl. We'll have a grand old time playing dress-ups,' she said.

Amaranta reached over to the pile of garments on the

bed and pulled out a dress. It was made of a fine, green, silky cloth and Bridie felt her hands tingle with pleasure as she rubbed a piece of the fabric between her fingers. She looked across at her new mistress, amazed at her generosity. Suddenly, Bridie realised that Amaranta was not much older than twenty, barely out of her teen years, and had probably had few servants of her own.

'I think the green would complement your eyes,' said Amaranta. 'They're a lovely colour, you know.'

'Thank you, ma'am,' said Bridie shyly. Amaranta reached out and gently tugged one of Bridie's black curls. They had grown quickly over the past two months and now reached down to her collar.

'A wild Irish rose unfolding, that you are, Bridie O'Connor,' said Amaranta, and Bridie blushed, the colour rising from her naked chest.

The green dress was several sizes too large, and Bridie immediately asked for a pair of scissors and needle and thread. Amaranta was impressed by how quickly she cut the dress down to size and altered it to fit.

'Where'd you learn to sew with such a deft hand?' asked Amaranta as Bridie stood before the cracked mirror, smoothing out the green fabric.

'My mam was a fine seamstress. I'll be happy to tend to all your clothes, ma'am. I love to sew and to cook and I'm not afraid of hard work.'

'I can't imagine that there's much you are afraid of,' said Amaranta.

The next morning, Jacobus came tottering into camp and eased himself down onto an upturned bucket by the fire. He carried Marmalade inside his shirt. Neither Eddie nor Amaranta had emerged from their tent but Bridie had been up before dawn, setting the fire, bringing water from the forest and preparing breakfast for her new employers. Jacobus looked wan but the old mischievous spark was back in his eyes again. Bridie offered him a cup of tea from the billy and went on kneading the damper she had prepared.

'You're a wise child, St Brigid,' said Jacobus. ''Bout time you got yourself out of those trousers and back into a skirt. And latching on to Eddie Bones might serve you well. Stupid fool that he is, never could pick the devil in a blue dress from an angel of mercy. You'll be bringing him the bad luck he deserves, I hope.'

'And what sense am I to make of that?' asked Bridie, snatching the tin cup back from Jacobus and pouring his tea into the dirt. 'Sure enough I brought you good luck, bringing you back from the dead and you not deserving a scrap of kindness. And why should you be calling a curse on Mister Bones? It's no small thanks you owe him for paying for your medicines. Get out of this camp and go to the Devil!'

Jacobus pulled his pipe out of the inside of his jacket and began packing it with tobacco, humming softly to himself as if Bridie wasn't even there. Bridie glared at him, wishing she'd left him to rot in his tent.

She went about her work, ignoring Jacobus and quietly fuming. When Eddie Bones finally emerged from the tent, Jacobus was still sitting on the upturned bucket, gazing silently into the fire.

'Good morning, Alf, Bridie,' said Eddie, nodding at each of them. He stretched sleepily and smoothed his yellow hair flat. 'Come to visit your granddaughter and see how we're treating her, old boy?'

'He's not my grandfather,' snapped Bridie.

'No, of course,' said Eddie. 'I did know that. And there's no family resemblance, is there? So to what do we owe the honour, then, Alf?'

'No honour among thieves, Eddie,' said Jacobus. 'It's Mrs Bones I've come to have a word with.' Eddie Bones grimaced.

'She doesn't want to speak with you. Best if you move along now.' He reached down and grabbed Jacobus by the arm, dragging him to his feet. Jacobus took a moment to steady himself and then looked up at Eddie and suddenly, inexplicably, he grinned.

'It's a tangled web you've woven for yourself, Eddie,' he said, glancing at the tent where Amaranta lay sleeping.

Bridie watched the old man shuffle down the dusty yellow road until he disappeared among the sea of tents. When she turned to ask Eddie Bones if he'd like breakfast, he was gone too. Bridie went back to the fire and waited for Amaranta to wake.

The mornings were always slow with Eddie and Amaranta. As the long, hot summer unfolded, Amaranta spent a lot of time lying on the red satin bed, reading novels and complaining of the heat, refusing to help with any of the practical work involved in keeping the camp. Eddie would emerge early and go straight to his 'business'. What exactly that business was, Bridie had some difficulty establishing. In the late afternoon, he'd usually come back with at least one person in tow. Some days it was only a boy wheeling a barrowload of mining equipment that Eddie had purchased from the latest round of disillusioned goldseekers. Within a week there were four cradles, a dozen sharp pickaxes, crowbars, water-lifters, zinc buckets, shovels and axes strewn around the inside of the big tent. Bridie couldn't keep track of the flow of men and equipment.

Gradually, Bridie began to realise that Eddie had business with miners all across the goldfields. In exchange for equipping them and paying their licence fees, Eddie would take a cut of whatever they found. In the evenings, dusty, bearded miners would come into camp and sit at the long bench that Eddie had paid someone to build for him, and Bridie would be kept busy making tea and damper. Or sometimes, mysteriously, a puncheon of ale would arrive in the camp along with Eddie, and then there would be laughter and loud conversation until late into the night. Bridie would keep in the background, sitting in the tent with Amaranta, repairing or adjusting her vast collection of dresses. Bridie loved handling the soft rich velvets, and carefully repaired any tears in the fine lace that edged the collars and sleeves.

Occasionally, Amaranta would go out and join the men, but never for long. Later, when Bridie was lying on the low camp bed inside her little tent, she would listen to the voices ebbing in the darkness. And in the small hours of the morning she would hear Amaranta berating Eddie when he finally joined her in bed. Sometimes their voices would rise to angry shouts and then, the next morning, Bridie would discover Eddie asleep by the campfire.

On a dry, hot February morning when dust was whirling around the goldfields, driving grit into everything, Amaranta sat at her makeshift dresser in her white lace undergarments, shaking a bottle of lotion and cursing under her breath.

Bridie sat in a corner of the long tent, repairing one of Eddie's shirts. The collar was damaged and the buttons had been torn from its front. Bridie had heard him arguing with Amaranta in the small hours of the morning and she was fairly sure that Amaranta was responsible for the damage to his clothes.

'Brigitta, you can stop that now. Eddie has far too many shirts, he can wait. I have a pressing task for you. I want you to mix me a few potions.'

Bridie folded the shirt up and watched as Amaranta wrote out a list of instructions.

Bridie glanced at the sheet and then handed it back. 'I can't read, ma'am.'

She was ready for Amaranta to grow irritated, but the woman looked at her with a mixture of interest and compassion that made Bridie more uncomfortable than if she had laughed.

'Well, perhaps if I explain it to you, you'll be able to remember the recipe. The sun here is cruel and my skin is suffering from the heat and dust. So I need some *Crème de l'Enclos*. You must take half a pint of new milk, a quarter-ounce of lemon juice, a half-ounce of white brandy. Then you must boil it and skim the surface. I will use it to wash myself with each morning. But it must be fresh.'

'There are no lemons to be had on the goldfields, ma'am.'

'What are you talking about! Of course there are lemons. Why, there's a man selling lemonade at a stall only three tents away.'

'But he makes it with acid, ma'am, not real lemons.

I could order some real ones from Mr Mallop's store, but it could take a long while before they arrive from Melbourne.'

Amaranta scowled and then threw herself down grumpily on the bed.

'Everything takes for ever in this wretched hellhole. Eddie should never have brought me here. This isn't how I should be living my life. If I don't go back to the stage soon, I'll go mad.'

'Mister Bones is sure to strike it lucky any day now,' said Bridie.

Amaranta looked at her sceptically. 'I'm sure he'd be pleased to know you have such faith in him. Eddie's no miner. He pretends that all is well as long as he has a fistful of cash. He'll be bankrupt before he knows it, the fool.'

Suddenly, her mood changed again, as some new thought came to her.

'Brigitta, where is old Jacobus camped?'

'He was down near Chinaman's Gully. When I was caring for him, that was. I think he's working as a shepherd, minding a claim for someone up on Golden Hill now that he's well again.'

'Help me with my clothes,' said Amaranta, leaping up off the bed. She stood before the mirror, winding up her long black hair and pinning it into place while Bridie pulled the stays of her girdle tight for her.

Bridie watched as Amaranta walked off into the dust storm, her skirts whirling around her.

That evening, Eddie came back earlier than usual and sat down beside the campfire with a disconsolate look on his face.

'Is everything all right, sir?' asked Bridie, pouring a cup of tea for him.

Eddie sighed. 'No, everything is not all right, Bridie. Four of my men working a claim have gone and done a bunk on me, and the other claim isn't yielding an ounce of gold. If our luck doesn't turn soon, I'll be ruined.'

Bridie hadn't wanted to believe Amaranta when she'd suggested that Eddie was bankrupt, but hearing it from Eddie himself made a chill creep up her spine. If the Boneses had no money, she would have to leave them. The thought of being alone on the goldfields once more or having to make her way back to Melbourne again made her shudder.

'Where is your mistress?' Eddie asked Bridie.

'She's gone for a stroll up Golden Hill. I think she was hoping to find Mr Jacobus.'

Eddie sat up abruptly as if he'd been slapped, letting his stool fall over in the dirt. Without saying a word, he set out quickly in the direction that Amaranta had taken.

When Amaranta returned, she looked very pleased with herself. She went into the tent and Bridie heard her singing as she changed out of her red dress. Bridie put her head around the tent flap.

'Mr Bones is looking for you, ma'am. I told him you'd gone up to see Mr Jacobus and he went after you.'

'Bloody fool!' she exclaimed and then seeing the expression on Bridie's face she said, 'Not you, Bridie. It's not your fault, but you must take a note to Eddie immediately.'

Amaranta finished writing, blotted the ink and folded her note in half.

'I want you to find him as quickly as you can. It's very important he gets this note before he does anything stupid.'

'But I don't know where he's gone.'

'Go up on Golden Hill, near where you told me to find Jacobus. He'll be on his way up there.'

Bridie didn't understand the urgency in Amaranta's voice until she reached Golden Hill. Eddie Bones had Jacobus by the front of his clothes and was shouting at him.

'She's not yours any more, Jacobus. She's mine. My wife. And she'll do as I wish. You're nothing to her any more and I don't want to catch you stirring up trouble again.' He lifted Jacobus clean off his feet and threw him to the ground. Jacobus lay with one hand raised to shield himself from the sun and Eddie's fury.

Bridie put her hand across her mouth to stifle a cry as Eddie drew back his leg and kicked Jacobus hard in the gut. She turned and ran through the city of tents, her mind whirling. The thought of Amaranta being married to Jacobus made her flesh creep, but seeing the old man on the ground and Eddie abusing him was no less disturbing.

'Did you give Eddie my note?' asked Amaranta, her eyes still steely.

'I couldn't find him, ma'am,' said Bridie, putting the note down on the upturned barrel that served as a bedside table. Amaranta crumpled the paper in her hand.

Bridie couldn't meet her gaze. She gathered up a handful of dirty washing and backed out of the tent. At the edge of the bush, she sat down with the pile of soiled clothing in her arms and sat staring into nothingness, puzzling over what she had witnessed. Eddie and Amaranta were the two most complicated, mystifying people she'd ever met.

In the middle of the night, Bridie woke to a strange and unfamiliar sound. She crawled out of her swag and saw Amaranta's silhouette, long and black, moving against the calico of the big tent. Her hair was loose but she was wearing a full-skirted gown. Bridie guessed it was the red and black lace one that she had repaired just the other day. As she glided back and forth, her shadow moved gracefully across the canvas. And as she danced, Amaranta sang, in a rich and honeyed voice. Bridie could imagine Eddie Bones sitting on the big bed, watching.

When Bridie turned away she saw a row of men at the edge of their camp, staring at Amaranta's shadow, mesmerised by her movements.

33

A troupe of stars

A few days later, in the early morning, Bridie returned from the bush with a supply of fresh water to find two men sitting on the long bench, poking at the embers of the fire and eating the damper that she had prepared for breakfast. One of the men was gigantic, with a thick black beard and a mane of untidy black curls, the other was bald-headed and fat, with a ruddy, clean-shaven face and blue eyes.

'And who do you think you are to be eating our damper?' she said crossly.

The fat, bald man grinned and stood up and made a bow. 'Alfred Wobbins, at your service, miss. Here by request, miss. To join the honourable company of thespians, miss,' he said, bowing again.

'Mr Bones doesn't need any more men to work his claim,' said Bridie, snatching the damper back from the big bearded man at the end of the bench.

'But, little miss,' said Alfred Wobbins, 'we're thespians! It's all the talk of the diggings that Mr Bones is keen to gather a troupe and what a very fine idea that is. My friend and I have discovered we're not miners after all. I've been here a month and not found a bleeding thing, so it's the fine old life of the thespian that I hanker for once again.'

Bridie didn't want to admit she wasn't sure what a thespian was, other than a thief like Jacobus, as he was the only other person she'd ever met who talked about them. Nor was she keen to confess that she'd heard nothing of the forming of a 'troupe', so she simply glared at the man, picked up a small tomahawk and set about splitting wood to make more kindling for the fire.

Eddie looked as surprised as Bridie had been when he emerged from the tent.

'Freddy Wobbins!' he exclaimed as he stepped out into the bright morning sunshine.

'Your lovely wife said you'd be very glad to see me. And I'm certainly glad to see you, Edward Bones!' said Wobbins. 'Someone should take that man Hargraves and string him up for the line he's spun that brought us humble folk in search of gold! Your Amaranta tells me it's a different type of gold you'll be mining from now on.'

Eddie laughed, and ran one hand through his hair. 'Bridie, fix our guests some tea and then run up to the butcher's and buy a pound of sausages for their breakfast. We have a morning's work of plotting and scheming ahead of us, and our companions will need sustenance!'

Word spread that the camp on the turn of the Ballarat Road was a meeting place for performers of all types. Bridie had never met anyone like the people that began to arrive. The big, black-bearded man turned out to be a bluff Scotsman called Robbie McRobbie, who was nowhere near as fierce as his appearance suggested. Most evenings he would get drunk and recite poetry in Gaelic and sometimes the poems would move him so much that tears would course down his face and drip from the end of his beard. Bridie loved the sound of his voice, the rolling warmth of his words, so close to the language she'd known as a small child.

A week later, an Italian fiddle-player called Marconi joined the camp. Marconi could also juggle knives and catch them in his teeth. He tried to persuade Bridie to be part of his knife-throwing act, but she politely declined.

One morning Eddie came into camp with a slim, curly-headed boy called Thomas Whiteley. Bridie heard his laugh before she saw him. His voice carried through the camp, a warm inviting sound that made her look up from her work as if someone had called her name.

Tom's chestnut hair fell in snarly tangles around his collar and over his eyes. He had to push a thick hank of curls away from his face to see who he was being introduced to. Freddy Wobbins was so incensed by this that he demanded Bridie's sewing scissors, set Tom down on an upturned crate, and immediately began cutting his hair. Bridie thought the stranger might be offended, but Tom smiled as if he was happy to humour them all.

Tom was nearly sixteen years old and had come to the goldfields with a gang of boys hungry for riches, but they'd had no luck panning for gold. Eddie had found him outside the post office playing a tin whistle and dancing to earn a few coins, and easily persuaded him to throw in his lot with the thespians. It didn't take long for everyone to understand why Eddie had invited him to join the troupe. He had a handsome, good-natured face, brilliant blue eyes, and he loved to laugh. Tom even laughed when Marconi threw knives into the ground around his feet as he danced, which seemed a rather dangerous form of amusement. No one could help liking him.

Bridie enjoyed the company of all the new arrivals, with one exception. One afternoon Jacobus came drifting back into camp and sat down on the long bench, making himself at home. Every day from then on he'd be there with Marmalade tucked inside his shirt, playing his concertina, showing Tom his magic tricks or chatting with one of the other men. He became a familiar part of the backcloth of her life, yet he made her uneasy. It wasn't simply that he'd stolen Sugar, nor the fact that Eddie Bones obviously disliked him. Sometimes, when Jacobus looked at her, she felt he knew exactly what she was thinking. It was as if he understood all the lies she'd ever told and every promise she'd broken.

Some nights she dreamed of Gilbert coming into camp and discovering her in this company of thieves and thespians, and she would wake in a cold sweat. And then she'd wish that she could will Brandon into her dreams instead. She knew he'd like everyone in the camp. But she could hardly make a picture of Brandon in her mind any more. It was as if her old life was slipping further and further away, as if it had all happened to someone else.

On a sweltering February afternoon, Eddie called a meeting of all the performers. They sat crammed inside the big tent on upturned crates with the canvas flapping around them as Eddie announced his plan to open a theatre.

'Now some of you men know that I've made application to Melbourne, but the government says it won't grant us a licence as the diggings is too wild a place. There aren't enough police on the fields as it is and they think we'll be stirring up trouble. But I've seen the magistrate and he's on our side.

Where there's theatre, there's civilisation, and he's keen to see the goldfields civilised. If we can get enough signatures on a petition, he'll forward it to the government and we'll have our theatre. So here's the rub, boys, I need you all to scour the fields and secure every man's mark you can. The sooner we get the licence, the sooner we'll be in business.'

The actors set out to every corner of the diggings, explaining the plan and getting signatures on the dusty sheets of paper that Eddie Bones had given each of them. Bridie and Tom trudged from one camp to the next with a pencil and the petition, asking each miner to make his mark to secure support for the theatre. Eddie took the list into every makeshift store in the canvas town and quickly gathered hundreds of signatures.

Bridie was sitting at the entrance of the big tent, darning a pair of Tom Whiteley's socks, when Eddie Bones came into camp, whistling. He had a thick envelope tucked under his arm.

He tweaked Bridie on the cheek and called out to Amaranta. 'We've got it. We're in business, my songbird,' he said as Amaranta came out of the tent. He put his hands around her slim waist and lifted her into the air.

Amaranta laughed. 'Ah, Eddie, I knew they wouldn't be able to resist you! You could sell fire to the Devil himself.'

Bridie watched them with bewilderment. That same morning, Amaranta had called him the greatest fool she'd ever known, and their angry words had sent Bridie scurrying from the campsite. She hated hearing them argue, but here it was, not three hours later, and they were like newlyweds again.

'We're official squatters on the Ballarat Road,' laughed

Eddie, unrolling the new licence. 'Official! Right here, to be precise, at the heart of the goldfields, "the site is to be used as a place of amusement for a term of one year, on condition said place of amusement will only be opened three nights per week; that each night's performance will terminate at ten o'clock; and that no exhibition will be given that would tend to lower the morals and good behaviour of the inhabitants of Ballarat".'

'That shouldn't be difficult,' said Freddy Wobbins, slapping Eddie on the back. 'If you consider the morals of this place, we can't make 'em much lower.'

They set to work the next day. Men appeared from nowhere, tools in hand, to help construct the new theatre. Eddie and Amaranta's tent was dismantled and moved further back on the site, along with all the other small tents that had been erected by the new thespians. Teams of men and horses towed saplings and great trees that had been felled in the nearby bush. Bridie loved the sharp, heady scent of the fresh-cut eucalypts.

Once word had spread that the theatre was to be erected and that Amaranta, the Songbird of the South, would sing in it three times a week, support came from all corners of the diggings. Storekeepers donated old lumber, pieces of sheet iron, tin and zinc, packing cases and rolls of calico and paint. Even the government officials who'd been so reluctant to begin with arrived with bags of nails. Bridie was kept busy making tea and baking damper, and cooking up big pots of stew and soup for all the workers, who would often arrive in the early evening after a full day working their claims. They laboured late into the night, under a big, bright autumn moon. It was a strange scene, the theatre coming into being by moon and star and firelight, on nights crisp with the promise of cold weather.

'We'll call her the "Star",' said Eddie Bones, looking up at the huge swirling mass of stars above them. 'The brightest star in the Southern Hemisphere, that's what our theatre will be, with the most beautiful star within!'

When it was completed, the building looked more like a giant cabin than a conventional theatre. It was made of huge logs, odd pieces of cut timber and canvas. The orchestra pit was just that, a hole dug into the ground, with seats made of logs and planks. The seats for the audience were made of packing cases and boxes, and at the rear, a giant felled gum tree. In the centre of the theatre, suspended from the bark roof, was a big hoop of iron with dozens of sockets for candles. Big Bill, who'd been a blacksmith before he became a goldseeker, had made it, lured to help by Eddie Bones with the promise of a free ticket to the opening night.

'Our own chandelier,' said Tom, laughing, as he jammed candles into the rough black holes. Bridie saved all the fat she could from her cooking and set it in pots, storing them up for when the theatre was completed and they'd use them to light the stage.

Bridie sewed the stage curtain from every scrap of fabric she could gather. Every morning after she'd finished the chores of feeding the camp, she'd sit on an upturned box in the theatre, stitching stray pieces of fabric that she'd been able to beg, borrow or steal. There were fragments of fine cloth mixed with rough hessian potato sacks. When she finished it, Tom helped her thread it onto the two young saplings that he'd whittled smooth to act as curtain rods.

For Bridie, making the scenery was the best part

of the whole season of building.

Everyone in the troupe worked as a team while the other helpers finished the structural work. Robbie McRobbie rolled out the great big sheets of calico that the storekeeper had donated, and then Tom helped nail them to a frame. There were to be two scenes, one set inside a palace and the other set outside. Tom painted the two scenes on opposite sides of the screen. There seemed to be no end of things that he could turn his hand to. Bridie watched him admiringly as he painted a high balcony on one corner of the backdrop.

'You see, when we have to change the scene, we'll simply turn it about!' said Tom. Bridie laughed. Eddie Bones had already explained the procedure but she liked the way Tom was always so keen to tell her things. Sometimes, she knew he watched her, waiting to think of something clever to say. It made her feel as though everything around her was changing, exactly like the backdrops in a play. One moment, Tom looked like any other boy on the goldfields, with his worn boots and grubby face and hands, but then she'd catch sight of him from a different angle and feel astonished. When he hooked his thumbs into the belt of his trousers, tipped his hat back and laughed, he was the handsomest man she'd ever set eyes upon.

One bright autumn morning she realised that more than anything she wanted Tom to look up from his script and stare straight at her, Bridie O'Connor. She wanted him to gaze at her alone and not stand there acting as if Amaranta was his princess and the only focus of his interest. She looked down, and seeing a bright pinprick of blood on the tip of her finger quickly put it to her lips, tasting the blood and wondering at the strength of her desires.

34

Broken promises

Bridie knelt beside Tom and watched as he painted the advertisement on a big sheet of canvas, with little flourishes. The lettering was perfectly shaped, black and bold.

'You've a fine hand, Tom Whiteley,' said Bridie. Even if she couldn't read every word, she knew elegant writing when she saw it.

'Can you read it all right?' asked Tom, beaming.

Bridie took a deep breath and then confessed. 'I never finished learning my letters.'

'That's something else I'll have to teach you sometime. It's not so hard as it seems. Here, I'll point to the words as I read,' said Tom, sounding even more pleased with himself. 'Grand Opening Night of the Star Theatre on Government Road, Under the patronage of Captain Worthington, Gold Commissioner, When will be Produced the thrilling musical drama of *The Princess of Patagonia*, Supported by the Full Company and featuring the Songbird of the South, Amaranta El'Orado. After which, the National Anthem with full band and chorus, and the whole to conclude with a grand vocal and instrumental concert of songs, duets and dances. Doors Open at 7 o'clock. Admission: Boxes 10s, Pit 5s.'

'How are we going to manage a full band?' asked Bridie, a little worried by the extravagant description.

'Eddie already has a big list of volunteers for the band. I've heard him talking about it. There's an American miner called Jake who can play the banjo, there are two fiddle-players as well as Marconi, and I'll play the tin whistle – when I'm not on stage playing the Princess' guard, that is – and there's a Cornish miner called Charlie Peat who has a trumpet. Oh, and Jacobus will play his concertina after he's finished doing his magic act.'

'And all will come to our rough temple of drama to worship at the shrine of the beautiful El Ave Chant D'Oro,' said Jacobus, leaning over their shoulders. Bridie jumped. She hated the way Jacobus always sneaked up like that.

'C'mon,' said Bridie, ignoring Jacobus. 'Don't we have to hang this up somewhere? I'll help you.'

'Eddie said to take it down to the old gum tree in front of the new government building.'

Bridie took a corner of the big poster and Tom took the other and they carried it down the road together.

'You don't like the old wizard, do you?' said Tom when they'd got out of earshot of Jacobus.

'What's there to like about him?' said Bridie.

'Well, he knows some fine tricks and he treats that crippled dog of his well. I feel sorry for him. Besides, I heard that you nursed him when he was sick, but now you won't even talk to him.'

'And what's it matter to you, Tom Whiteley?' she said, starting to feel annoyed.

'It matters because I'd like to know you better, Bridie, and if you don't trust him, there must be a good reason,' he said, blushing a little as he spoke.

Bridie couldn't reply. She didn't want to talk about Jacobus. A hundred questions were whirling around in her head. Why did Tom want to know her better? Did he think she was pretty? Or did he like her like a friend or a sister? What was it that he saw in her?

They pinned the sign up outside the post-office building and stood back admiring it. There were dozens of other small signs and notes pinned to the wall of the building. Some were tattered and worn with age, some were on new parchment.

'What are all those other signs about?' asked Bridie.

'They're a bit like lost and found notices,' answered Tom. 'See, this one is a note from one miner to his friend telling him to look down Chinaman's Gully when he arrives at the diggings. This one is from a woman looking for her husband: "Mrs Emily Durbridge seeks news of her husband, Henry. Anyone knowing of his whereabouts, please write or send word to . . .", and then it's got an address in Melbourne. Eddie Bones says that sooner or later everyone in the world will come past the Ballarat Post Office.'

'I wish that was true,' said Bridie. 'It's three years since I've seen my brother Brandon. Sometimes I feel frightened that I wouldn't recognise him if he did come to the diggings. He'd be more than twelve years old. I don't even know what he looks like now. He wanted to go to America but I promised I'd bring him to Australia. I promised I'd send for him, but I don't even know how to find him, even if I had the fare. I sent him two letters from Melbourne but there was never any answer. He could be anywhere in Ireland, anywhere in the world.'

Tom reached over and touched her lightly on the arm. 'Everyone is coming for the gold from all around the world. Maybe he stowed away on a ship or got himself a job as a cabin boy. He might be like the lads I came with. Teddy Raggan was only twelve. Maybe your brother will come to the diggings one day, Bridie, just as you have.'

Bridie tried to laugh, but the sound came out as a small broken sob.

'I'll tell you what we'll do,' said Tom. 'I'll put a sign up for you. You never know, you might get news of him, and even if he doesn't come himself, there are enough Paddys on the goldfield, one might be from your part of the country, one might have even been in the same workhouse as you.'

Back at camp, Tom pulled out his pen and ink again and read out each word as he wrote it in his elegant, curling handwriting.

'If this should meet the eye of Brandon O'Connor who may have come to the goldfields from County Kerry, Ireland, or any person from County Kerry who knows his whereabouts, his sister, Miss Bridie O'Connor of the Star Theatre Troupe, is most anxious to hear news of him.'

They walked back along the dusty road to the post office and Tom nailed the note up alongside the raggedy older signs. Bridie touched the clean paper with her fingertips, tracing over her own and Brandon's names, the two words she clearly recognised.

'It's hot as hell today, so of course the ink dries quickly,' said Tom, taking off his cap and wiping the sweat from his forehead.

'Sometimes, when it gets this hot, I go up to the water-hole,' said Bridie.

'You know somewhere good to bathe?' asked Tom, his eyes lighting up. 'I thought the creek was too shallow or too filthy hereabouts. Will you take me there?'

Bridie led the way across the hot, golden ground and into the scrub. When they reached the waterhole, Bridie looked up at Tom. He was much taller than her, almost a man, and she was overcome with embarrassment.

'I'll just sit and have a rest while you swim,' said Bridie.

Tom didn't argue with her. He threw off his shirt and untied his boots, but when it came to taking off his trousers, he blushed and then laughed at himself.

'It's hot enough that my trousers will dry on the walk back,' he said, buttoning them up again. He dived into the waterhole, sending sprays of silver water up into the air. The bush was still and shimmering in the afternoon heat.

Bridie watched his red-brown hair and the white arc of his arms as he swam out into the heart of the deep waterhole. Then he turned and called to her, 'Bridie O'Connor, you can't sit there in the burning sun. I promise, I'll not look at you, but you've got to come into the water.'

Bridie swallowed hard. There was nothing she wanted more. 'You promise you'll keep your face turned away from me?' she called.

'I promise!'

Bridie stripped down to her underclothes, shyly, all the time watching the back of Tom's head. The water had turned his hair a rich, dark mahogany. The bush was still, with only the echo of bird cries against the surface of the billabong.

Bridie dived into the cool water and gasped with

pleasure. Her shift clung to her skin and her bloomers filled with water and billowed around her. She dived under and her hair swirled as she parted it with her hands. When she surfaced, Tom was watching her, grinning.

'You promised to keep your back turned,' said Bridie, splashing water into his laughing face.

'You'd not deny a man such a vision of loveliness as yourself.'

'A lie on my soul if you're not the worst flatterer in the whole Colony, Tom Whiteley,' said Bridie. She tried to sound cross but the words came out full of warmth. Tom dived deep into the tea-brown water so she couldn't see him, but she felt the swish of his body as he moved past her underwater. He came back to the surface, spluttering. For a moment, he rested his hand lightly on her shoulder, as if to steady himself but Bridie felt the caress of his fingertips like fire on her bare skin. She turned quickly, and swam away from him, her shoulder tingling where he'd touched her. The water was like liquid silk against her skin and she opened her mouth, savouring its sweetness.

35

The living and the dead

Bridie worked late into the night, sewing furiously to finish everyone's costumes for the grand opening. The troupe had rehearsed the play countless times and Eddie Bones said that they would open on Friday night, but here it was Monday and there was still so much to do. When Bridie went to the store to buy more thread, Mr Pescott was happy to give it to her. A group of boys followed Bridie down the road, calling out questions.

'Are you in the show, miss?' called one boy.

'I betcha she's the Princess,' said another, elbowing his friend. 'She's Tom Whiteley's girl.'

Bridie spun around on her heel and glared at them. 'Off with you, you pack of half-wits,' she shouted. The boys laughed at her flash of temper, but they slowed their pace and let Bridie stride ahead. She couldn't help feeling a thrill of pleasure at what they'd said, even though she wondered how they could think she looked like a princess in her threadbare green dress, her hands red and raw from hard work. And who had told them she was 'Tom Whiteley's girl'?

In the theatre, Freddy Wobbins and Tom were on stage,

working through their lines, but they were constantly distracted by the argument Eddie Bones and Amaranta were having in the orchestra pit. Bridie stood at the theatre entrance with the princess costume in her arms, waiting for Amaranta to notice she was there.

'But this *is* what you wanted,' shouted Eddie Bones. 'We're back in the theatre, just as you insisted.'

'Eddie, you told me that we would stage this show for no more than three months, and then you'd sell your interest in the Star and we'd both go back to Melbourne. Now I discover you've signed a one-year lease and commissioned some fool to build us a bark hut to live in! One year! What folly! I will not waste my life and ruin my chances in this dusty hellhole while you play the great man among the barbarians!'

Bridie wanted to cover her ears. After all the work they'd put into the theatre, she couldn't bear to hear Amaranta speaking ill of it. To Bridie, it was the most exciting place she'd ever seen. She didn't care about the rough bark walls or the dirt floor. She knew that the Star Theatre was a place of magic for all its shabbiness.

Bridie sent a worried frown in Tom's direction, wishing he would intervene, but he shrugged and shook his head. One by one the actors left the theatre, leaving Eddie and Amaranta to fight it out alone. Bridie took the costume back to the tent and laid it out lovingly on the red satin quilt, admiring her work. It was the finest thing she'd ever made in her life and she couldn't wait to see Amaranta wear it on opening night. It had taken Bridie countless hours to sew the dozens of layers of feather-white silk into place. On each fold of fabric was a cluster of tiny seed pearls and silver and white brocade gleamed on the bodice. Carefully she gathered up the dress and placed it in Amaranta's trunk, where it glowed like a fairy's gown. Bridie was sure that Amaranta would change her mind about Ballarat, once she'd worn the costume on opening night and seen how much everyone in the audience admired her. Maybe the show would be so successful that Eddie would be able to build a real house for them all to live in. Then Tom could write letters to help her find Brandon and she would save up the fare and send for him. The world seemed full of endless possibilities. She stepped out of the tent and sang to herself as she set about preparing the evening meal beneath a clear, bright afternoon sky.

The evenings were becoming icy. In the middle of the night, Bridie woke up feeling the chill against her face. There was a glow of light from the nearby tent. Bridie crawled outside and looked to see who could be awake at so late an hour. There were angry voices coming from Amaranta and Eddie's tent. Bridie was used to the sound of their muffled arguments but this time there was a third voice interwoven in the heated conversation. She lay in the dark, puzzled by the interplay of the voices. Suddenly there was the crack of a gunshot. Shivering, Bridie reached for a blanket, wrapped it around her shoulders and ran over to the big tent. Tom was standing by the entrance looking uncertain. 'What's happened?' said Bridie. 'Why are you just standing there?' She tore open the tent flap and rushed inside.

There was chaos everywhere. Everything had been swept from Amaranta's dresser and the big looking-glass was smashed in pieces on the dirt floor. Backed into one corner was Jacobus, with his hands in the air, and on the other side of the tent, Eddie Bones and Amaranta were struggling for possession of Eddie's silver pistol. Suddenly, the gun went off again. Bridie smelt the sharp tang of burning gunpowder. For a split second, everything in the tent, in the whole world, became absolutely still except for the gentle swish of Bridie's blanket falling onto the dirt floor. And then Bridie felt it. It was like being seared with a burning coal. She looked down and saw a flower of red spread across her nightgown. Everyone was staring at her and she couldn't think why. Bridie touched the red flower. Her hands came away wet with blood and then there was a strange high wailing sound that filled her ears, a cry from far away, like the cry of a banshee, and her legs gave way. The tent swirled around her and Tom reached out to catch her as she fell.

Bridie opened her eyes and shut them again quickly but the agony was just as fierce with her eyes shut tight. She gasped as someone touched her skin and pain flared. She was lying in the middle of the big feather bed and all around her were the murmur of voices and a sea of floating faces. It was hard to focus on anyone, the pain in her side was all the time pulling at her, demanding she give it all her attention. She was wrapped in Amaranta's deep blue velvet cloak and the black fur trim brushed against her cheek. She tried to raise a hand to push it away but it made the searing pain in her side even worse.

'She's conscious,' said Amaranta, her voice tight with anxiety. 'Bridie, girl, are you in much pain?'

Bridie could only whimper in reply.

Doctor Halibut stood beside the bed, washing his

hands in a basin, and the water ran red from his fingertips. 'It's a messy wound, but mostly just torn flesh and a chip off one rib. Two of the ribs were cracked by the impact. A little more to the left and things would be different. She's a lucky child.'

'No, the luck's ours. If we'd killed her . . .' said Eddie, putting his head in his hands.

'Not we, Eddie. You,' said Amaranta angrily. 'It was your pistol.'

'If you hadn't intervened, she never would have been hit,' said Eddie, defensively.

'If I hadn't, you'd have the old man's blood on your hands and the troopers would have you for murder.'

'And now you've both got Bridie's blood on your hands! Why the hell are you two still fighting?' shouted Tom. 'Can't you see where your stupid arguments have led!'

Bridie tried to speak but Dr Halibut lifted her head and spooned something thick, white and sweet between her lips. Darkness came to her quickly.

Bridie woke the next morning, aching. Her head felt heavy and her side was throbbing. There was a flurry of movement beside her. Painfully, Bridie turned her head to watch Amaranta silently gathering up her strewn clothing and jewellery from across the dirt floor. She folded up her dresses and scarves and hurriedly packed them into the big black trunk.

'You can't go,' said Bridie in a small, broken voice.

'I have to do this,' Amaranta answered, not looking at her.

'You told me you loved Eddie. How can you leave him?'

'You're just a child. You can't understand. Things will only get worse.'

'I understand,' said Bridie, turning her face away. 'You're a coward,' she added, unable to contain her bitterness.

Amaranta came over and stood next to the bed. 'You could come with me, Bridie,' she said softly. 'Or you could follow me when you feel up to the journey. I'll leave money for your fare so you can meet me in Melbourne.'

For a moment, a vision of herself and Amaranta riding in a carriage down Collins Street flashed through Bridie's imagination, but she pushed it away.

'Can't you see? We were making something special, something that no one has ever made before.'

'I can't be a part of that any more,' said Amaranta, turning away from the bed. She walked over to the trunk and pushed the lid down, snapping the lock into place. 'I don't have time to argue. The dray leaves in half an hour. But my offer to you still stands.'

Bridie felt a great wave of exhaustion wash over her. It hurt too much to talk. She wanted to roll over and turn her back on Amaranta but every movement sent a ripple of pain through her body. She covered her face with her arm and wished Amaranta would hurry up and leave. She didn't have the strength to fight any longer.

It felt like hours before the flap of the tent lifted again and Tom entered with a mug of warm billy tea and a bowl of milky gruel. He helped Bridie to sit so she could sip the sweet black tea.

'Tom, last night, when I fell, I heard the banshee wailing,' she said, too frightened by the memory to meet his gaze. 'When the banshee wails, it means an O'Connor is about to die. I heard one the day my father died.'

'That was your own voice you heard last night, not a banshee,' said Tom. 'There are no banshees in Australia.'

Bridie lowered the tin cup.

'Maybe I brought it with me and everything will be ruined here, like everything was ruined at home.'

Tom glanced around at the wreckage of the broken looking-glass. Smashed bottles of lotions lay in the dirt among the shards of mirror.

'Don't you worry, Bridie. I'll clear everything up later. Everything will be fine.'

'Oh, Tom, you know that's not what I mean. How can the Star open without Amaranta?'

Tom shrugged. 'I know all her lines. Eddie says I can play the Princess and that boys always used to play the girl's part. They still do in lots of places. Eddie says women probably shouldn't be allowed on stage at the diggings. It's much better that I do it.'

Bridie winced. The notion that Tom could play the beautiful princess made her want to groan. She looked into his earnest, unhappy eyes and knew he was putting on a brave face.

Bridie slept fitfully throughout the afternoon. Each time she woke and looked at the debris around the tent, she had to bite her lip to stop from crying. Just when things had seemed so good, when she'd found her place in the world, when she'd found all these people that she could belong to, everything was falling apart again, crumbling to dust around her. The pain in her side didn't seem anywhere near as difficult to bear as the pain in her heart.

It was early evening when Bridie woke and found Jacobus sitting next to the bed.

'What are you doing here? Go away,' she said, wearily.

'Now, child. I'm here to keep vigil. Can I get you some water?'

'I don't want anything from you. I hate you. It should have been you that was shot. It's your fault Amaranta's gone.'

As she spoke, a shudder coursed through her body and she let out a small cry. She felt as if she was falling. Jacobus stared down at her with a stricken expression, his face shadowy and unfocused in the fading light.

'Bridie, girl, you're burning up,' he said, resting a hand on Bridie's forehead.

Bridie tried to push his hand away, but another wave of shivering overtook her.

'Here, let me look at you,' said Jacobus. Gently, he turned down the big red satin quilt and loosened Bridie's nightgown. 'You're all swollen under your arm and these dressings need changing. Has Halibut been to see you today?' Bridie shook her head and clenched her teeth. Jacobus folded back the dressing and raised a kerosene lamp above her. He caught his breath.

'Bloody Halibut. The wound is poisoned.' He covered her up again and set the lamp on the end of the bark dresser.

'I'll be back in a moment, child,' he said.

The dark seemed to come down quickly and the night was full of strange moving shapes. Through her fever, Bridie imagined a wind had picked up and was sweeping across the valley. The sides of the tents seemed to billow and swell, and the figures moving in and out of the lamplight looked strangely distorted. Bridie heard voices and felt hands touching her burning body. Faces came close to hers, and stroked her cheeks: Jacobus and Tom. Both their faces seemed to swirl above her head, and then in the middle of the night, came a stranger's face, with golden skin – the Chinese doctor.

The tent was full of strange scents and the lamplight flew up in white arcs all around her as she writhed in pain. Then more faces came close to her and she felt hot breath against her skin. The living and the dead all came, Caitlin and Brandon and Gilbert, baby Paddy and her dad, each of them seemed so close to her that she could almost reach out and touch them. When she opened her eyes, they swirled above her head and called out her name. Bridie recognised her mother's voice and saw her face again, luminous in the dark folds of the canvas tent. When her body was so burning hot that she felt she would be consumed by the flames, her mother's hands seemed to move across her like cool water and draw the heat from her burning skin. Day and night merged into each other as Bridie fought against the fever.

Bridie woke and stared up at the roof of the tent. Judging by the light, it was late afternoon. Something had happened to her. She felt light and yet incredibly weak. She raised one hand from under the blankets and realised the pain had subsided. It didn't hurt to breathe any more and the throbbing under her arm was gone.

At first, she didn't notice that Jacobus was sitting beside the bed. He packed and lit his pipe and the warm scent of tobacco filled the air.

'Ah, you're back with us, St Brigid,' he said. 'Is there anything you'd be wanting after your long journey?'

'I haven't been anywhere,' said Bridie. Her own voice sounded strange to her from lack of use.

'Three days you've been away with the fever. You fell sick on Monday and today it's Thursday.'

'Thursday! That means tomorrow the Star will open!'

'Aye, they're all over in the theatre rehearsing the show,' said Jacobus.

'Amaranta came back?'

'No, young Tom's galumphing about like a great young heifer, playing the Princess of Patagonia. It will be a fine comedy, that's for certain. Hope the diggers don't pelt us with rotten fruit.' He drew on his pipe and chuckled to himself.

It was hard for Bridie to speak. There were so many questions that she needed answers to.

'Was Mrs Bones your wife?' asked Bridie.

Jacobus laughed. 'Now where would you be getting an idea like that?'

'I've heard and seen things. I saw Eddie Bones punch and kick you and tell you to keep away from his wife. Was she married to you before Eddie?' asked Bridie.

'My little patron saint Brigid,' he said, laughing. 'Now are saints meant to be such busybodies? And martyred eavesdropping busybodies at that!'

Bridie scowled in reply.

'Well now,' he said, weighing his words with care, 'let's just say that men with beautiful wives sometimes get peculiar ideas in their head. Can't believe the man's lived with her for so long and doesn't know his own wife.'

Jacobus laughed again until tears sprang to the corners of his eyes.

'I met Amaranta El'Orado when she was a plain and grubby little Irish convict's bastard, a waif, no older than you are now. Found her singing on a street corner in Old Sydney Town. Amargein O'Donahue she was then. Bit like you, a girl with a boy's name. Amy, I liked to call her. I took her in, saved her from the gutter. Four years I cared for her, taught her, fed her. That's when Eddie Bones "discovered" her. I had a magic show in a music hall in Sydney, "The Wizard Jacobus and his beautiful assistant El Ave Chant D'Oro". Amy sang her heart out for me then. And Eddie Bones saw her one night and stole her from me. Took her off to Europe with him and I never heard from either of them again, more than three years gone, until you brought him to my tent.'

Bridie pursed her lips. 'You must have kept her prisoner. She never would have stayed with you. The devil take your lies, old man. Eddie Bones must have rescued her,' said Bridie.

Jacobus laughed at her again. 'I have many vices, some of which you're familiar with, my dear. But young girls is not one of them. More trouble than they're worth. Amy was never my wife or my woman in any sense of the word. I loved her like a daughter and for all her wilfulness, I know she's loyal to me still. That's what sticks in Eddie's craw.

Eddie likes to think because she's his by law that I've no claim. But it's a mysterious thing, the ties that bind people together. Once you brought me back to life and then, when you were on the brink of death, I did the same for you. Me and that young Tom Whiteley, we never left your side. Hauled you back into this world by your heartstrings.'

Bridie pulled the red satin eiderdown up over her head. She didn't want to have to listen to another word.

'Well, it seems you're well on the way to recovery, St Brigid. I'd best be getting you some soup so you can get your strength back to hate me properly.'

She watched him leave the tent, then slumped back deep under thc eiderdown. Tentatively, she touched her chest, just above where her heart lay beating and wondered at all the invisible threads that spiralled outwards from it, binding her to Tom and Jacobus and this strange new world.

36

Starry, starry night

By evening, Bridie was so restless, she wanted to get out of bed. When Tom came to see her, she made him help her up. Amaranta had left her blue velvet cloak behind and Bridie wrapped it around her shoulders and, leaning on Tom's arm, went outside to join the rest of the troupe by the fire.

Eddie Bones looked up across the flames and smiled at her, but it was a weary smile. 'It's good to have you back with us, Bridie. We've missed you. It's been a hard week without your help.'

'Och, lassie, but it's too cold for a wee ailing mite to be out,' said Robbie.

'No, I'd rather be here than anywhere,' said Bridie.

Marconi grinned, put his fiddle beneath his chin and struck up her favourite melody. Bridie felt a glow of warmth that was more than the heat of the fire and it flowed into her like a dark, warm channel of strength.

The next night, there were hundreds of diggers waiting outside the Star an hour before the show was to begin. Bridie had walked to the theatre with Tom's aid and sat in a chair in the wings, doing last-minute alterations to one of Amaranta's abandoned costumes so that the dress would fit

Tom. When she'd finished adjusting the pink satin gown, she helped do the actors' make-up, rubbing burnt cork onto Marconi's cheeks to turn him into a black minstrel, making Eddie Bones' fair eyebrows dark and exotic for his role as the Patagonian prince, and using chalk and paste to whiten Tom's face and transform him into the 'fair princess'. Tom watched her intently as she applied the paste to his skin and she couldn't help blushing. It was so strange being this close to him, their faces only inches apart. He tipped his head a little to one side and she had to keep straightening his chin so that she could apply the make-up properly. When she had finished, he looked into the mirror and grinned. His teeth looked very white against the bright red lipstick, and a twist of dark curl was poking out from under the long wig he wore. Bridie leaned forward and tucked it gently into place. It was such a small thing, but for a moment she felt that strange fiery current run between them, just as it had the day at the waterhole.

The band of volunteer musicians struck up the tune that signalled the Princess' entry and Bridie watched from her chair, in the shadow of the curtain, as Tom minced on stage and curtseyed to Freddy Wobbins, who was playing the role of the King. Tom's long limbs poked out at all angles against the fabric of his gown. When he turned to move downstage for his big opening speech, he tripped on his skirts and sprawled across the rough stage, flat on his face. Tom looked straight at Bridie, his eyes wide with distress. The house was in uproar as he got up, clutching at the folds of his dress.

Bridie knew Tom would persist. He would never give up. He would recite every one of his lines, sing every song, no matter how badly, but the audience wasn't going to be kind. The play was simply a disaster. Beside her, Eddie Bones stood with his head in his hands. Then, out of the corner of her eye, she saw a shimmer of movement, a swish of white satin, and suddenly Amaranta was beside them in the gown that Bridie had worked so hard to perfect. The feather-white folds of fabric floated on the evening air and the myriad seed pearls gleamed like dewdrops.

'Bridie, quickly, are all the hooks fastened?' she said, standing close so Bridie could adjust the gown for her.

The next instant, she was on stage, berating Tom as an impostor, making up lines which not only made sense of the story but completely stilled the audience. They were in awe of her from the moment she stepped onto the stage. When she turned with arms outstretched to the audience and burst into song, Bridie heard a gasp of appreciation sweep through the crowd. From that moment, everything fell into place. Even though Bridie was exhausted, the sheer excitement of watching the play unfold kept her lucid enough to make all the last-minute alterations the costumes needed.

When the curtain was drawn on the final scene, the crowds roared and showered Amaranta with small nuggets in appreciation. As she stepped out to accept their applause, Bridie shouted and stamped her feet with joy. It made her side ache but the pain meant nothing compared to her happiness.

At the close of the show, the band struck up another piece and then the diggers all got up and danced with each other on the dirt floor. Amaranta danced with Eddie as if they'd never fought, and Bridie managed to dance a single tune with Tom before sheer exhaustion overtook her and

Tom had to guide her from the dance floor. She was sitting in the orchestra pit, watching the dancers contentedly, when Amaranta came over and sat down beside her.

'I knew you'd come back,' said Bridie.

Amaranta laughed. 'And here I was, worried I'd find you dead, girl! A rider overtook the dray on his way to Melbourne and he told me that you were on your deathbed. I was ashamed I'd left you in that state, ashamed that I'd let down everyone in the troupe. And my Eddie. He drives me mad with his schemes and his mad dreams, but you were right, Bridie. We're making something special in this place that's new and fine and worth fighting for.'

After the last digger had left and they'd extinguished all the candles, Bridie and Tom walked out into the cool night air. It was a relief to breathe deeply, to get away from the smell of greasepaint and smoke and burning fat. They walked slowly up the hill, over Golden Point, to where the black bush edged the fields. Tom flopped down on his back, looking up at the night sky and Bridie sat down beside him. She wrapped the blue velvet cloak close around her and drew up the hood so the black fur trim tickled her cheeks. Tom looked across at her and smiled.

'It was magic, wasn't it?' he said. 'The show, the crowd. The Star. It was probably the best show any of those diggers ever saw in their lives. All because we made it happen. And Amaranta came back, as I knew she would. I knew she wouldn't let Eddie down, or me!'

Bridie laughed. 'So you're vying to be one of the great loves of her life, are you now? She's a fiery spirit, that one. You be careful.'

He turned and grinned at her.

'She's a grand lady but she's not as fiery as the girl I truly fancy. Nothing can put out the spark in my girl. Why, they can't even shoot it out of her!'

Bridie could feel herself blushing in the darkness.

'Between the two of us, Bridie, we'll set the world on fire, like those little burning fires down there. You'll make beautiful costumes and one day people will come from all over the world to see how fine they are. And I'll be the grandest thespian in the Southern Hemisphere – the greatest actor under the Southern Cross; and the Star Theatre will be the most famous theatre in all the New World!'

Tom reached out and his fingertips brushed against Bridie's and then their fingers entwined. Bridie looked up at the stars. The Southern Cross blazed bright above them and Bridie knew there was nowhere else in the wide world that she would rather be than under this sky, with this boy, and her whole life ahead of her.

Author's Note

This is a work of fiction and Bridie O'Connor is an imaginary girl, but her experiences are based on fact. Between 1848 and 1850, over 4000 girls were shipped out to Australia as part of the 'Earl Grey Orphan Scheme'. Earl Grey was Secretary of State for the Colonies and the girls were victims of the great Irish potato famine. The famine, or *An Ghorta Mor*, as it was known in Ireland, was a terrible event in Irish history that left more than a million Irish dead and drove almost two million people away from their homeland. I am not descended from one of the orphan girls, but more than 30 000 Australians are, and their influence has echoed down the generations.

The history of Ireland and its struggle to regain its independence from Britain is part of the history of Australia. Over 30 per cent of Australians have at least one Irish ancestor. Throughout the nineteenth century, the Irish made up 20–30 per cent of new arrivals. The impact they had on their new country, the stories and ideas they brought with them or put behind them when they left their homeland, influenced how Australia developed and helped create who we are now.

Famine orphans like Bridie lived through the heady days of the goldrush and they bore witness to huge changes in Australia's history. In writing *Bridie's Fire*, I tried to merge the experiences of a generation of Australian girls.

All the characters in *Bridie's Fire* are based on a combination of personalities that I came across in my research. Although none of the main characters is a historical figure, their experiences parallel those of real men, women and children of their times. I borrowed the name of the Wizard Jacobus from a real actor who performed on the early Victorian goldfields. Amaranta El'Orado's character was inspired by the actress Lola Montez. Studying the lives of these people was the most enriching part of writing Bridie's story, and I hope I have presented an accurate and true picture of the lives of the people who lived through that tumultuous era.

Even though we may not be aware of it, the past is with us in every moment of our waking lives. We are part of a continuum between our ancestors and our descendants. In writing CHILDREN OF THE WIND, I hope to shed light on the powerful link between who we were and who we are in the process of becoming.